HARMONY

A Pizza vs. Zombies Novel

Mairym Castro
&
Amanda Kelly

This is a work of fiction. Names, character, places, and incidents either are the product of the author's imagination or are used fictitiously, and any resemblance to actual persons, living or dead, business, companies, events, or locales is entirely coincidental.

Cover Designed by: Germancreative

ISBN: 978-0-578-74760-6

ACKNOWLEDGMENTS

I would like to thank friends and family who supported me in writing this novel. Bryan Thank you for forcing me to give you attention after hours on the computer. Your unconditional love & support. I want to thank my closest friends Miguel; Valerie & Francisco thank you for always supporting my ideas and listening to me for hours! But I honestly couldn't have done it without Amanda. Thank you for having patience. With awesome teamwork we wrote this novel! Oh, and also we could not have done it without that slow day in the Barnes & Noble Music Section, grabbing a book and looking at you with the famous phrase, "What would you do if there was a zombie apocalypse and you were just craving pizza?" Hope everyone enjoys it as much as we enjoyed writing it!

-Mairym Castro

CONTINUED

Thank you, thank you to my parents and sister. They're the best family anyone could have and are always there to bounce "crazy" ideas off of. Getting this book out there would not have been possible without Nieves, the best Beta-reader in the world, and Gabby, our star book promoter. Thank you both! Last but not least, thank you to my partner in (fictional) crime Mairym. Through both of us moving away, college, multiple jobs, and grad school we stuck it out and never let any of it stop us. Thank you for your constant enthusiasm and belief in our book. I'm grateful we took our zombie apocalypse and pizza joke so seriously we needed to write a book about it.

-Amanda Kelly

CONTENTS

CHAPTER 1

Deep Dish

There's just something about pizza. Other foods are great, sure. Burritos? Pretty solid. Cheese burgers? They're good every once in a while. But pizza? I'm always in the mood for pizza.

No, I'm always craving pizza. And 95 percent of the time when I can't have it, is when I want it the most. It's kind of like my last three boyfriends. Wait, who was I kidding? My boyfriends were never as good as pizza.

Anyway, on a long day like this one, I've been craving it. Badly. The pizza, that is. It's that perfect mix of melted cheese, red sauce, every topping, and extra anchovies. I sigh aloud just thinking about it.

I'm sitting, waiting at the only decent pizza parlor in town, my foot tapping away under the checkered table. I've got my family's drink orders but no family. Even worse? No pizza. Service is so damn slow I have half a mind to jump behind the counter and make my order myself. Except I'm off the clock today and I don't work for free.

Georgia probably won't even care. She knows I'm her best customer as well as her best employee but if I go back there then everyone will need me for something. Plus, if I move I'll lose my table. Then my mom will complain *whenever* she decides to show up.

Waiting for my family is becoming a mission and the thought of having a friend with me through this dreaded family dinner doesn't sound that bad. Then again, I have no friends.

I look around the crowded pizza joint. It's filled with the same people I had to deal with growing up, before I was shipped off. The kind of kids who didn't have to spend most of their teenage years in a secret military base, preparing for a war they never got to fight in.

It's also the same kind of people who are my peers at the local college. They seemed fine before I left. Now, not so much.

I'm glad what they've started calling World War III is over and all but, in a way, it kind of sucks. I would've loved to kick some Russian butt. Not to brag or anything but I was ranked first in my class of elite soldiers. Well, not officially because my commander was a sexist jerk but unofficially, everyone knew it.

Now I'm just considered a 19-year-old outcast in lala-land. I live at home but I work here part-time so I can save up to get my own place. I go to the local college, change my major about every other week, and last of all, I keep to myself.

My mom promised me that I could have a normal life now. I did everything my parents asked of me. Now they were giving me the space to be just like everyone else.

The flaw in this plan? I'm not like everyone else. I'm not normal. I'm not going to forget all that I've seen and done.

I scan the room discreetly. Yeah, with their shiny hair and

perfect smiles these kids are soft, vapid, and normal. I change my mind about having a friend. It's better to be alone.

I honestly am going to slam my head against the table if my parents take any longer to get here or if I have to keep waiting endlessly for this pizza. Patience isn't exactly my strong suit.

I watch as a waiter brings out a pizza. The guy is a new employee here. I think his name is Fred but I'm pretty sure I scare him so we don't talk much. I stare at him, hoping the pizza he's carrying is mine. Actually, I'm praying a little. He's holding it way above his head, so I can't be sure.

I try to make eye contact with him so I can try and convince him it's mine but he just walks right past me and brings the pizza down to the table next to me. My eyes fly to it even though I know for sure it's not mine.

Ugh cheese? Are you kidding me? That's the worst kind of crime. These people seriously need to rethink their whole lives if they're just settling for cheese. I scrunch my nose down even as my stomach growls loudly at the site, it is pizza after all. It's just missing a few magic touches.

I glance up from the pizza. There's a girl at the table with long blonde hair and a stuck-up sneer.

She's sitting with an attractive guy who probably doesn't know what he's gotten himself into. He looks like he just took her out because she has a nice rack that happens to be popping out of her tight dress if his stare there is any indication.

I watch as he keeps trying to cut at the pre-cut line of the cheesy goodness but the plastic-looking chick keeps telling him to cut a smaller portion.

Is that supposed to be attractive? I find it ridiculous. There, in front of her, is the best human creation and she wants tiny crumb-sized pieces?

I roll my eyes and turn toward the guy. He seems to find her appetite ridiculous too by the annoyed look on his face or maybe it's in response to her constant complaining. I don't know. It's a tough one.

He catches me staring and I notice he has dreamy eyes. He winks at me, which immediately causes Plastic Chick to turn her bitching my way. "Want to take a picture? It'll last longer and you can go drool somewhere else, freak!"

I turn back to her to see her giving me a dirty look.

Dreamy Eyes starts laughing. So, he was a jerk after all. They deserve each other.

Soon other people are turning around to stare.

I grit my teeth. I could snap this chick in two in a battle but here in lala-land I choose to stare down at my hands like an idiot. Sadly, kicking civilian ass is frowned upon, especially at my workplace. "I don't want Dreamy Eyes. I just want my damn pizza," I mutter under my breath.

"Baby, I'm sorry we took so long. Traffic was horrible," a familiar lilting voice says, stopping me from my detailed imaginings of annihilating the snobby couple in front of me.

I look up to see my mother. My father and my brat of a little brother are trailing behind her.

"Finally," I say, rolling my eyes.

"And don't call me baby. It's H, Mom," I add, annoyed. Mom just rolls her eyes and doesn't reply.

I used to be fine with my parents calling me pet names before the whole war broke out and I was sent off to become a human weapon thanks to my dad, the great freaking General. After that experience, I don't let anyone call me by my real name or anything cutesy.

"Here you go, H," Georgia says as she pulls up to our table. "Sorry for the wait. We're swamped today."

"It's fine," I say quickly, digging in before anyone else. I'm pulling the slice to my mouth and burning my hand in the process, but heck, I don't care. I blow on the pizza and open my mouth.

"Helgason?" My boss asks with a narrow in her eyes. I hear Dad choke on his soda and Mom giggle. I snap my mouth closed and bring the slice down for a minute. I almost feel bad for saying no but mostly I'm relieved she hasn't guessed it.

Still, she was so sure this time. I shake my head of dyed white hair, a look that I totally rocked.

"I'll get it next time," she says as she bustles off.

"Good luck," Dad mutters with a smirk.

"You really won't," I holler after her but she just waves us off. I've assured her countless times that she won't guess my name but she still tries every time she sees me.

I lift the pizza again. My mouth waters as the cheesy goodness just brushes my open lips then-

The sirens ring out, piercing my ears.

No. It can't be.

Bomb sirens. They get louder and louder. I spring to my feet in a fighting stance and check the exits. My beloved, uneaten slice falls and lands near my black combat boots.

This was really happening. It was my worst nightmare and secret fantasy coming to life. A shock of adrenaline runs through me. After two years of peace and everyone thinking the war was over, it looks like it wasn't as over as we thought.

I look at my dad and he just gives me his reassuring nod. Then I turn to look at my mom cradling my brother, hot tears already beginning to stream down her face as what this could mean dawns on her.

I know I have to help get everyone to the nearest bomb shelter. There are 233 in the D.C. area, where I live. If my incessant studying is right, and I know it is, then there should be a shelter less than a block from here.

As I walk to the front to get everyone's attention something honed deep in me tells me to look back, and I do.

I see two figures running full force towards the pizza parlor with eyes shockingly white, pupils nowhere to be seen. I bolt for

the door to lock it.

The figures keep on running. Moments later the piercing sound of shattering glass surrounds me like a flood as they crash through the storefront windows. I instinctively block to cover my face and head but my feet are already moving towards the first figure I see.

Over the shattering and screeching one woman's voice seems to break through from somewhere in the distance.

She yells, "Dear God!"

Suddenly I'm pulled from behind. I try to fight off my attacker but feel a sharp pain all over my body. I push past the pain and elbow him in the head. As I'm freed I take a giant step forward and feel my feet slipping beneath me on some shards of glass.

I'm falling and everything starts to fade. My last thoughts are of blinding white eyes and the sound of horrified screams ringing in my ears.

CHAPTER 2

Margherita

"Wake up, you weak degenerates!" Colonel Croft screams at the top of his lungs, waking us all up to racing hearts and full attention. It doesn't matter though, I'm certain my adrenaline is shot to hell by this point so this wakeup call is only preparing me for the day of constant anxiety and alertness ahead.

I nearly fly off my newly appointed top bunk and my feet scramble to find purchase on the hard floor. I'd already fallen from my bed during the wake-up ceremony earlier this week and the bruise around my ribcage is still yellow and tender. Everyone had laughed as I cried from the pain zinging down the right side of my body. I hadn't cried since.

Along with the pain and humiliation of falling I'd also been punished with extra time in the training facility, without food or water. None of those things were something I was eager to repeat. I'd only been here six days.

In a matter of seconds, we all stand straight and tall in front of our bunk beds waiting for our orders. Eyes straight ahead. Aching bodies from training, all pretending to be ready. I swallow loudly to get past the lump in my throat. I'm just relieved to be in position with the rest of them as the Colonel walks by me.

"Today at 0600 you will be training in combat and have a physical test," he screams at us.

"You have 5 minutes to get ready and meet in the mess hall, maggots!" he yells as he walks away.

Waking up to this every morning is a nightmare and all I can do is wish I could just go home and snuggle up to my nice, soft, pink blanket that's waiting in my room. I let out a breath knowing that it's so far beyond my reach now, it's stupid. I'm stupid for wanting it. I realize I better get my ass in gear. I turn quickly to get my toothbrush but end up slamming into a hard surface.

I rebound off someone's chest. As I begin to right myself, a hand pushes me down hard.

"Watch out, you idiot," a shrill voice barks.

I fall on to the floor only to look up and see Bran. I cringe inwardly but I don't know why I'm surprised. My life is hell now. Bumping into him just makes sense.

If the Colonel is Satan-and he is-then Bran is his fire breathing hellhound. On top of his unreal amount of muscles and the ability to thoroughly savor the pain and weakness of others, Bran is also a stone-cold killer. He'd come here straight from juvy and he wasn't shy about saying all the reasons why. If he were dumb like the rest of the meatheads here I might've felt better but in his blue eyes you could see that he was sharp, hard, and calculating.

Then again, I didn't underestimate any of these kids. I didn't know much about this program, Project Aries, hardly anyone did. I knew that everyone here was handpicked and under the age of 18. Some of these kids are highly intelligent. Others are insanely strong. I'm technically in the first category but the best reason I could figure I'm here is that my father is a General and a war hero. I didn't sign up for this but I'm here and I can't let my parents or my country down.

My father literally told me not to bother coming home if I didn't make it through the program, that I was lucky to even get in. My mother calls it tough love. I call it child abuse but no one is going to listen to me because no one ever has. It didn't matter why I was here, it only mattered that I made it through.

Bran is unfortunately a nasty side-effect of training. With everything combined he scared the shit out of me. I stayed as far away from him as I could but in a small cabin it wasn't exactly possible. Besides, he picked on others as a show of his dominance. Having watched him the last few days, I figure out that bumping into each other hadn't been an accident at all. I'm 15 and while I'm not the youngest, I'm one of the smallest and weakest people here. This was a game for him and I was the new target.

"Just because you're some General's daughter you think you're going to get it easy here?" he says, smirking along with his two buddies. They're nearly as big as he is but not nearly as intelligent.

Others walk by and are busy getting ready for training.

They pretend not to see. That's how it is here. You keep your head down and you stay alive. Even I've figured that out.

"If so," he continues, "think again, you little skank."

He picks me up and pounds me head first into the wall, making my bones rattle. My face takes the brunt of the impact and my mouth begins to bleed. As I pull back I also feel my left eye starting to swell because it hit the corner.

He turns me over to face him, his meaty hand bigger than the size of my head.

"You worthless piece of shit," he says once again, kicking me in my abdomen, making me wish this could all stop. I try to fight him off. I use everything I have, clawing and scratching, but it does nothing. I cry out, knowing my recently bruised ribs can't handle anymore.

The pain is so great, I sink to the floor and know there's nothing I can do but cover my head with my hands in protection. I'll have to wait till he gets bored with me.

"Dude! What the fuck? Stop it!" a guy shouts as he comes running in. Out of my working eye I see that he's completely stunning. He's got blond hair like Bran but it's longer, slicked back and to the side, and his blue eyes are warm and kind. He's also taller than Bran, less muscular but no less intimidating. His arms, covered in tattoos, reach for me.

Bran tries to block him but he can't. I watch in fascination but can barely hear over my own harsh, ragged breathing.

"Why do you care, Adam? It's none of your fucking business. Now get out of my way or you're going down with this skank," Bran says, spitting out the last word.

Distantly, since most of my focus is on trying desperately not to pass out from the pain, I can't help but wonder why this boy, Adam, is helping me. I want to hope he has no ulterior motives but it's just too hard for me to believe that someone else with their humanity still intact found their way here.

"What the hell did she ever do to you? Huh, Bran? Not a damn fucking thing. And did you forget that Croft is waiting? Now get out before I break your face and your little buddies' too."

"You'd break our alliance over some spoiled princess?" Bran grumbles, not backing down.

"I would. I'm not telling you again." The guy Adam gestures to me and it's all I can do to stay conscious through the pain but I watch as Bran huffs and leaves without another word, his cronies trailing behind him.

"Are you all right? Shit. What the heck am I saying?" Adam mumbles in a panic, making me think my injuries are worse than I realize.

"Don't move. I'm going to take you to the infirmary."

I cry out as agony sweeps through me again when his arms move me tight into his chest. He picks me up as though I weigh nothing and carries me down the plain, bright white halls.

With confusion and gratitude at war in the part of my brain that isn't screaming in pain, I consider his deep blue eyes. All I find there is concern.

"Thanks," I manage to get past my lips as he puts me down on the hard cot. At this point I've been jostled one time too many and the pain and darkness take over.

BEEEEEP BEEEEEP BEEEEEEEEP

I wake up from my nightmares of old memories with a throbbing headache, ears ringing from nonstop bomb alarms, and the sting of cuts all over my body, but what really bothers me is the overwhelming stench of rotting garbage, blood, and death in the musky air. I gag and reach up to the nearest table ledge, leveraging myself into a seated position. At least the sirens are no longer blaring.

Finally alert, I scan the pizzeria frantically. My parents are gone, my little brother too. I'm alone.

At least that's what I thought. I try to get up and I see all the others. There's a group of people just standing there on the far side of the restaurant. I quickly note my family isn't among them. There's no one I recognize either. They probably need me to guide them to a shelter.

Still, they look odd. They have torn clothes and look awful but it's the way they're just standing there that's bothering me. They're probably shell-shocked.

Flashes of memories come back to me and I remember the

men crashing through the windows. Where are they now? Where's my family? What's going on? I swallow my panic and try to stay calm.

Then I notice Plastic Chick. She's looking around the restaurant now, seeming to be just as confused and lost as I am. “Hey!” I yell at her. “What happened?” I ask, walking towards her as I shake the glass shards off my clothing.

She stops, makes a strange sound and stares at the floor, her blonde hair hanging around her face like a rag doll. Alarm bells are going off in my head. This isn't right.

Then out of nowhere she charges straight for me. How she's running in those heels, I have no idea. Still, I bolt away.

“Hey, calm down! I know your boyfriend checked me out and all but I thought we had no hard feelings," I say.

Then I see it, her eyes are white like the figures that crashed in through the windows. Jesus, her eyes are just gone. If they were white contacts, then I was Little Miss Muffet.

Shivers run through me even as I try to tap into my training. It's been a few years and I'm a little rusty but some things tend to stick in your memory, no matter how hard you try to forget them. I get a whiff of her stench and gag again. She's definitely contributing to the putrid garbage smell.

Luckily, I notice the others haven't moved. They're not coming to help me but they're not attacking me either. She keeps coming for me though, and I try dodging her by using the tables as shields.

"Are you even okay?" I scream as she jumps over the table in one leap, landing right near me.

I scurry back and swipe a steak knife from off the table behind me. Plastic Chick catches up to me easily and growls at me while trying to take a bite of my shoulder.

"Oh, hell no!" I punch her in the face and with a sickening crunch of bone, her nose snaps left.

There's no blood. None. I blink in shock but she keeps coming for me like she doesn't feel it. She probably doesn't.

Whatever she is, she's no longer human. This thing wants to kill me and in a game of kill or be killed, I know where I stand.

She comes closer, snapping her jaws like she's possessed and I slit her throat right then and there. Brownish ooze spurts out and I dodge it like a pro. I'm not about to find out if that shit is contagious. With my hands covering my head, I hear a loud thud and turn to see Plastic Chick's lifeless body fall to the floor.

I look beyond her and see that the others are just standing there, except now they're facing me. It's clear to me now that their eyes are just as blank as Plastic Chick's were. I don't know why they're not chasing me too but I don't want to stick around to find out.

I decide very quickly that getting the heck away from whatever these people have become is my newest priority. So, I run to the bathroom, steak knife in hand.

What is going on, I think to myself for the hundredth time along with a few choice curses as I lock the door. I turn on the sink and wash my face. Maybe this is all a bad dream? Except I know it's not. Unfortunately, all my dreams are just memories from my life and I definitely don't remember this shit happening before.

I take a good look at my face and I'm arrested by the sight of my eyes. They're purple. As in indigo purple. What the...

Considering my eyes are normally dark brown, this is strange. I toss my head from side to side, checking out the new color. Not going to lie, it does contrast amazingly with my dyed white hair but seriously, am I going to die or something? Will my eyes eventually turn white and I'll turn into one of them? Why haven't I turned into one already?

Now that I have time to think about it, I kind of feel like I just partied a little too hard and have a raging hangover. Maybe this is all a drunken delusion?

Okay get it together, H. I decide it doesn't matter if I'm delusional. As of right now I'm still me, albeit a purple-eyed me, and I need to get out of here. There's no time for monster theories or picking out outfits to go with my new eyes.

I take out my cell phone to call my dad which, silly me, I was actually expecting to work, and it has no service. I'm stuck in this tiny bathroom with whatever the heck that is out there and no service? I'm about to start acting like a brat and cry about it when I hear a familiar growling right outside the door. Great, more stinky creatures have decided to seek me out.

I look around and find the window just to the left of the last stall. I silently thank Saint Margherita, the patron saint of pizza. Not wanting to make much noise I crack it open, jump through it, and hit the ground running.

The streets are pretty clear, not much around except random bodies on the floor. It's like a post-massacre ghost town and I wonder how long I was unconscious for. I check my phone for the time. I figure I've been out for about two and a half hours. I kind of want to start freaking out but I know I have to hold it together until I'm safe. I ignore the bodies.

Then from the corner of my eye, I see a beauty, a 1969 Mustang Fastback, all black. It's a car I would only dream of touching, and if there's anything I love besides kicking butt, hot guys, and pizza, it's definitely cars.

I can't take my eyes off it. There's no one alive around that I can see or sense. Besides it wouldn't be stealing. I would just be borrowing it to get to safety. I think the owner would be proud. I put the steak knife under my belt and sprint towards the classic beauty.

It's still daylight, but from the looks of it and the time on my phone, the sun is fading fast. I should try to get to a safe place to stay the night. I don't know what those things are and I don't have the time to find out right now. I get close enough to the car to see a body in the passenger seat. It's definitely moving and is looking worse for wear. Could it be another person? I check the eyes.

Nope. It's a stinker. I make noises to see if it will get out but all it does is move its head. Is it stupid, I wonder. Probably.

I walk up to the Mustang, trying to hold my breath, and the

thing just stares at me. At least it isn't trying to chase me like Plastic Chick.

"Hey, want to let me get a ride?" I ask with a smirk on my face as I open the door. Hopefully this thing doesn't kill me for being an idiot.

"Is that a yes?" Still no answer. I guess it isn't much of a talker or its brain isn't working.

I spy keys idling in the ignition. Jackpot. Looks like this guy tried to get away before he turned into whatever he is now.

He leans forward and tries to bite my hand. I move it back just in time.

"I guess so, but sadly you can't come with me, Mr. Stinks."

I grab the creature by the hair to pull him out but he begins struggling like a madman. His limbs are flailing and one hand manages to claw at me, striking hard across my neck. It begins stinging in the way that I know it's bleeding. I take a second to hope the scratch is shallow. Suddenly the stinker finds its footing and uses its body weight to lunge at me.

I try to avoid him but I know I can't so I slit its throat as we both tumble onto the hard asphalt. I roll out from under his limp form and stand up, ripping off my jacket as I do to frantically wipe off the gunk his neck spewed at me.

"Damn," I mumble as I stare down at the thing. I'm not opposed to destroying before I'm destroyed, and I definitely don't feel right letting these things walk around my city, but it seems like a waste.

I look around at the eerily quiet streets and the urge to get off them hits me hard. The stinker isn't moving but the car is free and clear. I throw my now gunk-covered jacket over the body and hop in.

I get in and turn on the ignition to hear the beautiful purr of the engine. Smiling, I hit the road. As I speed along, I rummage through the glove compartment searching for something to wipe up the dried blood on my neck but it's a no go. I do however find some fast food napkins in the middle console. I look at my reflection in the rearview mirror and I'm grateful to find nothing but a thin scratch underneath the blood.

The only places I can think to go are home, a shelter, or Costco but I'm better off going home. That's where my dad would bring Mom and Justin. It helps that we have our own underground bunker at our house.

As I pass the familiar streets, I notice that they're also empty. This scares me too but I still don't care. I was knocked out for a while so I don't know what I expected. I just need to find my family.

I speed because hell, I want to see a police officer give me a ticket. In fact, the police would be ideal right now, so of course, they're nowhere to be seen. I watch with exhilaration as the dial ticks past 110 mph. I mean if they honestly care about my speeding at this point, I might as well feed them to a stinker. Nobody gets in the way of me finding out what the fuck is going on.

I finally get home and decide to at least be civil and park the beauty in the driveway. I take my keychain that's thankfully still in my pocket and unlock the front door to my house.

"Mom? Dad? Justin?" I call out, hoping to get a response. I get nothing in reply. Absolutely nothing. I silently walk around and make sure the house is clear. When I find that it is, I lock the front door and make sure every exit is closed so nothing gets in.

I run to my dad's room and find a couple of his guns with enough ammo to last me a couple of weeks but I don't feel relief. All the weapons are still here. The house is just like we left it. I was kind of hoping I wouldn't find any of this because this would've meant that my parents would've made it home at some point.

At the same time, I know Dad wouldn't have risked putting Mom and Justin in danger. I didn't think they would leave me behind either but I can't think about that. I trust they're safe. That will have to be enough for now.

I grab some clothes and toiletries I'll need from my room and stuff it all into my black backpack. Then I stash the weapons in my navy, oversized duffel. From there I make a run for it to the secret door to the bunker. I know I'm alone but I can't shake the feeling that fact can change at any minute. I want to be locked up in the bunker. It's secure and equipped with enough food to last me a couple of years. I can take on whatever comes my way but I need time to think and plan, and I need to be safe to do it.

I finally manage to open the intricate safety locks on the bunker and walk down into the tunnels.

"Mom? Dad? Justin?" I yell into the darkness. I sigh in relief as the lights turn on, thankful there's still electricity but bummed all the same as my last hope that my family might be here dies. No answer and no sign of them.

Sulking, I put the duffel with the guns I got from my dad's room on the bed. Then I turn on the TV to see if there's any news about what's going on. I mentally thank my dad for the wonderful idea of an antenna TV now that the WIFI is out. I'm surprised that it picks up a signal. Thankfully it shows a few news channels. I choose Channel 5 News at random and a fancy looking woman in a business suit is midway through her sentence.

"... The president and his family are safe and in an undisclosed location. They took off in Air Force One as of yesterday, officially closing the borders behind them. I will be speaking in his place." A bunch of shouting emerges from the crowd around her.

The politician looks up from her notes at the podium with a staying hand.

"All questions will be taken at the end of the announcement," she says with a raise of her eyebrow. The name Senator Milano, Virginia, U.S., flashes on the bottom of the screen.

She looks so serious as she pauses dramatically then dives back in.

"We, the United States, are in a state of emergency. According to the Center for Disease Control, our nation's capital is officially under quarantine. Three days ago, what appears to be a virus began spreading through the area. The virus is said to be extremely contagious. The cause is still unknown. While details are still emerging, the severity of the issue is clear. Still, it was with great relief that all of the riots we have been reporting on have stopped and the fires have been put out. The area has been evacuated. The quarantine walls have been put in place and the government is confident they've gotten everyone to safety."

Multiple clips show on the screen of tanks rolling through the streets of my city. People in hazmat suits are collecting people to bring them to safety. Behind them the streets are burning. Above them there are helicopters everywhere circling the area. The bomb sirens are a constant sound adding to the havoc around the scene. Bomb shelters are lit up and men, women, and children, many holding house pets, are walking toward them in droves.

My first thought is of course that this woman is insane. I'm still alive and so she's a big fat liar about everyone being safe. Then something else strikes me.

"Three days?" I shout out to the TV. "What the hell?" I don't believe this. I don't understand how it's possible. I passed out three days ago and am somehow alive? I missed this, the craziness, the panic of humanity. How could I have missed it all?

I stare at the screen for the millionth time and notice that yes, it does say Monday. I clench and unclench my hands rhythmically to keep calm. I went to Georgia's for pizza on Friday. Even with the reality of the situation staring me in the face, I still can't quite grasp it.

A male reporter's nasally voice comes from somewhere in the crowd.

"What about the people who aren't in shelters? Are they safe? There are reports that thousands of people are unaccounted for."

The senator narrows her eyes at the reporter but then she straightens to her full height.

"As I've stated all questions will have to wait until the end. However, the authorities are confident that any person who is unaffected by the virus is safe and inside a shelter. We've been doing everything within our power to make it so. Even with a population over 600,000 and the commuters and tourists, we are still certain that those who could have been taken to safety, have been.

"We ask that you keep in mind that the census is still being counted everyday with the amount of people in each shelter. In addition, it's difficult to know just how many people were unfortunately infected.

"As a caring senator to this great nation, I personally will be staying in and overseeing the border walls. We'll make sure every citizen is in a shelter. Hypothetically? If someone were still out there, I'd warn," the senator continues with a purposeful deepening of voice, "that they must seek shelter immediately. For those listening from their shelters, if you know anyone who's still out there, there are military personnel in your building that you can notify. Do not try to leave your shelter. For those on the outside the borders, you have nothing to fear. Luckily, we, your government, have contained the threat. As of 5 o'clock this morning, nobody has been or will be able to get in or out of the posted area until the threat is terminated. For safety reasons, in addition to a physical block from the outside world, all cell towers have been blocked for the time being in these areas."

A map appears on the screen of Washington D.C. There are red lines right over the diamond shape that completely encompass the capitol. These lines indicate where the border walls are located. Hell, it even blocked off the Potomac.

I live in the Northwest quadrant, in a neighborhood called Chevy Chase right within the border walls. Whatever was happening it was happening here and only here. How they managed to barricade us and this so-called virus within the 68 or so square miles of D.C. I couldn't begin to guess, but it was happening.

The politician comes back on the screen once more and she looks right into the camera.

"May God be with all the survivors and may this all end soon," she says with a serious, sad look on her face.

I hit the power button on the remote and throw the thing across the room.

"Bullshit, Senator Cookie. This is no virus," I yell at the monitor.

"This can't be happening...but that explains the no service on my phone," I say, a little annoyed.

"And I didn't see any damn tanks when I was outside." In fact, I was the only living thing for miles besides the stinkers, if they counted. I decided they really didn't.

"I bet those authorities inside the shelters aren't doing shit to help any of us who are left out here," I mutter. Great, now I'm talking to myself. Alone. Underground.

My mind starts racing with the news. They probably don't want us calling out for help because no one can do anything anyway. I'm sure they've given up on us. I have my theories about what's happening but they aren't thoughts I can even think to myself without feeling completely insane.

I sit on the bed and immediately realize I smell like garbage. I need to shower now. I run to the small bathroom and turn on the faucet.

Finally, I put my head under the running hot water and enjoy the peacefulness of the moment and take a breather. It doesn't last long though. I still need to find my parents, my brother, and get the hell out of Washington D.C. somehow. The senator said there are borders and I saw the pictures but I don't care. With my dad's authority, we can get out of here. Heck, maybe they've already gotten out. I don't know if I want that to be true or not.

This may seem like a negative situation and all but I have to think positive. Rule number one in combat training: You can't win a fight if you don't believe you can. I remember I'm a badass chick and guess what? I'm going to make shit happen. I reach out to get my towel and pull on my Transformers Pjs. I walk over to the bed and literally knock out from exhaustion

●○●○●○●○●○●○●○●○●○●

I'm sitting in the mess hall eating my disgusting chowder

with a smiling Adam. His smile is great and helps make me overlook the insurmountable negatives of being in the camp.

He doesn't talk much but he's sweet and perfect to look at. The art on his arms, the only colorful thing in this godforsaken place.

Today has been about mental warfare techniques and weapons. If it wasn't clear before that we're here to be more than just your average soldiers, it was damn obvious today when we learned the intricacies of chemical compounds in the latest technology.

No, we wouldn't be soldiers.

We would be assassins on a massive scale. From our superiors pinning us against each other and denying us meals and basic needs on the daily, they were making us killing machines.

Luckily, learning information was something I could actually do and I had to help Adam with it in secret. He was embarrassed that he didn't understand most of the lesson today and so we kept the reason for our meeting private. He'd helped me out and now I was happy to help him.

"It's almost curfew. I'll see you tomorrow," he says, getting up and giving me a quick kiss on the cheek. He's always so gentle with me. He's two years older than me but he doesn't treat me that way because I'm younger or a girl. He's just a kind person. I smile and wave goodbye.

I go back to playing with my food and am deciding

whether to go to my bunk or not when out of the corner of my eye I see Bran walking over. I remember that Bran had asked to spar with Adam during dinner break as usual-since they were a good physical match for each other-but Adam declined so he could spend time with me instead. Apparently, Bran didn't like that, or anything about me for that matter. He, like everyone else expected me to be weak, but somehow, I've been surviving. I'm not the strongest but like I said, I'm a quick learner.

He was alone and I was alone. This wouldn't be a random show of dominance. This would be personal. This was so not good.

"You think now that Adam has an affinity towards you everything is going to be fine, skank?" he begins slowly. His words are always slow, creepy. I don't answer and try to get up quickly. Even though my body isn't as exhausted today I'm still sore from every other day before, and I'm not quick enough.

I feel a tight pull on my scalp and I'm rammed into the table.

"Look at me when I speak to you," Bran commands with a smirk while holding me up by my brown hair. He leans in and whispers,

"I've had just about enough of you getting in my way." He pulls tighter and I struggle uselessly. Tears start to fall uncontrollably and I feel pain everywhere.

"You want to cry now? Well, you can cry about this," Bran continues in a gruff voice. Instantly I feel a sharp coldness

slice through the skin over my rib cage. I scream from the all-consuming pain, hoping for someone to come help, knowing no one will.

Warm liquid starts to gush out. I fall on the floor blindly, sobbing uncontrollably as he walks away and spits at the floor next to me.

"Go back to where you came from, skank." I touch the place where the liquid is coming from and lift my hand to see blood. Everything starts to turn black, and I think maybe this is how I'm supposed to end.

CHAPTER 3

Ultimate Pepperoni

I wake up from nasty nightmares about the first time I almost died, to a growling stomach. I wish for the millionth time that my nightmares were just figments of my imagination. I look down at my scar and trace it with a fingertip as my stomach growls again, louder this time.

I groan from both. One thing I wanted to ignore but the other I could take care of. I completely forgot to eat yesterday with all the shenanigans going on...and guess what? I'm craving pizza. I didn't even get the chance to take one bite four days ago and thinking about it again totally depresses me.

I get up, feeling the cold floor under my feet, and walk to the small kitchen. A quick search tells me there's nothing but canned foods and non-perishables. I'm so not in the mood for that.

I grab a gun and walk the tunnels to get to the house, hoping it's still clear. Even hoping that my family showed up during the night. I look through the peephole and open the door slowly. It sounds quiet.

I do a quick recon to make sure the whole house is white-eyed freak free. Once I make sure it is, I'm able to calm down a little and put the gun on the elastic waist of my *Transformers* Pjs. A sinking feeling settles in as I realize my parents haven't come back yet.

I get to the kitchen and pull out the bread, peanut butter, and jelly and slather it all together with three layers of bread before stuffing it in my mouth. It's not my extra anchovy pizza but it fills me up. I grab the orange juice from the fridge and start to drink straight from the bottle.

I slowly put it down as I realize my mom isn't here to bitch at me for my bad habits. It makes me smirk and at the same time it makes me worry. Suddenly the mix of PB and J with O.J. doesn't feel so good in my stomach, but I ignore it. I knew it was happening because I haven't eaten in four days, that was why.

Once I'm done I make my way back to the bunker and head down the cold tunnels. These bunkers remind me a little too much of the training camp I was sent to, but hey, there's no place like home, right?

I sit down and realize I need a real plan to get to my family. With no service this is nearly impossible but guess what? I'm H and I'm so good it hurts. No one compares to me and If someone has to free this city of these stinkers it's me, not the government.

I decide to check out the shelters nearby. First thing's first though. I need to stop being lazy and put some actual clothes on. I look down at myself and sigh aloud. Even though I love these Pjs I'm not going to kill anything with them on. They mean too much to me.

I glance at the clothes I threw on the floor last night and upend my backpack. I sort through the mess and decide on my black combat boots, a pair of Military green shorts and a holster belt my dad gave me for Christmas a few years ago that I never got to use. Thank God for having a dad in the military, right? I finish it off with a crop top that proudly reads, *Zombie killer*. It's vintage and come on, it fits the situation.

The nightmares about my almost death had snapped me back to reality and had me face the truth sooner than I wanted, but it's not like I could ignore it anymore. The stinkers were here. I'd probably have to continue to fight these things if I wanted to find my parents.

Senator Cookie could call it a virus but she herself said that the threat needed to be terminated. Well, been there, done that, and damn right I'm wearing the t-shirt. Though it's not like I have much of a choice. When something that used to be human comes at you completely devoid of pupils, with no other thought than to bite your head off, you better believe you need to terminate it, because kids, that's a zombie.

I know what you're thinking, what kind of attire is this to fight zombies? Well, I have an answer for you.

I'm H. I do what I want, when I want, and I look damn good doing it. I pull my bright, white hair into a French braid so it's harder to grab. I load up my guns and stick the knives in my boots.

I stuff a chocolate nutty power bar in a pocket and chuck a few more in my backpack where I'd thrown some other essentials in. I grab the keys and walk once more through the tunnels. I'm ready to roll.

I get to the peephole and look out. I see that the front door is open. Fuck. You can't be serious? These things got in? I grab my gun from my holster and open the door slowly making sure not to make a peep. I need to kill this thing now so I don't have to fight it once I get back.

I walk slowly to see where this little shit is and my head sweeps the area in confusion. I find the whole downstairs clear. I do, however, see that the fridge is open and someone stole the small amount of canned foods my mom had in the pantry. Great, now I have to worry about actual people stealing my stuff. Then again at least there were still other people around.

I walk out the front door to see my black classic beauty still parked in all her glory. I pull out the keys, get in, turn on the ignition, and hear the beast come to life. It brings a smile to my face. I would never get tired of that sound. I start reversing out of the driveway when a little light turns on. Ugh, really? I need gas.

On the corner just outside my neighborhood the typical teenagers are hanging around like they normally do near a fountain. I almost drive right by them but then I remember that normal isn't normal anymore.

Unfortunately, *they* aren't normal anymore either. I realize this as my quick drive-by gives me a crystal-clear picture of big ol' glaring white eyes and one too many rips in their clothes to be considered fashionable. The creatures that once were teens snap their jaws at me as I roll by, but otherwise make no moves. I find it odd that some creatures attack and some don't. Some just stand there, probably where they were infected. I find that pretty sad. Sensing no immediate threat, I decide to leave these guys for later. I have gas to get and a family to find.

I speed for the nearest gas station and find the streets of my once overcrowded city turned into a ghost town. Jeez, cue the tumbleweeds, I think to myself. Three days, now four, I guess...that's all it took to get like this? I don't know why but it's so damn hard to wrap my head around this. The traffic used to be insane, now there's only me. I hear the tires screech as I bank a fast right turn into the station.

I pop the gas cap and jump out the car door. Pulling my credit card from my pocket, I freeze.

One look at the pump's dim lights and I know I'm screwed. I have to head inside and see if I can get some assistance. Yeah, right.

I cock my gun and let it enter the building before I do as I sweep the area. The smell hits me first. Stinkers are here, and by the smell of it, there are a lot of them. I spy the cluster of them by the back door, near the beer aisle.

Slurping and other disgusting noises fly at me from their direction. I hope it's the beer they were sampling and not, like, leftover brains.

Since they aren't chasing me down the block, I figure they're the stationary, dumb kind, and I move on.

The shelves of the gas station have been ravaged and torn apart. Not one speck of food is left behind. I turn my head and find that I'm wrong. There are still three packs of raisins left. I can't really blame the ravagers. Raisins aren't worth the trouble of dealing with stinkers. Pizza on the other hand?

I pull up to the empty counter. "Hello?" I call out for kicks and giggles.

"Any chance there's someone here to get my sweet ride some gas?" When no one responds I nick a spare lighter from the counter and throw it on my belt.

"Help!" A faint voice cries.

I whip around toward the back where the bodies are collected. Could there be a human back there?

Another cry sounds, this one louder. "Please!"

I put my gun back onto the belt and opt for one of my knives. It wouldn't be good to accidentally shoot the poor guy yelling for help. I rush into the pile of bodies, and see glassy blue eyes pleading to me from beneath a pile of stinkers. I let those blue eyes, the first sign of life, guide me, my knife slicing away at the dumb stinkers above him. I cut everything in my path in a frenzy.

I cry out as one of the stinkers claws into my arm. Blood gushes from the wound and it only makes me angrier.

I redouble my efforts and go ham on the remaining creatures. As the bodies fall I'm also trying to avoid the nasty brown slush as best I can but it just isn't a priority right now. I kick a stinker's leg out from under it and then it stumbles and practically falls onto my knife perfectly. When I kick its body to the side, pulling my knife free, I finally see the body with the actual pupils lying on the ground.

He's an old man with grey hair almost as light as mine. His blue eyes look up at me in sheer terror and my only goal is to get him out now.

When the last body falls to the floor and lands on top of the old man, I take a deep breath and pray for some fresh air to get anything but that smell into my lungs. Then I crouch down to pull the zombie off my civilian. I offer him my bloody hand and he weakly holds on. He gasps wildly for air too and all I can do is drag him by the arm until he's free of the gunk and limbs.

"Angel," he cries.

I sit him upright and can't hold back my laughter as I gasp for air. "Never," I reply. I'd never been to heaven. Hell, on the other hand? I probably already had a reputation there.

"No, you are. You saved me," he says in between loud coughs. I eye his ripped gas station uniform and I smirk.

"Yeah, I kind of just need some gas, and I'm kind of in a hurry so it was entirely selfish, I promise. So..."

He gives me an odd look.

"What?" I ask with a shrug. Was I not clear? I've been told I have problems with that, what with my sarcasm and all.

"I need gas," I say slowly.

"The gas has been cut off. I'm...I'm sorry," he coughs out.

I groan and pat his back as gently as I can.

"It's fine." I decide I'll just have to jack a new car as I eye my current car mournfully through the store window. I turn back to the old guy. "Are you, you know, okay?"

"I don't know. Did they get me?"

"Get you?" I ask bewildered. There was something about the way he said it.

"I mean bite me. If they bite me, I'm done for. That's how it starts. I've seen it. I've been cooped up here for days but they found me. The biting. That's how it spreads."

I'm trying to process this information but he grabs my arm suddenly with a strength I wouldn't have expected.

"Okay, buddy, loosen up the grip unless you want to lose an arm," I say with narrowed eyes. I feel bad for him but not enough to allow him to cut off the blood supply to my hand.

He backs away a little and loosens the grip.

"If they bit me, please, you have to kill me. I don't want to be a monster," he says, his once cloudy blue eyes becoming clear and bright.

"Look, I don't think..." I begin then I pause. "Just check yourself for any bites before begging for death, okay?"

"Ok," he says earnestly.

"Maybe a bathroom mirror," I suggest dryly, my eyes heading toward the ceiling. I really don't want to see this old man undress and check for wounds. His clothes are half-torn already and he has blood and stinker gunk on him, which seriously isn't very pleasant.

"Of course," he says as he attempts to stand.

I help him up. "Thank-" he begins.

"Really, it's fine," I say, cutting him off abruptly.

Once he's on his feet and moving, I take a walk toward the window and try to see if there are any cars in or around the street that I can steal.

I hear the creak of the front door opening and I turn around, knife out and ready, but at the sight in front of me I drop it.

"Dad," I say in barely a whisper.

My father stands there, in the same army clothes he'd been wearing the night of the attack and with the aviators he's never without sitting on the bridge of his nose. At my whisper, his head whips toward me.

"Dad," I cry again.

I found him. No, he's found me. The relief that washes through me is so great I can barely breathe.

Before I can take a step toward him he rushes for me, hands out and coming for my throat.

CHAPTER 4

Florentine

As my air supply is suddenly cut off, I consider that this wasn't the kind of embrace I expected. My father's face comes toward mine, his lower jaw unhinged at an odd angle and aiming right for me. I pull my body back as far as I can with him holding me there as I try to avoid the bite.

His teeth chomp down an inch away from my nose, his spit flying out and onto my face. In case you were wondering, zombie smell has nothing on the stench of zombie breath. Even without the ability to breathe, that much was crystal clear.

Struggling against him, I bring my hands in a prayer position and not because I'm suddenly religious. I pull my clasped hands up on the inside of his outstretched arms in order for my elbows to break his chokehold. I manage it but the whole not breathing thing has me dizzy. Gasping for air, I use my hands to grab his head and push him back.

I run behind an aisle, putting a blockade between us as I manage to pull my gun back out. “Dad!” I yell. This literally can't be happening.

“You have to recognize me! It's me, H. Don't you know me?” I beg. I feel wetness running down my cheeks and I push it away.

The thing that was once my father growls and stalks me

through the aisle. I guess that answers my question.

I find myself at the end of the aisle and I feign going right then run left. My dad doesn't miss a beat and he pursues me.

He's smarter than the other stinkers, just like Plastic Chick, the first creature who attacked me. I wonder if his body remembers any of his army training because if it does, I probably won't make it out alive. I'm great but he has more years of training and experience on me. Plus, he wants to hurt me and even now I don't want to hurt him.

"Dad," I try again.

"Please. This isn't you. You can fight this. You have to remember."

I see a small freestanding newspaper cart behind me and I run toward it.

"Remember that time when you took Mom, Justin, and me to the circus?"

Dad chases me down and I begin to wobble the cart. It's heavier than expected but if I can push it enough I can throw it into him and get away while he's distracted.

"We sat in the front row. We got to pet the-" I get to the cart and wobble but it needs more momentum, "-elephants. Then I told you I wanted to be a flying acrobat. You told me I could be anything I wanted. That you love me. Don't you remember?"

It's one of my favorite memories. Justin was just a baby at the time. We were happy. Of course, it was before he shipped me off to the training camp from hell, so he didn't really mean it, but I think at that moment he did and that's what stuck with me.

Before I can blink, Dad growls loudly and charges at me once more. I push the cart but he pushes it back. I scramble but I'm not quick enough and a blinding pain goes through me as I'm crushed from the chest down.

"Dad," I cry desperately but deep down, I know there's no mercy for me.

He pounces on top of me like an animal, digging the shelf even further into my legs. I grit my teeth and pull out my gun.

"Please," I say one last time.

I manage to lift my gun and the only place I can reach is his chest. My hand trembles wildly as I hold it there. I know I can't do this but he doesn't hesitate at all. He lets out a bellowing growl and claws at me. I feel my skin opening over my skull as he tears at me.

I try to move but can't. I already feel the blood trickle down my stinging arms. With the force of the gun I push up on his chin and knock his aviators so they're askew.

This isn't him. His eyes are sickeningly white.

"I love you, Dad. I'm sorry," I say with hot tears streaming down my face.

I pull the trigger.

He claws at me even harder.

"Damn it!" I yell. I pull the trigger again and again. As the fourth-round pumps out, his body slumps over me.

I can't move, can't breathe and I don't want to. My father...I just...I...my brain can't even finish its thought. Tears pour down my cheeks and I just lie there. I'm unable to process what I've done. I want to curl up in a ball. I want to die. Maybe I will, I wonder absently. I'm still stuck under the cart and his body.

Suddenly I hear another door open and close. I hope it's a smart zombie that comes in and not one of the idiots. If death is coming for me I want it to come quickly even though it's no longer what I deserve.

"Angel," a voice calls out. "Can you hear me? I'm going to pull the newsstand off you."

I look up to see the old gas station attendant standing above me. I notice his eyes are still blue and not glaring white. So, he didn't go stinker on me yet. I guess that's good. I can't find the will to care.

He leans over, kicking my father's corpse out of the way. I hear myself whimper but I feel disconnected from it.

Then the old man tries to lift the cart. He pulls and pulls. I just lie there, staring at him. He stands back up and wheezes, grabbing onto his chest. I was already tired of watching this.

I sigh and release my gun at an awkward angle so it clatters to the floor. I've functioned as a hollow shell before in order to survive. I suppose I can do it again now.

"This is ridiculous," I say in a voice I don't even recognize. "Hold on," I continue. I grasp the cart with both my hands and try to slide out from under it. It takes me a few tedious minutes but somehow I manage it as the old man feebly pulls at it from above.

Once I'm free, the old man stares at me. I stare back. I

instantly realize this is the last place I want to be.

"Do you have somewhere safe you can go...um...I didn't catch your name," I say as I wipe at my blood and pick up my weapons, careful to avoid my father's body.

I push down those thoughts and push them down hard. You can't think about that, H, I remind myself.

Block it out, kid. Block it out or you might as well lay back down and die, my brain repeats. I focus completely on the man in front of me like my sanity depends on it, and it does.

"It's Bill, and no, I'm afraid I don't. I live in the apartment above the store," he points up.

"I've lived here alone since my wife died. I usually do take-out. I have no food at home and I don't have a car. The survivors ransacked the store. I can't say I blame them but I haven't wanted to move for fear of the biters. Plus, I have nowhere to go."

I wipe at my clothes and realize it's pointless. I need another shower stat. The smell is definitely rotting away my brain cells.

"Did you think of trying a shelter, maybe?" I ask with what I think is an enormous amount of restraint on my part to hold back my sarcasm.

"You mean a deathtrap? No thank you, young lady. I'm better off out here than being herded like a sheep in there."

I roll my eyes. Why do I bother holding back my sarcasm, I wonder?

"You're one of those," I say.

"You're one of those people who don't trust the government. So, where's your tin foil hat? The aliens might be listening in, ya know."

"Listen here, I've lived a long time and I've earned the right to be skeptical after the things I've seen. Why aren't you in a shelter?" he asks as his eyes narrow on me.

Ok, so he had a point. I didn't trust much either, especially not that Senator Cookie lady. Maybe I could use his assistance. I want Mom and Justin to know I'll be back if they find their way to the house while I'm out.

"I'll take you somewhere safe. It's a secure area and it has food and weapons and is not sanctioned by the United States government. In exchange you have to look after the place while I'm gone."

"Of course! Anything you need," he replies. "Where will you be?"

Oh me? I'll be searching for my mom and brother who are most likely either dead or stinkers but if they aren't, I get to tell them what I've done.

"Don't worry about it." I give him a withering stare.

"You need to do a better job of fighting off the stinkers and thieves. Can you do that, Bill?"

"With weapons and sustenance? Absolutely."

"Fine. I'll hold you to your word. Let's go now." I wipe my brow on my arm and as I'm heading toward the door something stops me. "Do you have paper and a pen?" I ask.

Bill nods. “Behind the cash desk. In the drawer.”

I hop over the desk and get what I need. I scribble out my address and write the words, *Safe haven only. Ravagers will be shot*, on the top.

A little of my blood has dripped onto the page but at least the words are clear. The blood just makes it seem like it was a blood oath but heck, I was giving these people a place to stay.

I stick the note over the three bags of raisins.

I take one last look at my father. I'll come back for you, I swear it, I vow silently.

I turn to the door and don't look back. “Come on, Bill,” I shout.

“I saw what you wrote,” he says softly. “Do you think people will come?”

I honestly didn't know but I had to try to help somehow. Finding Bill just proves that there are more of us alive out there and it was clear that the government was done trying to reach us. These people were defenseless and probably about to go hungry sooner rather than later. Like it or not us humans had to stick together if we wanted to survive this. I shrug, ignoring his question. “Come on, Bill. We've got a hot car to steal.”

Bill Stares at me in amazement. “What do you mean steal?”

I smirk and shrug. “Just what I said,” I say as I keep on walking. I take a last look at my black beauty. “I’ll never forget you!” I scream at her direction and Bill laughs.

We walk for a good 15 minutes till I see a parking lot with a good number of cars. “Can we please take a break, H? I'm too old for this.”

I stare at him and laugh. It's a hollow laugh but it's hard to feel anything at the moment. “We’re almost there but stay here and I’ll go get something nice.”

He stares at me as he hunches over, hands on knees, and begins huffing for air like we just ran a marathon.

“Okay. Sounds great!” He puts his thumb up and I walk away.

I look through the parking lot trying to find something but so far nothing is worthy of me putting my butt on the driver’s seat. I keep on walking until I stumble upon a white BMW M3. Holy mother of cake, I think my heart just healed from my Mustang.

I run to it, gun in hand, just in case there's a stinker inside. I reach the M3 and go for the door. Yes! It's open!

I look around the car to see if the keys are inside or if a stinker had them.

Nothing. Just my luck these days. Some stinker out there was a real bastard.

Thank God I’m the most amazing person in the world because I would’ve been screwed with a major S. I look for the wiring under the steering wheel. I finally locate the wiring harness connector. I pull aside the battery and ignition wire bundle. Then I strip about 1 inch from the battery wires and twist them together. I connect the ignition wire to the battery wire and BOOM! The baby comes to life.

"Yes!" I sigh aloud and put the baby in reverse.

I belatedly hope a stinker hasn't gotten to Bill because that would've made me a horrible babysitter or in this case old man-sitter.

I see Bill still trying to catch some air. I honk at him and watch him react like he's having a heart attack and is about to die on me, which by the way, is hilarious.

"Get in. We don't have a lot of time. I don't want to be out here while it's dark."

He opens the door and gets in. His eyes flick over the ignition in surprise. "H, how did you turn on the car if you don't have the keys?"

I glance in his direction and lock the doors. "Bill, sorry to tell you but I'm a convict. I escaped during the outbreak and this gave me a chance to be free." I smile brightly.

His eyes get so big I swear to God they're going to fall out.

"I'm kidding. Jesus. Don't die on me." I turn back to him quickly. "But seriously, don't worry about it." I put my eyes back on the road and speed away.

We finally get home, passing the same teenage stinkers on the corner. I wave as we go by and they snap their jaws. Bill shrinks himself down in his seat and looks at me like I'm deranged. He's probably not wrong but he has no room to judge. On the way here, Bill filled me in on what he'd seen since the attacks.

The day after the bomb sirens, tanks led by the armed services began filling the streets picking up survivors to bring to shelters and clearing the roads of any cars or blockages. Bill said they came into his home to collect him but he saw them coming and he hid downstairs in the store. I told him that was insane but he didn't seem to hear me.

He also heard the ravagers that ransacked the gas station two days ago. That was the last he'd seen of anyone. The men and women came in with weapons so he stayed hidden. They were saying they'd been to Reagan airport but all the planes were either gone or damaged. The airport itself was filled with people infected with the virus.

They said the union station was overrun with the virus too. The walls were preventing them from getting out. He didn't know what happened to them after they left. The only thing he knew was that when he got hungry earlier today he risked getting bitten by going to the frozen aisle for food. They caught him and that's when according to him I saved the day, or whatever.

I park the car on the driveway and manage to turn it off. "Wait here, Bill," I say, taking out my gun and walking towards my house.

I know there's nothing wrong but it doesn't hurt to be safe. Plus, I have this stupid hope that Mom or Justin will be there.

I open the door and make sure the house is empty. I try not to attach any emotion to the fact that it is. I come outside and see Bill sitting in the car.

"Come in, Bill," I shout.

He walks over. "I seriously need to get you some clothes

and you need a shower," I mutter. Bill follows me over to the bunker and I show him the complicated way to get in. I give him one of the spare rooms that are down here and tell him to wait as I head upstairs to find him some clothes.

I go up to my parent's room and stand right in front of their closet. With shaking hands, I open my dad's side. I search blindly through the clothes because all I can think of is his lifeless body on the ground with those white eyes.

I killed my father. I didn't have much of a choice and I know him, I know he wouldn't want to live like that but still, that was my dad. I just have to live with it somehow. I don't know how I'll deal if Mom or Justin were bitten.

I needed to find them. I grab a bundle of clothes that look like they would fit Bill and run downstairs.

I really can't bear the memory of my dad and the fact I killed him. I renew my vow to go back and give him a proper burial. I open the bunker and find Bill immediately. He's just where I left him. He's got this constant deer in the headlights look that almost makes me want to laugh.

"Here you go," I say, throwing the clothes on his small bed and then moving to leave.

"H, that man you killed at the gas station, did you know him?" his voice asks curiously as it follows me.

I feel hot tears starting to form in my eyes. I don't dare turn around to face him. "I don't want to talk about this," I say and walk out.

I go to my room and take a long shower. I wonder if I can live with what I've done. If my family is somehow alive, how can I face them? I start sobbing with my head under the running water.

I know better than to let my emotions control me but this is my family. My little brother is only 10. I might never get to see him get his first girlfriend and freak her out until she dumps him. I might never see him graduate. Our father would never see that either. My mother, if she's even alive, will go to bed alone every night. This is reality. I wait under the hot spray as sobs wrack my body. I cry until there's nothing left.

I get out of the shower and put on a lame t-shirt I find along with some comfy sweats. I lay down on the somewhat comfortable bed and indulge in my thoughts. I really hope my mom and Justin are alive but after tonight I no longer have hope for anything. I need to accept that I'm alone. I finally close my eyes and drift into oblivion.

I swerve out of arm's reach and then elbow my opponent hard in the face. This is street fighting on our lunch break. There are no rules here. His nose starts gushing blood and I hear a gasp or two from the crowd around us but I don't care.

Seeing my opportunity, I go in for the kill. I've kicked him back and now he's under me, my hands around his throat. His sweat-slicked body is pinned beneath me and I can practically feel the pain he's in radiating off him. I look over his bloodied face and when our eyes meet, he gasps as if he's seen something beyond comprehension. Maybe he has. I have no emotion now, no fear. No weakness. This is how I am now.

The second that blade went through my body, I changed. I may not have died but it was too close. When I woke up, my world had tilted on its axis and everything became clear. I was no longer content to have my life messed with so easily. The sweet little teenage girl was gone.

I would be stronger. I would fight harder. I would never give in. I decide that since I'm in hell anyway, I might as well learn how to fight and win. I know I've gone over the edge and there is no way back.

After wishing I had died, I realized that maybe I could use my new emotionally bankrupt persona to do something good. I know I can help the people who need it. I can help end this war. That's the ultimate goal for me now.

It's what I think but it's never what I say because in here, it's all a game. To win this game I have to pretend I'm a sociopath like the rest of them, and so far, I'm pulling it off nicely.

I'm H now. I'm alive now. Nothing else matters now.

On top of him, I lift up, squeezing his neck tighter, and use my knee to dig into his solar plexus. His hand immediately flies to the side and taps the ground. Understanding the signal, I pop up and wipe the blood off my hands, ready for more.

"Who's next?" I yell to the crowd.

I look down at my opponent. He's still lying there.

I offer him my hand to help him up but when he sees me coming he scrambles away. I laugh because I'm able to do this now, strike fear into men twice my size.

I know they think I'm insane and I'm glad. I will survive like this. I'm going to be the best assassin this world has ever seen. It's the only thing keeping me from crashing in on myself now and never crawling back out.

When no one comes forward to fight me I scan the crowd and spot Bran, the cowardly stabber himself. Without warning I bolt towards him, determined to take him down. I pounce and with my knee over his throat, I use a maneuver he once used on me and hold his head still by grasping his hair. With my other hand, I pull out my knife.

"What the fuck?" he shouts as he gasps for air with shallow breaths.

I dig my knee in deeper. I could kill him but I wasn't a monster. One of us was, but it wasn't me. I wouldn't let him take that from me too. Besides, in social warfare there are worse things than death.

"Make a truce with me or I'll succeed where you failed with your knife, asshole!" I threaten. He pushes and he's damn strong but I haven't given up most of my sleep and any free time to train with Adam for nothing. Brute strength isn't everything. I'm not budging.

I spy Adam running through the crowd to get to us but I wave the knife hand out to him to tell him to pull back. I almost died because of this scum. I deserved this. I was doing it. I poise the knife over Bran's face.

"Fuck you, skank. You don't have the balls," he spits out. His blue eyes blaze and in their depths, I swear I see amusement. He's enjoying this.

"Wrong answer," I say and slice cleanly over his eyebrow. Not too deep but enough to sting and scare the hell out of him. I smile as he cries out in pain and shock. I stare into his eyes, waiting, and I see when he notices the change in mine.

I continue waiting, unblinking, until he finally opens his mouth. "Fine, princess. Truce. Now get the fuck off me."

"Gladly," I say and wink at him. I walk away, letting everyone know that I'm not afraid to turn my back on anyone, not even Bran. I've got this shit on lock.

Adam follows me and stands against the doorway of my cabin. He stares at me for a while before he reaches out and takes my hand. "You did good, H. Just be careful. Okay?"

I nod. Adam has changed since my stabbing too. He wasn't handling shit as well anymore.

He's been even more quiet, more distant, except when he has random outbursts of rage. He's always been intimidating but now he's bordering on unstable.

He scared people as much as I did. He started taking a lot of walks on his own too.

I didn't blame him. I had to be strong enough for the both of us now. I would be.

CHAPTER 5

Five Cheese

I wake up to a faint knocking on my door. “H?” I hear Bill’s quiet voice call out.

“Ugh I'm coming,” I say sleepily. I look in the mirror to see dry saliva on the side of my face and my hair looks like it needs a good brushing. I scrub my face but leave my hair a mess. My growling stomach has other plans.

I open the door to find Bill still waiting on the other side. “And what is it you need that you had to summon me from my slumber?” I ask, staring down at him.

Now that I have a minute, I notice that Bill is such a small old man. Now that he's showered he's kind of adorable. I wish I could put him in my pocket and pet his head. Something about him seems different though.

“Why are your eyes purple?” I yell out as it occurs to me. They had definitely been blue before. The color wasn’t so different now but I couldn’t ignore it when my eyes were the same shade of purple too.

“I don’t know. I was hoping you would tell me,” he answers softly.

I scoff. “How should I know?”

“Well, you have purple eyes. I don’t know. I thought maybe you...I’m not sure.”

“I haven’t done anything except save your life. What? Are

you accusing me of putting food coloring into your eyeballs at night?" I laugh. "You're a treat, Bill."

"Well, why do you have purple eyes?" he asks, not wavering from his purpose.

I frown. Never mind about the adorable comment.

I have no idea what's happening to you or me, I want to shout but I don't. Above all things I hate thinking someone could get the best of me. I'm H and the day you make me admit to being wrong or ignorant is the day I might as well just throw in the towel.

"You woke me up to ask me that stupid question?" I sputter out.

"People have different colored eyes. Get over it. As for your eyes? I haven't got a clue. I've done nothing but save your ass from a horde of stinkers and considering how early it is right now and your bizarre line of questioning I'm starting to wonder why I bother to do nice things at all."

He continues to stare at me and I make a move to brush my hair out of my face so I don't have to look at him anymore. That question shook me to my core. I didn't know why his eyes were suddenly purple. How the hell could I explain that if I didn't have the answers myself?

"Actually, I woke you up because I made breakfast and I thought we could go look for survivors or anyone we could help."

That didn't seem like a bad idea and it was something that had been rolling around my mind since I figured the government wouldn't be helping anyone not in a shelter by now, but I had other plans. I needed to find Mom and Justin. Maybe I could do both?

I give him a menacing look for good measure and then walk out. "Food now. Talk later," I say walking past him out of the bunker and towards the kitchen of my house. Someone had done some exploring. I stare at the plate of PB&J sandwiches. At least the old man had a good taste in food.

I sit down and grab my sandwiches. "Number one, you're not leaving here," I say.

"Number two, I'm going to go do whatever you said but I don't need a sidekick. You stay here. I'll leave you a knife but just stay here, okay? If anything happens, lock yourself in the bunker. I need to find my mom and brother and then I'll come for you." I can't believe I just admitted that.

Normally I don't reveal anything of myself or my plans but there's something about this old man that makes me feel like I can trust him and that I should reassure him.

He stares at me and shrugs. "That's fine, I guess," he says.

I finish my food and chug down my orange juice. "Okay then." I get up and walk to my room.

I run through my daily exercise routine, keeping my body honed and on point. The routine helps me feel like myself and frees me from thoughts of purple eyes or feelings of crushing guilt. After that I finally manage to brush my hair and make it flawless like it always is.

Then I look at my pile of clothes and weapons as I think about my plans. I really need to do something to get my head together. I get dressed and walk toward the house's entrance. Before I leave I teach Bill how to open the door to the bunker and make him show me at least three times before I'm satisfied.

"Bye, Bill. See ya later," I say while looking out the peephole, gun in hand.

"Bye, H. Be safe," I hear faintly.

"Yeah yeah yeah," I mutter under my breath. I open the door quietly and walk out. I get to the M3 and manage to hot-wire it again. I seriously needed a new ride with keys. If a stinker was chasing me, taking time to hot-wire wouldn't cut it.

I sit in the driver's seat for a good five minutes just staring into nothing before I realize that I haven't listened to any music in what feels like forever. I turn on the radio and, of course, static comes on. Talk about radio silence.

I click on the audio button and notice the previous owner had a CD in. I press play and guess what song comes on. Come on, guess it. "Three Little Birds" by Bob Marley. God damn it was I in I am Legend? All I needed was a dog. Come to think of it, I realize there are no pets wandering the streets either. I saw some in the footage with their owners but I'm still a little worried about any animals that might be left out there.

I put the car in reverse and realize I'm not quite ready to face Mom and Justin. I doubt I'll find them right away but there's a chance I do, and I can't do that just yet. Yesterday was too hard. If they're alive then I can't face them and if they're zombies then I don't want to have to face that either.

I need to calm my mind. An idea sparks and I smile.

I'm going shopping.

For one thing it's a girl's instinct and for another, everything's basically free. I speed down the roads till I see a small comic book store. "Jackpot!" I say as I pull into a parking space.

I take out my gun and open the door. A little bell rings as I slip inside. If there were stinkers I wanted to see them before they saw me. The damn bell kind of made that hard, though.

When nothing comes running at me, I figure I'm okay. Plus, the place smells decent so there's a good chance it's stinker free. There are blood and gunk stains on some parts of the floor, but I do my best to avoid them.

I walk in and grab a couple comics. I just love these things. Then I notice a katana scabbard right there, right behind the register. It has a carrying strap and everything.

"Oh yes," I say, making little grabby hands.

I jump over the counter and slide it out of its scabbard to examine the blade. It worries me that it's still here. Either I'm really lucky or there were less humans alive than I figured because this should have been pilfered by now.

I hope I'm just lucky. I run my fingers down the shiny steel and realize I really want it. Mom would never let me buy one of these. She thinks I'd probably decapitate Justin, which is true.

I sigh at the thought and swing the strap over one shoulder and let it hang around on my back. It's heavy and kind of impractical if I need to grab the thing quickly for a fight but it'll do.

I grab the comics on the counter and leave. As I'm exiting the small store I see my reflection. "Damn girl, you look good," I say, winking at myself. This kick ass, take katanas and comic books life was really working for me.

I get in the car, take the time to re-hot wire and hear the Bob Marley CD for the millionth time. Okay, I loved him but I needed something new. I'm about ready to choke myself. There was literally one beat in the entire song.

I pull out from the parking space and head onto the main road. I quickly get to the mall that's about 5 minutes from my house and pull up to my favorite bookstore. I get out of the M3 and basically run to the entrance as usual with my gun in hand. I also realize I need to get some more and should stop by the Bass Pro Shop or a weapons store to see what I can scrounge up.

I open the doors to the wonderful wonderland of books. Even with this shitty stinker invasion on the outside, everything in this place is still amazing.

I walk in slowly to make sure the area is clear. To my right, two stinks stand around. I immediately assess that they are the dumb kind though, so I know they aren't going to be a bother. I walk through the Teen Fantasy and Adventure aisle to find a couple of books and I stick them in my bag.

I keep strolling around, enjoying the smell of the books and from the corner of my eye I see a young guy with his head down, pacing the store. He looks awful and his clothes are pretty torn up but I'm not judging. I'm just happy to find someone around my age to talk to.

"Hello?" I call out, keeping my distance and analyzing him. I slowly get close enough to see his torn clothes are also splattered with blood.

He looks up sharply and his piercing white eyes are on me. I open my mouth to say something but can't gather the words. I turn to run only to realize I'm too late.

I thump to the ground with his weight on me and try to keep him from snapping my face off. I try to push him off but for some reason he seems much heavier than he looks. I manage to scramble back and on a nearly forgotten reflex, pull out the trench knife in my boot.

"I don't want to do this again," I cry out with a saddened tone as I get to my feet. This is so totally my fault. I should've just grabbed my books and CDs and gone on my way.

He charges at me causing me to lose balance but I quickly regain it and snap into battle mode. I take a swing at him and miss since he's much faster on his feet. Why stinkers have this ability I don't know. It makes me feel like I don't have a chance and maybe it's time for me to give up. Then again, if I gave up I wouldn't be H, would I?

I groan and swing the knife, dodging his advances. Then I manage to plunge the knife into his leg. He drops to one knee and growls. "I'm sorry, you sort of deserved it," I say and somehow he gets up, his eyes even more calculating as he pulls the trench knife out of his leg. He drops it on the ground and charges at me like the injury didn't happen. He viciously grabs at me, managing to wrench my arm badly. I groan, freeing my arm from his grasp. Then relying on the instincts that have been ingrained in my mind, I ignore the pain and pull my gun from my belt as I'm dodging his advances.

I take a shot and miss.

Damn it, I did it on purpose. I don't want to shoot him. Yet that won't stop him from attempting to kill me, nothing will now. I steady myself and as my mind goes blank I stare back into his white eyes, matching his cold determination. I hold my finger on the trigger calculating the right moment to end this.

He pulls himself up and runs right towards my gun. I manage to get the shot I've been waiting for. Then as if in slow motion, I watch his body fall to the ground.

I put my gun down and look at his lifeless body, unable to rationalize what's going on. Part of me knows if I left him alive, he would attack someone else. He was a monster. I couldn't save him but I could save the next person that walks in and can't protect themselves the way I can from becoming one too.

As much as I'm trying to run away from my mind and not be this killer I was trained to be, this is a game of survival. I just can't believe I hesitated at all. I'm still not emotional in any sense of the word, that was stripped from me long ago, but I've let the past two years of civilian life soften me up some.

I breathe in and realize I have to toughen up. There's no room for weakness anymore. This guy, whoever he was, didn't deserve this. None of the affected did but moping around won't help them or me. It will only get me killed faster and I have no intention of going down. I will find my mom and brother and I will get them back safe.

I walk quickly, making sure I haven't forgotten anything and making sure there's nothing else creeping around and ready to pounce. I gather what I want and stick it all into my bag, especially all the CDs I came for in the first place. As I'm walking away I look behind me, telling myself I shouldn't feel guilty for pulling the trigger. As I look at him I see a lanyard sticking out of the guy's pants right next to my nearly forgotten trench knife.

Given the current state of affairs, potential car keys are too tempting to pass up. Quick as lightning I get close to him, avoiding the dark pool of goop coming from his rotting body. I hold my breath, hoping he doesn't suddenly come back to life and end me. Then I pull the lanyard out.

There are keys attached just like I suspected. I clench the lanyard in my hand, grab the trench knife and run to the exit so I can take a deep breath full of clean air. I walk outside to the parking lot trying to clear my mind and start clicking the emergency alarm button on the car. I follow the sound to a dark red Mustang GT sitting under a tree.

Jackpot.

I sure love exotic cars but nothing fulfills me more than American muscle. I get in and fix the seat to my new ride. I decide to deem her Daredevil.

I turn the ignition on to hear the beauty roar to life and

then I see it. A full tank...finally, something is going my way.

I start adjusting my mirrors and catch a glimpse of my appearance. As I wipe off the grime and blood off I see tears rolling down my face. I take a deep breath and pull myself together. I can't keep fighting my mind.

Whatever is going on got to my dad, got to too many citizens, and ripped their lives away. I can't feel guilty. I can't let my emotions get in the way. The only way for me to justify what I've done is to get answers. I finish adjusting the mirror and nod at myself. My dad would've done the same for me. He would've found answers. He would have fought to keep living so he could get help.

I can't let him down.

I also didn't lose years of my life and endure torment just to cry and mope in a car now. I throw my head back into my seat and close my eyes. I grip the steering wheel tightly, trying to calm my racing mind.

When I feel resolved, I reverse out of the parking space and speed off just to feel the adrenaline boost. I know now that someone needs to fix this shitshow. So, it's going to be me.

I'm on what usually is a major highway and see that some cars are stopped, abandoned in the middle of the street. I race around them for the thrill until I'm bored and take the next exit.

I wish I could lure stinkers out into the roads and just run them down like bowling pins too. It didn't sound like too bad of a plan, actually. I notice the burned down buildings and the wreckage that the fires I heard about left behind. I can even smell the lingering stench of smoke through the air vents as I drive by. It makes me a little queasy to think about all the chaos that's happened and what my city has now become.

I also notice the giant walls that surround D.C. in nearly every direction I drive and I know it must cover every square inch of land that could lead out of here. I don't even have to be close to see them either. The walls are huge and stick out like mountains from miles away.

I'm driving along aimlessly, lost in my thoughts when I realize what street I'm on. The rusty red brick building catches my eye.

Before I know what I'm doing, I stomp on the brakes and the car screeches at me with the sound of rubber on metal as it careens to a halt. "Holy hot wheels, Daredevil," I laugh as my body jerks forward roughly. Thank God for seatbelts. I pull my gun out of the cup holster and thank God for guns while I'm at it.

Normally, I wouldn't have ruined such a beautiful joy ride but this was kind of an emergency. I'd found myself in front of Georgia's Pizzeria.

I stare at the storefront in awe from the inside of my car. All I'd been craving in these past two days from hell was pizza. Now it was right in front of me.

I nearly get out and run but then I remember the whole stinker thing. I check to make sure the coast is clear. Of course, it's not. There's a stinker standing a few doors down by the bank. I didn't know if he was the smart or stupid type but with pizza on the line, I'm willing to take my chances.

Leaving the keys in the ignition, because who's going to steal it, I slide my katana from the passenger seat where I have to lay it down while I'm driving. Then I pull it to my back as I get out. It worries me more than I want to think about that I haven't seen a single human except for Bill. There were some ransackers, sure, but they might be gone or bitten too. Who knew?

Was this going to be my existence now? I was banking on the shelters having actual humans in them but I couldn't think about that right now.

"Pizza, H. Think of the pizza," I remind myself out loud. If Georgia's alive, I'm going to ask for a serious raise for coming back to work during a zombie apocalypse.

I saunter past the stinker, giving it a wide berth. I found that any distance where I couldn't smell them was the perfect distance for me. The man moved closer to me. He looked to be about in his 30's and his skin had a grayish-greenish tint to it as though it were truly rotting. Yuck!

His white, blank eyes whip toward me and I can't stop my cringe but I keep my gun hand steady. He growls and snarls and throws his hands out to grab me. I pull the gun back, not wanting to waste ammo and pull out my katana.

With a heave, I hack at his grabbing arm. Knowing the drill now, I back away before the brown ooze can splash me. He makes a squawking cry like a crow and reaches with his other arm. I slice that one off too. His cry pierces my ears and I stab him through his chest until he's down and stays down.

I wipe my katana on his clothes and glance down to check my own outfit. Still clean. I laugh and run to the door of the pizzeria, avoiding the glittering glass of the broken windows that covers the surrounding area. “Nice try, sucker,” I yell with a look back.

And suddenly I'm tackled to the ground. “Oh, damn it!” I cry as the breath is knocked from my lungs. I manage to lift my head and feel the weight of what has to be five stinkers converging on me until my cheek is pushed down hard to the ground.

I feel grubby hands all up on me, and all I can do is move my katana around as I hope that I won't become a stinker too. After frantically moving my katana around like it’s the end of the world, I find purchase and shove it in deep until the movement stops. I drag myself out from under the bodies and stand up.

Breathing harshly, I fold over myself and notice I was literally squashed by one really large stinker. I laugh so hard my intestines start laughing with me. I take in one deep breath, facing away from the stinker, and hope Georgia somehow found her way back here.

She can just make me a sweet slice or eight of my favorite pizza. I open the doors to the pizza place and the horrid smell hits me like a brick to the face.

I make my usual check of the area. Remember Plastic Chick? Yeah, she’s rotting in the corner where I left her. Insane guilt hits me but I push it back.

I walk over some of the dead bodies, avoid the huddled stinkers in the corner, and start to look for Georgia. I can save her, like I saved Bill. I had to at least try.

"Georgia, where are you?" I ask with my katana in hand, paying extra attention to my surroundings. I'm dead set on not getting squished to death by a fat stinker. It's a bad way to go.

I walk around getting a little anxious and out of nowhere I hear the glorious noise of pans clanging together in the kitchen.

"Yes! There is life!" I say to myself as I cautiously walk over.

"Georgia!" I scream out, walking into the kitchen as I open the double doors. I notice an old woman with grey hair I don't recognize standing by the sink but not moving. I hope it's an actual person. I can't tell because the whole place smells as it is. Plus, I am so not accepting the fact that all I have is a defenseless old man to keep me company. I'll die from hearing back-in-my-day-stories long before a stinker can do me in.

"Hello, ma'am. I don't know if you've noticed but Washington D.C. is under attack and I'm pretty sure it's not time to be doing dishes," I say. The lady turns around and she's a stinker, but worst of all she's Georgia.

CHAPTER 6

Extra Anchovies

The front of her apron is splattered with brown gunk. Her hair is down and matted to her face and scalp. I'd never known it was grey because she always wore her hair net and chef hat. Her eyebrows had been dark. How would I have known?

I stand there with millions of emotions going through me. "Oh my God. Georgia, no," I say feeling kind of teary-eyed.

"You knew how to make the perfect pizza. Please tell me this is a joke," I beg, approaching her.

All she replies is "Grr-err-ahh-rgg."

Well damn.

I back up and stare at her. "Seriously? Is that what your vocabulary consists of now?" I know I'm being irrational, fighting with a stinker but I have literally had it up to my eyeballs with bad news and I'm losing my patience.

She growls and walks towards me with grabby hands. I hate that she's a stinker. Yes, I wanted pizza but she was kind of also one of my only friends, if you could call her that. I was pissed at her for letting herself get bitten.

It was shitty for both of us but it was a fact. She was a damned stinker. I knew I owed her something even if she wouldn't understand it.

Still, before I say it, I make sure no one is around. I'm sad, not stupid. "Georgia, my real name is Harmony," I finally confess to my boss. Yes, Harmony. A stupid name given to a girl who's the violent type. It's hard to go through military training with a name like Harmony.

You don't see girls named Peace or Love in the ranks so I sure as hell wasn't going with that name anymore. Her white eyes stare back at me, unblinking, the usual creepy stinker status in full effect. I don't know why I bothered.

I wonder if I have to kill her but I don't think she'll hurt anyone. I think she's the dumb kind of stinker. For some reason, some of the stinkers are violent and vicious and some just...aren't.

I don't want to kill her if I don't know that she really is a threat. Then again, I doubt she wants to live like this. I'm not sure and I really haven't been feeling right about playing God and deciding who or what gets to live or die thus far. I decide to trust my gut on this one.

I move past her cautiously and head towards the huge fridge, fingers crossed that I can find something to salvage from inside. I open the fridge and sag in all too real relief. Beautiful dough, reasonably fresh assorted toppings, and jars of her famous red sauce stare back at me. It's like I found the holy grail. I stuff all I can into a bag I find, along with one of the brick oven pans, careful not to turn my back on the stinker that was Georgia.

I find some bottled waters from the mini fridge, apocalypse

gold, and shove them in my bag too. They'll be a good resource to keep in Daredevil while I'm driving around. Plus, I'm pretty thirsty. Still, they would in no way make up for the fact that I still had no pizza in my stomach.

When I'm satisfied with my bag, I look back at her. "I'm sorry," I say, grabbing the ingredients, ready to get the hell out of here. It's not much but it's all I can think of right now.

I shudder as I yank open the door to Daredevil and get in. I place my bag of goodies in the seat next to me along with my katana and buckle it all up tight in a seat belt.

What am I going to do? I'm craving pizza like I'm craving my next breath. And while I have all the ingredients, I have no Georgia to put them together. I didn't even look for my mother or brother and lastly, I still don't know how to get out of D.C.

I know that I can't stay cooped up in my house forever and maybe it's Bill's paranoia talking in my head but I don't want to stay in a shelter either. I have a feeling that once I'm in one, I won't be able to leave and search for my family. Today was a bust on just about every level.

I put my darling in reverse and head back to the house. Once I'm in the driveway I breathe in the smell of the sauce for comfort. I realize I have to go see Bill. He had this way of making me feel bad for leaving him and I didn't know why. Hopefully he hasn't left and taken all of my food supply.

I knock on the door and hear Bill struggling on the other

side. “H, I'm glad you’re back,” Bill says with that old guy, wobbly smile of his.

“Anyone come by?”

“No,” he states.

“Hmm, take this,” I say, handing him the bag. “And be extra careful with it. I’m going to go shower. Rough day,” I mutter, walking past him. I begin my descent down to the bunker and into my room.

Out of curiosity I turn on the TV to the news, which we surprisingly still had. I start undressing, ready to put on some comfy sweats but I pause at what I see on the screen. Like before, all the stations seem to be featuring a clip they keep playing over and over again. I find a channel that looks like the beginning of the clip and tune in time to see Senator Cookie posted up on her stupid podium with a look of sadness and regret on her face.

“Yes, all Washington D.C. residents are safe and the bomb shelters are necessary. It is with heavy hearts that we announce the decision we’ve taken to bomb the nation’s Capital to eliminate the virus. In less than five days at 12:01 a.m. Monday night, we will do so. Due to the rapid rate of contamination and the growing number of residents affected by this as well as the residents still unaccounted for, it is imperative that we take immediate action while we still can. Again, it is absolutely urgent. If you’d like to send food or supplies to help the survivors, we will be delivering them to the government sanctioned shelters this week. While the shelters are well stocked, we can always use more to get them through the bombings until it is safe to go outside once more. Time is ticking to help those in need."

Less than 5 days? 5 days! I look at the time at the bottom of the screen. It was 7:13 p.m. but this announcement went live at 7 p.m. sharp. I had less than 101 hours until the city was bombed. Holy shit.

She turns to the crowd, her serious demeanor turning into one of sympathy.

"I understand how difficult this is. As a resident myself, I worry for my friends and family members back home but I believe in our government and I know their actions are entirely necessary and just. As a member and head of the emergency border patrol I am very confident that the residents are all in shelters and that they will be safe there. There will be no further questions at this time."

I quickly turn the TV off and forget the fact I was taking my pants off when I run out of my room screaming like a frantic lunatic. "Bill!!!!" I run into every room and he appears out of the kitchen.

"H, is something wrong?"

I stop and stare incredulously at him. He did not just ask that after I'd screamed like I was on fire. What was I going to do with this guy?

"No shit, something's wrong. The government is bombing the damn city in basically 4 days instead of getting us out of here," I say very loudly just in case he can't hear me. His blank stare remains on his face like a painting.

Finally, he says, "Oh," with no emotion whatsoever.

"Bill, are you okay?" I ask, knowing he's probably in shock.

He doesn't respond. Jeez. I need him to pull it together. I try another tactic. "I'm sure there are people holed up in their own houses who are too afraid to venture out to shelters."

Bill still won't even acknowledge that I'm speaking so I start to poke him with every word I say. "We. Need. To. Get. Everyone. Out."

"Out?" he says, starting to hyperventilate. His shallow breaths become wheezy and it makes me cringe.

"Bill, breathe. It's okay. I got it," I say sitting him down. Mentally I'm obsessing over the fact that soon my city will be completely obliterated. I haven't eaten in a while and I realize it's dark out. I've never really ventured out while it was dark. Well, I guess I'll just have to make tonight an exception and the food, unfortunately, will have to wait.

I leave Bill to catch his breath and I jog to my room. I look in the mirror and realize I have to pull my act together before Bill dies on me. I have to give the old man a break. He actually deals with my craziness.

I rush to the bathroom, turn the sink on, and listen to the running water. I sigh and splash my face, causing all the dirt and grime to disappear. I connect with my creepy purple eyes I'm still not used to in the mirror. I don't understand why this happened to me but in the grand scheme of things it just isn't that important. I needed to make a real plan here.

I've made it this far for a reason, and I can't let all my training go to waste. Deciding it's now or never, I grab my katana, who I've gotten extremely attached to after she saved me from the giant stinker. I load my gun with ammo and put it on my belt that I've re-secured along with my pants. I grab an energy bar and another pocket knife and stuff them into my black backpack, leaving just enough room on my back from my katana holster.

Then I make my way towards the bunker's living room.

"Bill, I'll be back. Calm down. Make some tea. Write a poem or something." I look back at his expression and hopelessness has entered into the lines of his face.

"I'll get us out. I promise," I add as I head to the bunker door. I look out the peephole and see everything's clear.

Before I run out the front door, I rummage through the kitchen pantry to find a small flashlight, which might come in handy. I open the door quietly and walk out.

I feel the soft, cold breeze I haven't felt in the past few weeks and stare up at the full moon in the dark sky. I smile and take a deep breath.

I run quickly to the houses nearby to see if I find any living beings but after I go thoroughly through all 44 houses in this neighborhood, I've got nothing but a dead goldfish. All the houses here are about the same. I live in suburbia and when I drive into the neighborhood next to mine, I'm not surprised to find these houses look the same too. They're also empty. There aren't any signs of anyone recently being home either.

I'm stumped and I can only pray that those shelters are chalk full of people. I decide that checking the shelters and asking around if people are missing is better than trying to go through every house in D.C.

It's eerily dark out now and the street lamps are my only source of light besides my flashlight. I'm thinking I should be extra cautious when in the corner of my eye I see a young woman around my age looking around and walking swiftly.

A person! A real person. Just as fast as I think this, I freeze. I've been fooled so many times. I had to stop reacting like life was normal and remember that some stinkers were more life-like than others. Even though I knew this I kept hoping for something different.

Then it occurs to me that if she is still a person, she may need help. She was walking alone at night and she may not know about the city's scheduled date with doom. I decide to stay where I am and call out to her from far away. Maybe she wasn't a stinker or if she was, maybe she wasn't the kind that attacked. Distance might be helpful just in case.

"Hey!" I scream out. She stops and turns her head just a bit as if trying to figure out what I'm saying. Maybe I wasn't loud enough. “Hey, over here,” I shout even louder.

She stays in that position for what I can say is an eternity and then I hear a soft clicking sound. Soon she’s heading toward me. It's not a minute before I’m staring headlong into her eyes of nothingness.

Just great. Why I keep trying to help I have no idea. She turns her face to the side and makes the clicking sound one more time before she starts sprinting toward me faster than I can comprehend.

I reach for my katana a little too late before her significant weight lands on top of me and she's snapping her jaws in my face, exposing the faded bite mark on her neck. She’s inhumanly fast. It’s not fair.

I manage to get on top of her and mash her head against the cold asphalt but it only manages to make her just a bit more enraged. The claws come out, literally. Her fingers are broken but it doesn't stop her from trying to attack my body with them.

I punch her as hard as I can, drawing some gunk out from her face but she manages to get out from under me. I crawl as fast as I can to reach my katana. She frantically slashes at my arm and takes a piece of my top with her.

“You jerk, this was my favorite shirt,” I say, pulling up on an elbow and turning around with the katana. I use the force of the turn to cut her head off in one powerful motion.

I fall back to my side and lie there, breathing heavily on the asphalt. I stand up on shaky knees, still trying to catch my breath, and realize I'm way too tired for this shit. I collapse back to the ground. I start to close my eyes. It feels good and cold but I know I have to fight to get my ass into my car, even though I don't have the fight in me.

I know there are other stinkers around. It's too dark out to see them and my flashlight has completely disappeared on me, but for once I'm grateful I can smell them. As a matter of fact, I should be starving but that smell kills my appetite too.

I make myself look up and through hazy eyes I see a two-story house in front of me. With every ounce of energy I can gather from the last bit of my adrenaline, I force myself to get up and race towards the door. I open it, grateful it's unlocked, and see the most comfortable pale blue couch. I collapse onto it and drift off into a deep sleep.

●○●○●○●○●○●○●○●○●○●

"Pack up, maggots. You'll be shipped out to the airport in 3 hours. You don't have to go home to your pathetic lives but you can't stay here," Colonel Croft spits the words out sharply, his face cold and assessing as always. He looks around the mess hall as if he could kill those of us left at camp with his lingering stare.

I hear the mutters all around me and they echo my own thoughts. We're leaving? But why? We were close to the end of training but we hadn't gotten orders to be assigned for the war. It sounded like we were just...leaving.

"When should we expect to get shipped out to our assignments, sir? When will we hear from you?" I ask loudly amid the many questions being asked.

"War's over. We won," the colonel barks out.

The room is silent as his words sink in. Then the room erupts in shouts and cheers. Beside me I hear the small sigh of relief from Adam and when I turn to him he squeezes my hand under the table. I nod but I can't find the words to say. The only other person who doesn't look happy or surprised, even, is Bran. Then again, he rarely gives away any emotions and hell if I care what that degenerate thinks.

Colonel again addresses the room at large saying,

"The president has recalled all troops and pulled our funding. Now, all of you, get the hell going. Now!" he shouts. "We may not be fighting but you will still obey my damn orders."

"Over?" I sputter as a flurry of motion begins around me as well as shouts of victory. The Colonel is already walking out the door. I jump up and run to catch up to him. "Sir, I don't understand."

"Not surprising, maggot," the Colonel returns acidly.

I ignore him and try again. "What will we do now? There are no reserves for this. We're out of jobs. You want us to be civilians? Why the hell did we go through all this training if we're not going to use it? What are we supposed to do?"

"Does it look like I care? You think you're the only one

this screws with? There are people far more important than you that made plans. Billions of dollars lost. Our government is run by idiots. There was history to be made. World domination. You don't see those people crying like pussies, do you maggot?"

"What people?" I ask, confused and intrigued. "What plans?"

"That's none of your business. You want my advice? Go find a man who's desperate enough to have you and pop out a few babies. That's what you're good for anyhow."

I pull on his arm and force him to stop. The look in his eye tells me he knows I can stop him. "I'm ranked highest at this godforsaken place. I know I am. Don't pull that sexist crap on me, sir."

The Colonel looks murderous as he takes my arm forcing him to stop and shoves it away. I let him. "Doesn't matter. You've lost it all and now you have nothing. Welcome to the real world, kid. None of it matters. Go home. It's over.

So, you've lost your soul? Oh well. You should be thanking me for all I've done." He laughs then as if he's said something clever. He hasn't.

He walks off and I stand still, knowing I should be happy but unsure what to do now that my only reason for living these past few months has been pulled out from under me.

CHAPTER 7

Meat lovers

I wake up to footsteps and the bright sun hitting my eyes. I get up alertly and look around for the source of the sounds. It's Thursday and definitely morning by the look of the sun. I've got till a minute after midnight on Monday before the bombing and I can't forget that. So, whatever I'm hearing I've got to deal with it fast.

My backpack is still snug on my shoulders. I find I also managed to bring in my katana but I have no idea how. I grab it and am thankful that for once no nightmares assaulted me during the night. Unfortunately, that was probably since I had been more or less forced into unconsciousness.

I look at my ripped shirt and the multiple bruises I have from the battle with the super stinker. Since there are no bite marks and since I'm still human, I figure I made it out okay. I start walking, looking at everything and anything, making sure I had just been hearing things earlier. I go up the stairs, yanking open all the doors.

I come to a halt as I reach one that's locked. "What the hell?" I mutter under my breath. I back up a little and examine the brown wooden door with it's simple metal handle. I try opening it again and it really is locked.

I move to grab my katana but decide I rather check out what's going on before drawing any sort of weapon. I take a deep breath and step back.

Well here's to nothing, I think to myself. I kick the door on the weakest part right near where the lock is mounted. I grunt, pushing through with my kick as the door swings open with a loud bang.

"What the hell?" shouts a man's voice, repeating my sentiment.

I grab my katana and walk in to find a guy, a real one, surrounded by comic books with a katana pointed right back at me.

I slowly inch toward him, analyzing every move he makes. As I'm going to open my mouth to speak I realize he's kind of gorgeous.

He's about 6'3. All I can see are his astonishing green eyes and a jawline that makes me feel all-woman inside. And those lips. Oh God, I just want to stick my tongue in his mouth and do dirty things to him. Sadly, this was not the right place or time.

I also notice the *Walking Dead* zombie killer shirt, straight legged jeans, and a pair Converse shoes. He's a bit different from my usual type but he has my attention.

I blink, trying to stop this line of thinking when he breaks the silence.

"Interesting. Is this kicking in doors a hobby?" he asks while holding an intense stare. It's then I find that holding eye contact while trying not to drool is hard.

I put my katana back in its scabbard on my back, taking a calculated risk. "I come in peace. I pinky promise," I say, only pretty sure he won't shish kabob me.

"Stay back or I swear I'm going to stab you," he replies a little shakily. It's kind of cute.

I eye his body language and his hold on his katana. I walk forward and smirk. "Go ahead."

He shoots me a glare but puts down his weapon. "You're either crazy or you're just used to getting away with having a smart mouth. Is it wrong I'm intrigued?" he says, looking me up and down, a smirk playing on his lips.

I feel myself slightly blush but I get out of my girly moment pretty fast.

"What's your name and how long have you been here?" I demand to know, walking completely into the room and inspecting him closer.

"The name's Jonah. I've been here for a while but that's none of your business. What's your name, Snow White?" He reaches out and grabs a strand of hair from my face.

I slap his hand away and push my finger into his forehead, moving him away from my personal space. Snow White, huh? I'm no helpless princess. I'm me and I'm the most amazing thing that has ever crossed his path and just like that, I've definitely snapped out of fangirling.

"My name is H, and don't you ever call me Snow White again unless you want me to decapitate you," I threaten lightly while smiling.

"H?" he repeats skeptically as if he hasn't heard my threats at all.

"That's right," I say.

"Interesting. Is your whole family named after the alphabet? Or are you just trying to be mysterious?"

"It's my name, kid. Sorry you didn't know before. You're obviously missing out but I'm guessing you don't know a lot of things. For instance, that you need to be in a bomb shelter right now. D.C. is about to be nuked. So, you should probably get going."

He looks me up and down. "I can take care of myself, thanks," he replies.

Ugh. Here I am trying to help and he's blowing me off? "Is that why you're locked in here all alone and you're holding your katana like a baseball bat?"

His face suddenly changes. The green irises seem to darken. "I don't know, H. You seem to know everything. You tell me."

I ignore him and walk out. Maybe he wasn't worth saving after all. I put my own katana in the scabbard and swing on my back strap as I walk quickly down the stairs.

"Hey! Where are you going? I'm not done here," Jonah's voice calls down to me. "You can't just break down a man's door. This is trespassing."

He's an attractive guy so it's a shame he's so stupid. I could kill him for God's sake. I open the front door slowly to make sure there aren't any stinkers. Then I walk out, closing the door behind me. Soon after, I hear the door re-opening and closing and the padding of footsteps.

"H, wait up seriously," Jonah calls from the distance. Was he actually following me? Of course, he was.

I keep walking. Suddenly something taps my shoulder. Out of instinct I crouch down grabbing for the hand that tries to tap me again and I throw it over my body, a great Krav Maga technique I learned as a military guinea pig a couple years back.

The body slams to the ground in front of me and I get on top. I look down.

Jonah smirks up at me. "If you wanted to be on top you didn't have to hurt me. All you had to do was say so," he says on a wheeze as he brings his hands to my hips.

I roll my eyes, push off his hands, and stand up. "Why don't you go back to where you came from, huh?" I say, giving him the stink eye as I cross my arms.

He stands up, righting his clothes. "Are you always so feisty?"

"Are you always so eager to chase your only salvation away?"

"Maybe if you hadn't knocked my door down like a savage we wouldn't have to deal with this unpleasantness," he says and one corner of his mouth lifts.

I walk away without saying a word. I know I shouldn't be such a bitch to him. He literally was my only other distraction besides Bill. Oh, Bill. He's probably worried because I didn't come home. I should check on him.

I'm on the move but quickly realize that Jonah is still

following. I wish he knew better and stayed away. I still might turn around and punch him. I decide to just pretend he isn't here.

It's about mid-morning and the stinkers are keeping to themselves. The only thing beating down on me today is the sun. I find my car a block away, pull out my keys from my backpack, and hop in. Before I can jet off, Jonah hops in the passenger side. I don't say a word to him the whole way home. I don't dare glance at him because I know he'll be smirking if I do.

When I finally reach my house, I open the door. I keep my gun ready and do a quick recon before heading to the bunker. I ignore Jonah behind me but I can tell he's impressed. I finally unlock the door and saunter in.

Bill's head pops out of the kitchen. "H, I was worried about you. I made brownies," he says, and before I can answer Jonah comes in.

"It smells so good in here...what is this place?" he asks, as he stops to stand beside me.

"Oh, dear God, H. Why didn't you tell me we were going to have company? I would've made breakfast," Bill says, acting like an embarrassed mother.

"Seriously? Let me just pull out my phone that so totally works. And he's not company. He just followed," I say making my way towards the brownies waiting in the kitchen. Brownies: breakfast of champions, and their stalkers apparently.

"Is she always this crabby?" Jonah asks Bill as he puts his hand in front of mine and snags the first piece. I want to give him one of my menacing stares but I'm ignoring him.

Bill doesn't reply but I can see him nod from the corner of my eye.

Um, hello. He should be grateful I saved his life. I swipe a brownie too. I bite into it and sink into a chair. Bill had told me he wasn't a good cook. I don't know if it's because I'm starving or because the recipe was easy but it tastes like heaven. I let myself enjoy it for just a minute.

"Anyway," I say loudly as I stand up again, "What have you heard of the bombing, Bill?"

Before he can answer, Jonah rudely interrupts. "Bombing? Is that what you meant by D.C. being nuked?"

Of course, he had to go hysterical on me. I can't ignore him anymore or he'll upset Bill. "Calm down...breathe. Let Bill talk," I say, waiting for Bill's response.

"They aren't going to stop it. We have about 86 hours."

"How do you guys know all this?" Jonah asks.

"It's all over the news. Haven't you been watching?" I reply.

Jonah shakes his head and then swears loudly.

"Exactly," I say. I turn to Bill. "The brownies are delicious," I begin. I watch his face light up at my words and it does something to the center of my chest. I try to ignore that and continue. "Do you think you could make a pizza with the stuff in the bag I brought home yesterday? Because that would be stellar."

Bill opens his mouth but Jonah steps in front of me, blocking my view of Bill, as well as my view of pretty much anything but his tall frame. “And you were just going to leave me in my house?”

“Hey, I tried to warn you. Plus, you followed me, didn't you? Don't have a cow,” I say trying to sound flippant but I can't help but notice how good he smells. Kind of like a forest and some sandalwood mixed together. That also reminds me that I could use a shower.

Unfortunately, there wasn't time. I really had to go to the shelters, find my family, and ask people if they knew of anyone who might still be out here, alive and unprotected. There was no time for a shower at all. The best I could hope for was to come home tonight still alive, and have an edible pizza waiting for me. Still, I could at least change out of my ripped shirt.

Jonah runs a hand through his dark hair. “I'm not having a cow, H. Can you just give me a damned second to process this, Jesus.”

I wave him away. “Take all the time you need. In fact, help Bill make the pizza while you process. And for the love of God don't screw it up, our supplies are limited.”

“And where are you going?” Jonah questions with a growl.

“I want to make sure everyone who's still alive is safe and I’ve got people to look for. I have a lot to do today and very little time to do it so if you'll excuse me.”

Jonah grabs onto my arm lightly. I ignore the heat of his skin. I almost bring him down to the ground again but I think of Bill and his delicate sensibilities. “I'm not making pizza. I'm coming with you," he says. "I know some people who might be unaware of the bombing."

"Can you fight?"

He turns away kind of sheepishly. I see right through him.

I duck into the next room, quickly change my shirt, and come back with a .45. "Can you shoot?"

"Yes," he says confidently.

I nod but still demonstrate how to hold it without making it obvious I'm doing it. "Great. Well, this gun's like any other, I guess. Here's the safety. Then you know the rest, point and shoot."

He watches me closely then nods. He was so going to get us killed. But heck, what other choice did I have for back-up these days?

I turn to Bill. "I like everything on my pizza. Please don't burn the bunker down," I say with a smile. I have to admit he's growing on me.

"I won't, H. You can count on me. Now, both of you take some water bottles and brownies to go. You've barely eaten."

"Yeah, yeah," I gripe but I shoot him a wink and do what he says, Jonah following at my heels.

"When will you be back?" Bill calls out, trying to force a smile. He knows it's dangerous. For some reason, I don't want to worry him anymore. I want him to have hope in me.

"Don't worry. Just be ready to leave when I do. We're getting out of this hell hole," I reply confidently. He can count on me too.

Five minutes later I hop into Daredevil and hit the road hard, tires screeching. Jonah automatically grabs the handle over his seat. “Nice ride. Can I drive?”

“Nope,” I reply. I tap my fingernails on the steering wheel then turn to him. “Here's how it's going to go down. You tell me everything you know about what's been happening and I'll do the same.” Honestly, he probably didn't know much but we needed to be upfront if I was going to let him into my life and into my house. Plus, the more info I had, the better. Especially since I had a feeling I wasn’t going to get rid of him any time soon.

Jonah leans back into the seat. “It's kind of a long story.”

I laugh. “Lucky for you we've got time. I'm heading out to the farthest shelter from us in the Northeast and then I'm working our way back so we don't get stuck too far from home when the time is up.”

He bites into a brownie and I can tell he's trying to avoid telling his story. It's trying my patience so I put a little extra oomph into my driving, speeding hard around road blockages-like other stalled cars in the middle of the road-for fun.

He turns a little green but I think it does the trick because he opens his mouth and begins.

CHAPTER 8

California Style

"I was at a comic book store downtown. I was pretty out of it, not really paying attention to anything but my reading. I heard some noises behind me and it was getting annoying. I jumped up to tell them to be quiet and saw this couple getting..."

His face turns a little pink. "Let's just say I thought they were getting frisky. The girl practically jumped this kid and she went straight for his neck with her teeth."

"So, you realized she was a stinker?"

"Stinker?" he repeats with a smile. I can see him thinking it over. He laughs. "That's a great word for it." He pulls a hand through his dark hair and his eyes lift a little as he goes back to his memories, which makes me want to jump his bones.

"No, I didn't realize what she was. Not right away. I just thought it was wrong that there was a hot girl trying to get frisky in the middle of the aisles of a comic store and the poor dude was screeching."

"Right," I say sarcastically. I'm so not going to mention the fact that I read comics. He'll probably start ripping my clothes off, which I totally wouldn't mind but we had a mission. I smirk at the thought. "Continue."

"Right," he repeats in the same tone. "Well, the guy, he started freaking out. He was all scrawny and flailing. So, I tried to help him out but the girl kept coming for him. I mean her head was shaking side to side like pulling some Emily Rose possession shit. So here I am, trying to drag him out of her grasp and she won't let go and I'm sorry but I'm not about to hit a girl."

"No, you'll just follow her home and annoy her to death."

Jonah only smiles wider. Ugh. I like his sense of humor and how he doesn't let me push him off balance. I melt and hope he doesn't notice.

"Are you going to let me finish my story?"

I turn toward him and the car bumps up fast. My head whips back to the road and in my rear-view mirror I see a bicycle. Whoops. I keep my eyes on the road this time as I say, "Continue."

I can practically feel him smirking beside me. "Well, the poor kid is bleeding pretty badly and so I focus on him and finally manage to pull him upright. We run and this girl starts chasing us through the shop. As I'm running I notice it's dead empty. Not even the guy behind the counter was there. Well, the kid trips, and as I turn around to catch him, I see the girl's eyes clearly for the first time." He stops and out of the corner of my eye, I see Jonah shutter.

"Blank, right?" I ask.

Jonah stays quiet. I don't know if he'll say anything at all.

"Yeah," he finally replies gruffly. "Blank eyes. No pupils, nothing." He frowns as if he still can't grasp it.

"Anyway, the girl just pounces on him. I swear she flew like 20 feet. I just got this feeling that I didn't want to touch this girl. I've seen documentaries on people who take substances and it makes them go crazy and eat the face right off you. Anyway, everything's kind of slowed down now even though it's all happening so fast, and I look up and see this weird display on the wall. You know the kind with two swords intersecting on it?"

I do know. I realize the comic book shop he's been in was the one I just went to. He had one katana and I had the other, but I wasn't going to mention it. Besides he's still talking.

"I manage to pull one off. I run at them still struggling on the floor and I'm about to try to separate them but then I see his eyes. I'm sure you can guess."

I nod. I knew the drill now. He'd been bitten so he turned.

"He starts going crazy too and they start fighting as if they both want to kill and be killed all at once. It was nasty stuff. There was this brown fluid everywhere that looked like jelly. I just bolted. I got in my car. Drove home."

"Where you've been holed up ever since," I surmise.

"We don't own a TV. My phone had no signal. Luckily my dad and sister are out of town. I wrote them an email. I don't know if they got it. There's been no response. I've been finding leads on the best way past the quarantine limits. They have gates and guards. I wanted to make a plan to get out of here but I needed a little more time."

Suddenly I turn toward him, feeling very excited. "So, you can get us out of the borders?" I try to ask nonchalantly.

"Possibly," he replies but his word is clipped.

I try something else. "So, you have a computer?"

"A few..."

"What do you mean?" I hedge.

"I build computers. It's a hobby."

"Ok, but how is it working? The WIFI and data service has been cut."

"You haven't heard of satellite internet? Guess you don't know all the answers. It's actually not that complicated. You can buy the portable router and it's cheaper than WIFI."

"Ok, Mr. Perfect. So what do you know about all this?"

"I can tell you I've been getting all my info on the, uh, stinkers from the government database. It's not exactly legal though. So..."

I laugh. "Who am I going to tell? Bill? He's like a hundred and six."

"Whatever. The files kind of indicate that the virus was planned but it doesn't say how or why. There's just too much information on it for it to be the first time it's happening."

"What do you mean?"

"I couldn't get most of it. It was in code but it lines up like an experiment. It's extremely regimented. They have too much information on it to be a freak event."

"What did it say?"

"Again, I couldn't crack it all but I know it spreads through saliva to blood exchanges. It takes anywhere from 30 seconds to 6 hours to take effect and it kills off the brain cells. It's almost as if the person inside is a vegetable. The body still works but the entire structure is different. Their eyes work best at night and their physical bodies feel no pain."

"What's the smell?" I ask.

"The stink is on account of the dying cells. Their biological makeup requires them to have the overwhelming desire to spread the virus. I figure it's like how humans have a need to reproduce but on a bigger scale because it's their only need. That's why they attack."

All right. So, I'm a little in shock over how much he knows, especially for being a kid dumb enough to hole up in his room during a virus outbreak. I wonder what else he knows. "Ok. Why are some stinkers still intelligent and lethal while others are full blown idiots? Some attack and some don't."

"Noticed that, did you?" he asks and peers at me from the side of his eye. I ignore him. "Honestly I'm not sure. There seems to be a link between certain factors of genetics and the way each person reacts to the virus. There was something about three possible results from the trials."

"What? Like dumb, dumber, and mineral?"

"I guess. I just know that some people for whatever reason have bodies that are able to stop the process of killing all of their brain cells. Those people still have their fighting and cognitive functions still intact. The others have no control. I don't know what the third kind does. Maybe they died right from the bite. Did you see anyone die from it?"

I thought about the bodies littered on the floor of the

pizzeria. Did they die from bites or just being attacked? I wasn't sure. "Maybe. I kind of woke up to the...situation." I don't mention I had been passed out for several days or why. "There were bodies but they could've been from anything. Maybe fighting each other. I was hoping there were other humans who got away and fought them off." I shrug. I honestly don't know but his theory makes more sense. Maybe the bite can kill.

I can tell Jonah wants more information about what I know but I'm not down with sharing too much so I cut him off. "So just to get this straight, you have a working computer and you still didn't know about the whole bombing thing?" I ask.

He frowns at me but answers anyway. "There's been no news on a bombing online. In fact, there's been nothing on the internet at all about what's happening except that there's been a virus outbreak and D.C. is fine but is being quarantined for safety. What you've been seeing must be a local newsfeed that the government is trying to make us think is being shown nationwide."

Shit. "That explains why there's only one feed on every station." I consider what he's said. "So, you think the bombing is real or fake?"

"I'm not sure but I'm going to go with real. It makes the most sense. That way they can neutralize the threat."

"Along with any other civilian casualties that they don't care about. Screw that. Our government needs to get off their asses and help get the humans out before they go and bomb us. Like fuck? Get your shit together, Senator Cookie!" I yell and speed a little more. I glance down at the speedometer and see 115. I am killing too much gas so I slow back down to the 90s. That I can live with.

"Senator Cookie?" he asks, puzzled. "Wait, you don't mean Senator Milano, do you?"

"Yeah. That's the one. Brown hair, bad highlights, fancy suits, boring shoes. She seems to be spearheading this whole quarantine thing. She's the pinched face of it anyway."

"I ran across a file on her in the database. Get me to my computer and I can check it out. It might help us figure out what we're dealing with."

"Aye aye, nerd boy. We'll stop by your place now since it's around the corner. So, one last question. You got any other family?"

"It's just my dad and my little sister. My mom died when I was 15. Anyway, Dad and Jess are in New York for the week."

I guessed we both went through some traumatic things at that age but I swallowed that thought down. "They're probably fine, then. You're lucky."

"Yeah," he says a little sadly. "I was using the database to find a way to get out of here and head there but so far I couldn't find any cracks in the quarantine borders. Hmm."

"What?" I ask.

"They just set up the borders too quickly. If I wasn't convinced before, I am now. This whole thing wasn't a mistake or if it was, it was something that they knew about but hoped would never happen. Still they had plans for it anyway."

"Yeah...funny how quickly they go from assessing this unknown situation to having bombs prepared to detonate less than a week from now. This is bullshit and we are getting out. I say we hit the shelters and we do what we can here before times up. Then we bolt."

"Why not just stay at your house? You have a shelter and supplies," he asks as I pull into his neighborhood.

"We don't know how long the effects of the bomb will be in play. We could end up stuck there for a few months or even years before we can expose ourselves to the air outside. I'm not sticking around for that one."

"You're right," he says and I smile at one of my favorite phrases to hear coming from his lips. "I'll look for information in the files I've hacked on the type of bombs," he continues, "but I'm going to focus on finding a way out of here either way. I swear I'm this close to cracking the plans for the walls. If I get those, I can help get us through. I know people, including the senator, are coming and going. You said she was in a press conference. Did it say from where?"

"The screen said she was in Virginia. I guess you're right. There must be a way in and out."

"Exactly, I've just got to get a lock on where that is. By the way, turn up here," he says pointing. "My house is the 5th one on the left."

I nod and slow the car down. "Your plan sounds good. I can't wait to get out of here." I don't tell him I want to head west.

I'm thinking California. Since he's heading to New York we'll just go our separate ways.

"I'm with you," he says as he opens the car door and makes a run for his house. I don't have the heart to tell him we won't be together long even though I doubt it would matter.

●○●○●○●○●○●○●○●○●○●

We stay silent in the car for what seems like an eternity but I've got my music and Jonah's constant tapping on his computer keys fills up the car plenty.

We've finally arrived at the outer limits of D.C. that are the furthest north from my house. Jonah has the screen of his laptop in front of him and he's directing me. I wanted to start with shelters that would be furthest away so we could work our way back and I also wanted to see what we'd be up against if we tried to leave. Just beyond the street I see a hill that I know leads out of D.C.

Up on the hill is a row of what must be at least 60 feet tall stone barricades. I start driving toward the walls. "That's the border to Maryland," Jonah states and I can only nod.

Slowly I drive the car closer to the border but not close enough to draw attention from the police cars and black SUVs that are lined up right beside the walls. "They have stations built and look-out towers already. How did they do this so quickly?" I mutter out loud in awe.

"The walls were airlifted in," Jonah replies softly. "Since most of the military resides around here, this is where they were all stationed, guarding the walls. The walls are open inside and they all connect to each other like long hallways. There is only one entrance in and one exit out surrounding all of D.C."

I process this and look up at the barricades that wind around the hill and go as far as the eye can see in a line to the left and right. And while it looks like I could just scale these walls, I know that this was made by the government, and it would never be that easy.

"They're enforced by snipers, barbed wire and chemical weapons that will keep us in and outsiders out," Jonah says as if he were reading my thoughts. I sigh and watch as Jonah closes the laptop.

"Does your magic computer have anything to say on how we can get through all that? I'm not opposed to using sheer force but I don't want to go in blind."

"I need time to decode the information but yeah, I think I can get us through by disarming their technological security. Again, I just need to get to the location where high-ranking officials are coming and going."

"And if you're wrong or you can't decode it in time?" I ask.

"We can stay in your bunker, eat pizza, and repopulate D.C.," he says with a grin.

I turn on him and assess my computer-nerd. "How about this? Pray you're right and can decode it in time and I won't kill you."

"Will I get...your pizza before you do it?" he returns quickly.

"Keep dreaming." I sigh aloud and stare one last time at the black military vehicles lined along the hill. “We should go,” I add as I turn around before anyone spots my car.

Jonah says nothing more and soon we’re at the shelter.

CHAPTER 9

Hawaiian

It's a school, Sequoia Middle. I always found schools to be especially creepy when classes were out of session and this was no exception. Very few cars line the parking lot and I hope that doesn't mean there's only a few people here. I park Daredevil and stare at the middle school sign.

I turn to Jonah. "Are you ready?" I ask, even though I don't know if I am. With a sigh, he shakes his head and gets out. "What am I supposed to be ready for exactly?" he mumbles.

I double check my weapons, deciding walking in with a giant katana attached to my back isn't exactly the best idea. I settle for a small knife in my shoe and follow him.

As we're on the path to the bunker I start to think of my mom and little brother and how I hope they haven't ended up like dad. I dread and hope they're here, alive and well. I sigh, realizing I finally have to explain what I'm doing here. "We're looking for Kate and Justin Booker," I say abruptly and turn away, hoping that's the end of that conversation. I really can't handle questions right now.

Just thinking of my dad is crushing me. I seriously miss him. Even though he had no emotions whatsoever, he was like a rock. He only showed Mom his emotions and that made me happy. Now he's gone.

I shake off my thoughts and keep on walking cautiously. So far, no stinkers anywhere. Jonah looks at me with a troubled expression. “Got it. Are you okay, H?”

I stop and I stare at him. “I’m better than ever. Now let's get this over with,” I say, sticking my tongue out so I don't seem cruel.

He smiles and keeps going. We finally reach the door and we both stare at each other. “Let’s hope for the best,” I whisper as I pull my shades over my eyes. I knew we were going inside but they gave me confidence. They remind me of my dad. Jonah gives me a look and I just raise one brow in challenge. He raises a brow too but says nothing as I open the doors.

We walk in and there’s no stinker smell, which is somewhat of a good sign but I know they could still be around. We see three guards in military uniform in front of another set of doors. “Eagle 1. All clear in zones 1 and 2. I repeat all is clear,” a short man says into a walkie-talkie. The other two men, one with a buzz cut straight out of the 80’s and the other with intensely bushy eyebrows look at each other and then walk back in.

Thank God they weren’t stinkers. I would’ve lost all hope completely. I sigh in relief and shove Jonah ahead of me. “Seriously, I have to go first?” he whispers.

“Yeah, just in case. You're the test dummy,” I say with a smirk on my face. We walk to the entrance and approach the guards.

"Welcome to shelter Zone 63," the short one says to us. "We're here to assure you that you will be safe from the virus and the subsequent bombings here. We need you to sign in and we'll need your fingerprints and a quick body scan."

Jonah looks like he's about to agree and takes a step forward. Ugh, he has so much to learn. Shorty was not in charge and we'd get nowhere with him. "Hi," I say loudly, grabbing hold of Jonah's shirt and pushing him behind me. "I'm here on assignment from my father, General William E Booker. He's part of the Air Force." I take a quick scan of the guards.

Buzz cut's eyes light up in recognition and he even stiffens a little. Bingo, he's my way in. "The General is here?" he asks in an anxious voice.

I'm the only one who knows how very wrong he is but I have no idea which shelters are open and working. I have to get information and go off the cuff. "If he was, you'd know," I reply, deadpan. "I'll be going through all the shelters for the next few days for him."

"Where is he and why would he send you?" Bushy Eyebrows sneers.

My eyes turn on him, quick and deadly. "As you can imagine he's otherwise occupied with this clusterfuck of a mess," I say, waving my arms around to show exactly what I mean. "I'd explain just how busy he is and what he's doing but that shit's above your pay grade.

"If you don't want to cooperate just say the word and get ready to feel the full force of your government breathing down your neck, and at the moment they're not feeling very reasonable. Suffice it to say that I'm here and I've got stuff to do and I'd like to keep it quiet.

"So, walkie-talkie your little buddies and let them know I'm coming."

Jonah presses a hand to the skin at my lower back and I shiver. "That we're coming," I amend with a sigh, so Jonah knows how annoying he is. "I'll take a list of your active shelters. No names, just priority admittance. You understand. You can go off our physical descriptions. Think you can handle that?"

"Ma'am, the walkies only reach the two surrounding shelters. The communication between shelters has been the biggest issue since the phone lines and internet has been cut. I don't advise this but if you need information from a shelter, you'll need to do it in person," Shorty says.

"I know that," I snap. I didn't but what else could I say. "Why do you think I'm here in person? Notify those two shelters if you can manage it, or is that too difficult? Will I need to report this?"

"No, ma'am. We'll do our part. We'll take you down now but, well, we need you to sign in and do a quick scan. It's government policy. No exceptions."

A thought hits me. The sign-in sheets? Perfect. I push Eyebrows aside to subtly show my strength and even with all his bulk and muscles, he staggers a little. "As for the sign-in sheets I'll need a copy of them ASAP."

Shorty runs a hand through his hair. "That's not possible. It's a pen and paper sheet. People sign in when they get here. We only have the one copy. We're just reporting the number of occupants as instructed. You can't take the census off the premises so if you need to see it, you'll have to go through it now."

"Fine. My associate," I spare a glance at Jonah, "will do so while you take us down to the shelter."

Looking even more disgruntled since I pushed him, Bushy Eyebrows turns on me. "You'll still need to get scanned. Like we mentioned, it's policy."

"I'm well aware of all government policies," I say with impatience, eyeing Buzz Cut, clearly the leader of the pack, meaningfully. "We won't be staying long. Besides if I were a stinker would I be here talking to you?" Jonah snickers, adding the perfect effect of disbelief.

After a moment, Buzz Cut nods once. His buddies back down immediately.

"Last thing. If civilians are still out of the shelter but might still be unaffected by the virus, will you be rescuing them?"

"No, ma'am," Shorty replies. "All rescue missions have been completed. I don't know if this is a test or what but everything is up to code here. We're following orders. People can come into the shelters but we won't be out looking."

I nod, disappointed at this failure on the government's part. "Fine. We need to peruse the sign-in sheet briefly as we check out the shelter," I say with a flick of my hand toward Bushy Eyebrows. "That'll be all."

I hold back my laugh as Bushy Eyebrows fists clench at his side. Buzz Cut throws a warning slap to his arm and walks off, hopefully in search of the sign-in sheet.

I know Jonah is missing out on the hilarious scene because I can feel his eyes zeroed in on me. I finally meet his intense gaze and find confusion and something else I'm not sure of waiting there. Thankfully Jonah knows to keep his mouth shut and we both follow as Shorty leads us where we want to go.

We walk through to a room that was clearly the school gym and from there we go down a flight of stairs. We finally get to the final stage of the bunker and open the last set of double doors.

Buzz Cut meets us down there, stacks of paper held in his left hand. Jonah reaches out with his long arm and with a strange fluid grace grabs the papers. He begins reading them at once.

I grab onto his shoulder to read the names with him, unable to stop myself from scanning the names. Without looking up he whispers softly, "I'm looking for Kate and Justin Booker, right?" Sudden tears choke my throat so all I can do is nod, my chin brushing his shoulder. That's when Shorty and Buzz Cut open the double doors.

A loud burst of noise fills the air. People laughing and talking, babies crying, children and small animals running around. I sag in relief at what I find. The room is buzzing and alive, packed to capacity with people. Actual people and living things.

After my initial shock, I take a better look around. There are tables of food, equipment, cots, and sleeping bags. There seems to be a semblance of order to the chaos but it isn't a place I want to stay in for long.

Jonah puts his hand on my lower back again and guides me forward as we walk, his eyes still glued to the papers. I don't shrug him off because I'm secretly grateful but I make sure not to lean into him either. I need to be on full alert and find my family-what was left of it anyway-if I can.

Both of us keep walking but our eyes are searching frantically, mine on the room and his on the sheets. This walking around thing was taking too much time and time is what we didn't have. I stand up on a table and I can hear Jonah in the background. "H, what the fuck are you doing? Get down!"

I ignore him, screaming, "Excuse me!"

Everyone stops and stares. “Is there a Kate Booker here with a small boy named Justin? Please be here,” I add with a slight sound of desperation in my voice.

The room goes silent but no one answers back. I keep searching the crowd but everyone goes back to their conversations. I sigh, adding, “Fine then. One last thing. If anyone knows of someone and they are still human. I mean you're absolutely positive they're still human and you know where they might be and are not in a shelter, come tell me and I'll try to help them get to safety.”

Many heads look up at that but again no one replies. The few guards however are looking at me with interest. I need to get out of here. I hop down and try to blend into the crowd with Jonah at my side.

A few minutes more and Jonah pulls me to a stop. He gives the papers a shake. “They’re not here,” his deep voice rumbles out softly. The kindness in his tone and in his green eyes makes me feel too much. I don’t need that so I just nod and turn away from him.

As we make our way to the exits I feel a tug on my leg. I look down and see a little girl with light blonde hair staring up at me. “Hey,” I say as I assess the little girl in her tie-dyed t-shirt and jeans. She only continues staring up at me. “Umm can I help you?” I ask.

“I’m Tessa,” she declares.

"Um, okay," I reply eloquently and exchange perplexed looks with Jonah. "Do you need help?" I pull my sunglasses up to better look at her.

Her eyes widen and she tugs urgently on my shirt to pull my face closer to hers and I let her. "You should put your sunglasses on," she whispers. Still confused but convinced by the firm tone of her voice, I pull my shades off the crown of my head and rest them at the bridge of my nose.

"Better?" I whisper back. I know some kids have trouble making eye contact. Maybe she's like that.

"Yes, if you don't cover them then they'll take you away like they took Tara away." I want to ask her what the hell she's talking about but I don't think I should say hell in front of a kid.

Jonah kneels down and puts a hand to the little girl's shoulder. He looks her in the eye like an equal even though she's just a random kid rambling nonsense. I feel the sudden urge to melt into a puddle.

"Who is Tara?" he asks with a teasing lift of his lips.

The little girl looks back and forth between Jonah and me. "She's my sister. I was going to ask you to help her but I don't think you can. They took her away. She got purple eyes like yours," she says, pointing at me. "They scanned her and it beeped. They took her."

I jump a little at her words, completely stunned. Then I lean in as closely as possible to her so no one will overhear us.

"Who took her away, Tessa?" Jonah asks calmly.

"The guards," Tessa replies in a shaky whisper. There's no mistaking the fear in her voice now.

"Why? What do purple eyes have to do with it?"

"I don't know," Tessa says and tears start to spill onto her little cheeks. "Everyone with purple eyes beeps when they get scanned. Anyone who beeps gets taken away. I don't want them to take you away. I want you to find my sister. You said you can help find people."

I don't know what to say to her. I don't want to lie to her but if what she says is true then her sister is with the government and out of my reach. Helping people on the street find a shelter is one thing but this is...something else. I stare at her, at a loss.

"We'll do our best," Jonah says.

"Good!" Tessa replies and wipes at her cheeks. "She looks just like me but bigger. Everyone says so. She's 14."

"Ok," I reply. Jonah stands up and I push my shades as close to my eyes as I can. "Thank you for the warning. We'll keep an eye out for Tara."

"Thanks," Tessa says and suddenly her arms are wrapped around one of Jonah's legs and one of mine, locking the three of us together. I try not to let this get to me because my emotions are locked up tight and they need to stay that way so I just pat her back awkwardly until she lets us go.

“We’ve got to go,” Jonah says and grabs my hand. Together we make it toward the exit and although all my senses are on alert, I walk past the guards confidently like I’m supposed to be here and demand the map of the shelters I requested before we go.

Once outside, my eyes meet Jonah's and he raises an eyebrow. I know he's going to ask about all this later. I don’t have any answers for him though. I start walking fast ahead of him, not caring if he follows or not.

He does follow and surprises me by only saying, “Their lack of communication will be helpful. I know it would be easier if there was a database to just see if the people you’re looking for are in a shelter, and where, but at least now word won’t get out about us coming and going.” I silently supposed he was right.

The rest of the day continues pretty much like this. I make sure to keep my shades on and tight to my face and I manage to avoid any and all scanners.

Though I wouldn’t admit it out loud, because I’m annoyed with him, Jonah helped too. After our first shelter visit he caught on quick and he adopted my attitude like he’d been born to it. He wasn’t exactly jacked with bulging muscles but he was tall and when he stayed quiet he appeared just as menacing as I was.

Things weren’t too bad. Plus, my dad’s rep continued to carry major pull. I was grateful I could still use the power of my father’s name, even though I no longer deserved it and I was tarnishing his memory with every breath I took. I didn’t think about that either.

The shelters were fairly close together and easy to get to, especially with the map given to us. Unfortunately, we made it through 8 shelters without so much as a lead on my family or word of those who are probably still human and probably not yet in a shelter. The 9th shelter, however, gave us the latter.

A woman told us that her sister's husband was crazy and more than likely they were still in their house without a clue or a care of the bombings. We took her directions and left. Jonah and I got through the neighborhood without any stinker sightings and as the woman described we'd found a family holed up in their house. They were the vigilante type.

I successfully avoided rounds from his shotgun, yes shotgun, and once inside, Jonah explained about the bombs. It took longer than expected but with pleadings to the wife that her sister was in a shelter, again mostly Jonah's doing, we got them to pack their stuff and their three kids in their car and follow behind us to the shelter.

In the 10th shelter all we found was lunch, but we were starving so it helped. By the 16th shelter we'd managed to find one old veteran, three sets of families hiding in different safe houses that were not equipped for bombs, and even a teenage boy who'd been trained by his family where to go if they got separated, and thankfully he was exactly where they said he'd be.

Unfortunately, there were also 10 people not where their friends and family said they'd be and we couldn't locate them. There were two we found where they were supposed to be but they were already stinkers. They were the dumb kind so we left them alone in their houses and Jonah told all the families what we found either way.

Now we're leaving the 16th shelter and I'm starting to feel sick when no one responds to my plea for my mom or brother. My stomach twists as I turn to see Jonah's face after he's gone through this list. We don't even exchange words in these moments. By now I know the look. Oh yeah and the stomach ache has not been helped by the government sanctioned slop we had for lunch. I'm seriously craving pizza like I'm craving my next breath but I know this is more important. Time is going by way too fast and we've barely made a dent in the shelters we need to get to.

That night, when we're both so exhausted it hurts, we break into the nearest house, meaning I break in while Jonah is the lookout, and then we pass out. Jonah doesn't even put up a fuss when I call dibs on the master bedroom. We only sleep for a few hours anyway. Again, I'm not sure if it's because I'm exhausted or not but my nightmares thankfully elude me.

Waking up to the sun in my eyes and the heat of the house I was kind of hoping that everything was over but unfortunately this is my life we're talking about. So I snap back into reality.

I check the time. We have a little less than 64 hours. As I adjust to being awake, I admit that I do feel better. Jonah looks like he can walk onto the set of a photoshoot, so he's got that going for him.

The whole day we go from shelter to shelter like we had the day before and it's still just as fruitless, maybe more so.

Now the sun is starting to set and I'm tired of the stupid dance of evading Jonah's questions and getting nowhere with the shelters. Luckily the next shelter is so close that Jonah and I decide to walk to it just to save gas. I could definitely use a walk to clear my head.

Plus, Daredevil is too awesome to give up and I haven't seen anything better since I jacked her. It's also kind of nice out and the fresh air has a crisp quality to it that reinvigorates me. Still, I decide on bringing my katana with me for the walk. If the guards take issue they can hold it for me but I'm not about to be out in the open like this without decent protection.

Jonah turns to me as we walk under the setting sun, the map clutched in his right hand. "I can't believe this is real life," he states.

"Believe it," I reply, keeping my eyes and nose peeled for stinkers. All I find is smooth, greying pavement that needs a fresh paint job ahead of us as far as the eye can see.

I feel Jonah studying me and it makes me twitch. With everything else going on, I'm unable to stop my paranoia from bleeding into every part of my mind because it feels like he can see right through me when he does this.

"This kind of stuff doesn't even freak you out, does it?" he says more than asks, his tone colored with a smug sense of knowing that I'm starting to realize is pure Jonah. "I mean, you know your shit when it comes to weapons, survival, and getting in and out of the government's hands."

"And?" I ask. I can tell he's been thinking about this for a while. I just don't know where he's going with it.

"And I'm thinking your dad really is a General. Is your grandfather one too?"

I don't want to go down this road but I have to say something. "He really is a general. I have training too," I add because I'm starting to feel bad that he doesn't know anything at all. Then I think back to his question. "What do you mean my grandfather?"

"Yeah, Bill. Short, old, same crazy eye color that could get you snatched by guards."

I burst out laughing. "You think Bill is my grandfather?" I double over in a fit of laughter. My eyes water and I'm holding my sides.

"You're not going to tell me he's your dad, are you?"

I put a hand out. "Please," I beg with tears in my eyes. "You have to stop talking."

Jonah stops in the middle of the road and crosses his arms. "Who is he, then?"

"I don't know. He's Bill. I picked him up at a gas station a few days ago. He was all helpless and old and he needed a place to crash. Eye color," I choke out on a laugh, "is a coincidence."

Jonah nods but doesn't move or uncross his arms.

I sigh in annoyance. "Ask him if you don't believe me. Jeez." Jonah stands there and eyes me like he does when he's reading me. I wonder, then if I've told him too much.

"You are kind of cute when you're mad," he answers suddenly. "You're always hot but the cute is new."

I open my mouth then close it. Then after giving him what I hope is an annoyed look, I turn away from him and keep walking.

I hear Jonah's chuckle somewhere behind me. I pretend he doesn't exist. Besides, according to the map and the big old sign in front of us, we're here.

"Bitlock Stadium," Jonah says as he reads it aloud.

I just nod.

CHAPTER 10

Spicy Italian

I draw my katana and motion for Jonah to do the same but he just shrugs, his weapon nowhere in sight. I roll my eyes but walk ahead as we wander into shelter number 17. Things are quiet. My mind is telling me that something's off. This is unlike every other shelter but I ignore it.

Whatever's happening I know I can handle it. I'm not scared of much. Jonah would crap his pants about anything, or at least that's what I used to think. Now I'm not sure.

He's been mostly quiet throughout our trip. Maybe it was seeing hope in some of the people's faces when we asked if they wanted us to find their loved ones out there and then the utter devastation when we'd tell them we found those loved ones, but they'd been turned into complete stinkers.

Jonah was the one that broke the news to them. He was kind-hearted and knew how to take care of the situation. He also hadn't mentioned the people he claimed he was looking for so I assumed he hadn't found them yet either. I could see in his eyes that it was starting to wear on him.

Still, we have to keep going. We walk down the musty halls and reach the doors that hopefully lead down to the shelter's inhabitants. The lights are dimmed because only every fifth light or so is on. I think it's the emergency lights. Unlike every other shelter there are no guards here. I'm grateful because they're annoying but it worries me too. Our footsteps echo down the barren halls and despite my bravery, the sound still gives me chills.

I shake it off and decide to woman up. Maybe this shelter is just empty. It doesn't make sense that it would be though because the shelters we've been to so far have been extremely overcrowded and it was on the list. Maybe this was an exclusive one for rich people, really quiet rich people, I muse.

I look at Jonah's worried face and keep going. I open the double doors and am grateful to hear the rustling and movement of others. The lights are really dim and again only the emergency lights are lit up. It's hard to make out anyone's faces.

It's barely 6 at night. Were they imposing an early bedtime or something? It seemed something the military would do. At least the military as they are now since the war.

Unfortunately, there's also a familiar lingering stench of rotting food and boys' locker room. I scrunch my nose in distaste. My poor nose has been through so much this week.

I rub it in sympathy and look to my right, where I find a light switch. I flip it. It's still dark. Damn.

I bring my shades up to rest at the top of my head because I can barely see anything at all. I have to risk it.

"Is there a Kate Booker here with a small boy?" I shout to the room, hearing my own words echo back to me. I feel a shiver run through my body but I press forward.

I see some movement in the distance and head-shaped figures in the dark. I rest my katana under my arm then pull off my bag from one shoulder and search through it till my fingers hit my flashlight and turn it on.

I flash it to the heads in the darkness to find white eyes staring back at me. White eyes everywhere.

Stinkers. All of them. A few hundred if I had to guess.

I should've known.

I feel Jonah close at my side now, practically plastered to me. "H," Jonah begins hesitantly. I look at Jonah's pale face and look back at the stinkers. They're making noises and zeroing in on my flashlight and on us. I can feel the tension in the air and am positive the stinkers are ready to strike at any moment. Our guns and katanas won't do enough damage to get us out alive. I know this and I know Jonah knows it too.

"At the count of three we run," I whisper, and out of my periphery I see Jonah's head move. "One...Two..."

Some of the stinkers start to shoot toward us.

"ABORT MISSION!" I push Jonah toward the double doors and we bolt. I hear the doors crash behind us and bodies thump loudly against them. Super stinkers.

I'm running faster than I can ever remember running. I hear the doors reopening and I chuck my flashlight into my bag then sling it onto my back as I turn around to watch the stinkers as I run.

Bodies are making their way through the doors. It's still dark and from what I can see their skin and features have decomposed so badly I can't even tell if they were once men or women. I'm so entirely engrossed by the sight. I turn around and realize my mistake immediately.

I'm about to crash into a wall. It's coming up too fast. By the time I recognize this I'm being jerked to the side and the corner nearly brushes my cheek and ear. It knocks my sunglasses off. They flail to the ground with a smash as I fall into Jonah's side, his arm tight around my middle as we run.

He just keeps going as he holds me up and once I find my footing, I shift my weight off him. I don't have breath to thank him but I squeeze his arm once before I move further away and try to maintain his spectacular break-neck speed.

"Keep running!" I yell to Jonah and to myself. I know better than to turn around so I'm not sure how close the monsters are but I'm not taking any more chances.

"Yeah," he shouts back. "I get that. Stinkers are chasing us!"

"Now is not the time to be a smartass. Run faster!"

I allow myself the briefest of seconds to note Jonah's smirk then I'm back to moving so fast I'm nearly flying.

We're gaining on the door and I can feel and hear Jonah's breaths coming hard, matching my own.

I watch his hand reach for the knob and relief floods me. We're almost out.

His fingers pass over the knob then slide back without warning. His grunt of alarm hits me as he's whisked away. I spin around, my katana swinging.

Jonah's in a full body grip from one stinker and three more are close behind him. Thankfully beyond them I see that the door holding back the rest of the stinkers has closed. I don't know how long it'll stay that way because I still hear the insistent banging on the walls.

I charge for the stinker attacking Jonah. He's huge and seems to be everywhere. I know I can just as easily hit Jonah if I try to strike out at it. I caution a thrust of my katana but the stinker backs out of reach and uses Jonah as a shield.

"H, behind you," Jonah shouts as he struggles and rams the back of his head into the face of the stinker holding him. I turn just in time to find a stinker on me. It pulls and tears at my arm and snaps at me.

I twist around and punch it in the side of the head. "Don't let it bite you!" I shout back to Jonah as I punch the stinker again, this time in the face.

"Got that too!" his voice yells back to me.

I want to roll my eyes but instead focus on the stinker in front of me. The brown ooze is spurting from its lip but it's not deterred. It's disoriented and wobbling but still standing.

I pull it by its stringy hair-this one was most definitely a woman once- and then force it back. I turn back to Jonah and he's thrashing hard against his captor. He's fast enough that he can't be bitten but not strong enough to break free of the hold.

I try to strike at the stinker once more but he pulls the same crap and pushes Jonah in front of my katana, and I nearly graze him. A low growl emerges from my throat in frustration. The stinkers behind the closed door are banging louder and I know it's only a matter of time before more converge on us. Time is running out for us and fast.

"Duck!" I yell out.

Jonah scrunches his body down best he can, given the tight hold, and I see the opening I need. I pull back to gain momentum and then slice through his captor's neck.

"Jesus!" Jonah gasps as the stinker's head rolls clean off and brown ooze splashes all over Jonah.

I pull back my katana and my arms feel so incredibly heavy. I know it's the feeling of adrenaline wearing off. Today's been too long and I haven't eaten nearly enough. I'm watching Jonah scramble back out of the headless stinker's loosened hold when a gaping mouth is suddenly hovering inches in front of me, taking over my field of vision completely. The smell is too intense. It burns my eyes. I gag and try to cover my face.

Two hands pull me from behind and I'm being dragged by my braid and my middle. My arms struggle against sudden holds, my hand is being twisted and the sound of my katana clattering to the floor just about destroys me.

I barely turn my head and see that the female stinker is back and she brought her two friends with her.

"Jonah," I yell," the gun!" They're panting and making awful screeching noises as they snap and claw at me. I elbow and kick and use every part of my body but it's no use. All of them are converging on me. I've been bested and I want to rage but I need to pull it together and save my strength.

My eyes find Jonah's as the stinkers pull me down, the items in my backpack digging hard into my spine. I don't know if he'll reach his gun in time. I don't even know if he has it on him. I know he left his katana in my car. Hell, I didn't know if he knows how to properly shoot the gun for that matter. With everything I have I struggle against all the holds on me but it only manages to get me pinned to the floor faster.

My eyes dart around until I realize one of my legs can break free from under a stinker's clawing hand. I quickly hook one stinker under his leg and he trips over it. All the air is forced from my body as he falls heavily onto me.

In panic, I fight through the pain and all I can think is that it's like a snake. I know it can strangle me or hurt me in other ways but I only worry about where its head is and I need to locate it. Now.

Then my head is jerked back and slammed into the linoleum floor as the female stinker falls to her knees and bends right over the stinker on top of me. She claws at my face until she grabs my hair and pulls my head back. Her cold, blank eyes pierce through me and I know my time's up. Her mouth opens and ooze drips from her face onto mine. I pull back as far as I can and spit on her but she doesn't seem to notice or care.

I decide I don't want to watch my own death. I close my eyes and bite my lip, bracing myself. I faintly hear Jonah calling my name.

Air is suddenly rushing into my lungs. The crushing weight has been lifted off me. I blink open my eyes and I'm being yanked by the hand to a standing position.

"What?" I cry as my world spins around me.

I'm yanked some more by Jonah and am being thrust toward the door by his left hand. I notice my katana in his right hand, covered from hilt to tip in stinker ooze. I dare a parting glance at the room behind me as we race out of the building and find the slain bodies of four stinkers in our wake. The door beyond though, is opening.

We bolt out of the building and down the long street. I don't even think of looking back and neither does Jonah. "Of all the freaking times to park away from the shelter," I call as I feel my backpack slamming into my back as I try to maintain my pace. Not surprisingly, Jonah is already ahead of me again because of his ridiculously long legs. He ends up grabbing my hand and pulling me to his speed, for which I'm so very grateful.

"Run now. Talk later, babe!" Jonah replies, his green eyes

laughing. It's a laughter born of narrowly escaped deaths and I want to hear it again and again. Then it dawns on me.

"Did you just call me babe?" I ask, appalled, between gasps for air.

Jonah throws his head back in another chuckle but doesn't stop running. "I saved our lives and that's what you focus on?" he asks huskily.

Right. That. "How the hell did you do that?" I cry. "I saw the bodies. That was no lucky mistake."

"I know how to fight. Unlike *some people* it's not something I enjoy or care to repeat, like ever, but I know how. I'm a," he runs out of breath then swallows, "pacifist. But yeah, I can fight. You think it's hot, right?" he asks like he's making another statement.

I glare at him over my shoulder. Then I turn back to the road with a start because I now have the car in my sights.

"Make love not war," he says with a wink.

I tear my hand out of his and pull out the keys from my bag. "Shut up and get in the car!"

I open the car and breathe heavily. I immediately seek out Jonah's pale face beside me and watch as he pulls in gulps of air. Content that he's here and we're both safe, I throw my open bag down at his feet and turn on the engine. Then only when the tires are screeching as I reverse and get us back onto the road do I let myself chill.

I have to roll the windows down because Jonah, my

weapon, and I are covered in nasty, brown stinker ooze. Jonah takes his time choosing a c.d. from the collection scattered in the back seat and then we're blasting it and driving around aimlessly.

After 20 minutes or so I force myself to ask where the next shelter is on the map. Jonah picks it up but only looks at me when he speaks. "We should've known that smell. It was familiar. I knew it," he says, sounding slightly panicked for the first time.

"I know," I respond and press on the gas even harder, making the engine roar. I did know that it was a possibility that a shelter could be infected but even having seen it, it's hard to believe. "Grab a pen and mark that one down," I mutter.

"Already on it," he says, pulling off the cap of a pen with his teeth. "Bitlock Stadium will now be known as Shitlock. As in damn, you better lock that shit up and throw away the key."

"More like Bitten Lock," I mutter.

"Good one," he says with a laugh as he's writing on the map. I smile.

He reads off the next shelter name and feeds me the directions. After a few minutes, I feel Jonah's eyes on me again. Seriously, his stares were starting to freak me out because I was already so used to them it was like I knew what mood he was in, and I wasn't even looking at him.

Right now, for instance, I could tell he was going to ask me stuff, and it wasn't something I wanted to deal with.

"Ok," he begins. "I think you've learned you can trust me by now. You've got to tell me what you know. Maybe start with who you are, for one. Your family. Anything."

I try to remain calm. "Can we talk about me later?" I ask.

Jonah continues staring. "No. I've helped you too, you know. Stop leaving me in the dark. It's bullshit. We just had to face a stadium full of undead monsters. I'm with you, H. Tell me something. I've earned it and I've waited long enough."

I bite my lip. "What do you want to know?" I ask, aggravation coloring my tone.

Jonah grins, surprising the heck out of me. "What's your whole pizza obsession about?"

I feel my eyes practically bulging out of my head. "That's your burning question?"

Jonah shrugs his wide shoulders. "I figured I'd start you off with something easy. The pizza?" he questions firmly but with a teasing tone. He's totally making fun of me.

I may or may not like it. "The day of the outbreak, I was in a pizza restaurant with my family," I begin. I end up telling him everything, except for the stuff about my dad. I'm not sure why but it all just comes out.

"So, pizza for you symbolizes getting back to that day? Taking back what was taken from you?" he asks, the teasing tone gone.

"What? No," I say immediately.

"I don't know." My voice lowers.

"Maybe." I glance at him then back to the road. "I just really wanted that pizza. It's amazing. Plus, it's great motivation to get here and fight off the stinkers, knowing there's something good at the end of all this. It sounds stupid but it's the small things that are getting me through this, okay? There's no guarantee that anyone I love is safe right now." I swallow hard. "I know for a fact that some of them are already gone."

Suddenly I feel Jonah's hand under my chin and he gently pulls me to face him. I take my foot off the gas and snap out of my head. "It's not stupid. We're going to get through this. And we're going to eat some damned good pizza. I promise," he says, his voice sounding like honey.

I stare at him, trying to find a lie in his darkening green eyes, searching out for something I know must be there but I can't find it. Something in my belly flutters and even as I feel it, I know there's no way in hell I'm giving a name to it.

"We need to talk about your eyes, H," Jonah says, totally breaking the moment.

"What are you thinking?" I ask as a way of deflection.

"That you and Bill are in danger for some reason. I know you don't want to hear this but I think you may have been infected."

"Don't," I say sharply. "There's nothing wrong with me. I'm perfect."

"H," he says firmly. "Look I obviously don't think you're a

stinker. I think there's something amazing about you, not something wrong with you but we have to talk about the possibility-"

"-No, *we* really don't," I say cutting him off. "*We* don't have to do anything, Jonah."

Jonah is silent and my breathing is harsh. I think I might be on the verge of a panic attack. "Fine," Jonah finally replies. "If you want to talk about it, I'm here. And you will," he says stubbornly.

I glare at him.

Finally, he nods and settles back into his seat. "Later," he begrudgingly adds. "For now, we need to buy you some new sunglasses before we hit another shelter."

I nod as I realize he's right and that for whatever reason Jonah really does have my back. I know it's odd to wear sunglasses at night and inside of shelters but I don't have much of a choice but to play it off. "Know of any stores around here?" I ask him.

Jonah pulls the map out of the glove compartment and glances at it for a moment. "There should be a mall not too far away. I remember I had a doctor's appointment around here once. I dropped off...someone at the mall across the street while I went to the appointment."

I frown at his tone. He sounded almost guilty. It was weird. "Ok," I say. I try to think of something to say. "Doctor's, huh? This is kind of a long drive for a doctor."

"Yeah, I got the Lasik procedure. Actually...Oh, man. I'm a

freaking genius. Let's go there," he says excitedly.

"What? why?"

"We'll get you colored contacts. No sunglasses needed. They had a bunch of samples that didn't have a prescription in them at the front desk."

I turn and barely contain my smile. Oh, he so was a freaking genius. I just wasn't going to tell him that.

"Not bad," I reply lightly.

He raises an eyebrow and I can't help it. I laugh. "Okay, okay. It's a great idea. Happy?" I give him fake applause.

Jonah faces forward and stretches out on the seat as his hands come up to link behind his head. "Why yes, H. I really am. It's hard to believe it took you this long to notice."

I groan and keep driving.

CHAPTER 11

The Works

The next shelter is filled with guards and people. My eyes look almost identical to the original brown they once were but it still feels off. Jonah assured me that he couldn't tell they were contacts though so I had to go with it. I pull up a chair, make my speech but nothing happens. No Mom, no Justin. No one is asking for our help.

We're able to snag clean clothes and wash off in the bathroom sinks. I meet Jonah outside the bathroom but only give him a slight nod. I'm disappointed with this entire day and I'm feeling done. We're probably going to work through the night as much as we can because time is limited. I make for the exit, hungry and exhausted, and I can feel Jonah's arm on my shoulder. He's already done with his list. "Maybe if we tell people that you're looking for your family, they would be more willing to help."

"And who are you looking for, Jonah?" I ask defensively mostly because I'm irritated that I haven't found them yet and I hate explaining myself. I noticed the way he searches the crowd along with the list of names but he doesn't know what my family looks like. He's obviously looking for someone else. He just stares at me in return.

I walk a little faster through the crowd of people. I feel hands grab me and all of a sudden lips on my mouth. For a second I think it's Jonah and I want to kick him.

I open my eyes and to my surprise it's Adam, my ex-boyfriend. I back up and stare at him. "Adam?" I ask in a hopeful daze. "Wait. What the fuck?" I sputter in confusion.

He looks at me. "What do you mean what the fuck? You're my girlfriend. I thought I was never going to see you again," he says, starting to get closer. "Suddenly I see you up on that table and..." He pauses and just runs a hand over my cheek. I can see he is happy to see me. Then he's staring into my eyes. I tell myself he can't tell the difference in the shade of brown. I'm being paranoid and I know it. I calm down as he says, "Listen, are you serious about helping people because babe-"

"-Girlfriend?" A voice growls from behind me. "What do you mean girlfriend?"

Both Adam and I ignore Jonah. I remember what was said and I start seeing red. I freaking knew Adam wouldn't remember. "Seriously Adam? I broke up with you 3 months ago," I say, baffled.

He only gives me a sexy, confused look. It almost seems posed but I knew it wasn't. He just had great cheekbones.

"I don't remember that, H. You never broke up with me," he says as if that would never happen, making me more enraged.

"Hello, is anyone going to answer my question here?" Jonah cuts in.

I just put my hand up and ignore Jonah's rambling behind me. Adam was about to hear it from me. I hated repeating myself but I'd made a great speech before and I wasn't letting him get away without forcing him to hear it one way or another.

"Look, Adam, you were great in a lot of things but recently all you've done is get high and play video games. And as much as I loved playing video games with you, it was just distracting. We never talked. You always had your shirt off and your abs are so perfect. We always ended up making out and never leaving your room..." I realize I'm digressing. I already forgot my perfect speech. "I deserve better than that," I finish.

"So?" he asks in confusion. That was the thing about Adam, he always seemed a little confused.

"So, I broke up with you and you were too high to even notice I left your house that night," I shout. "I haven't heard from you since so I assumed you got the message, dumbass."

I finally glance at Jonah. His eyes, a shade darker than normal, are scarily fixated on Adam.

"Wow. Okay. So, you're going to be like that, baby?" Adam replies.

I stare back at him, my badass glare turned up high, hoping he gets the picture.

"Can't you at least give me another chance?" he begs, sounding desperate.

My eyes travel his body and I have to admit Adam was one hot guy. I had a great taste in guys just like I had a great taste in cars and food. His blond hair went perfectly with his blue eyes and his perfect smile. Then there was his trail of tattoos that started with his full arm tribal sleeve, but it wasn't his looks that made me like him.

He was also an amazing person and had saved me multiple times from either dying or turning insane during our training. He was the calm in my storm. After we were released from camp because the war had ended, we ended up dating in the real world. Since then we were on and off again for the last few years.

By saying another chance, what he meant was the millionth chance. We always broke up because he wasn't the same guy when he was on drugs. Still I always ended up taking him back because before his addiction, he was probably one of the best guys I ever met. He cared about me and he'd kept me safe and it wasn't something I could just forget.

Plus, I couldn't quite blame him for his habits. Unfortunately, the kind of training that we went through-I shiver at just remembering it-never really leaves you.

I walk around with a bad attitude and my guards permanently up. Hell, I was a walking mental-case and ticking time bomb. I killed my own father a few days ago and I was functioning just like everyone else.

Adam's reaction to training was less violent but no less dangerous. Adam turned to drugs. He told me it was nothing hardcore but we both knew I only pretended to believe him.

I was glad he was alive but he didn't know how to be better. Could I blame him, though? Maybe I should give him another chance. I step toward Adam and grab his face.

At that moment, I feel myself being elevated from off the

ground and suddenly I'm thrown over Jonah's shoulder. What the hell?

"Put me down, you imbecile," I scream, punching his back and flailing like an idiot. I look up and look at the ever-confused Adam. Adam? Wait! Was I about to take him back? Was I the one on drugs?

He looks ready to pull me back but I shake my head. He knows I can handle myself and frankly he would slaughter Jonah in a fight. Then again, who knew? I didn't see Jonah slice through the stinkers earlier, I only saw the damage he left behind. It didn't matter though. If anyone was fighting Jonah it was me, and right now I didn't have the time.

I decide I'll deal with Jonah later. Adam sighs in understanding then gives me a quick pat near my hip in goodbye as I'm carried away. "Come with us. We're helping people," I yell out.

"I can't," he says with a quick shake of his head and his eyes flick sharply to the officers that are staring down at us. I get his meaning.

Even as I pound on Jonah's back he starts making his way back through the crowd, my weight not even deterring him. I find Adam's face in the crowd again and scream, "I'm sorry. It's not me, it's you," and go back to being owned by caveman Jonah.

Once the darkness of the night surrounds me and I feel the ground beneath my feet, I get in a fighting stance. With my right hand, I jab Jonah in the lower abdomen. Not hard, but enough.

He crouches down without air and wheezes out in a pained

cry, “What the-”

I roll my eyes. “Yeah, Jonah. You might want to think about what you're doing before you want to take me out of a conversation because next time, the punch will be further down south.”

Ignoring him, I pace and laugh. “What the hell was that, huh? Picking me up like I'm your property?”

He stays quiet, still crouching down.

“Do I look like your girlfriend, Jonah? Huh?” I say with anger in my voice. I'm suddenly pissed all over again. Where does he get off?

He stays quiet and stares up at me. Finally, his voice comes out strong as he firmly states, “No.”

I seriously want to punch him again. “Okay. Then why was that necessary?”

Again, he takes forever to answer. “Jonah!” I yell, focusing his attention back on me. Now was not the time to keep me waiting.

“First off, I was watching the guards and they were making calls,” he says, his voice sounding rusty and pained. “I know it won’t be far reaching but they’ll get the communication where it needs to go eventually and I think you were lying about your dad. I'm not sure why but I do and I figured if they found us out that shit would hit the fan so we had to make a quick exit.”

I take a deep breath, my lungs sore from screaming and I start to calm down a little. “Ok,” I breathe again and repeat myself in a quieter tone. “Ok. Let's get back to Daredevil then.”

We start racing to the car. I decide to ignore Jonah and turn back to the road, taking in the tension and the awkward silence.

“You really wanted to get back with that guy, H?” Jonah shouts suddenly. “That guy?”

Surprised at his outburst, I whip my head toward him. I'm rewarded with a priceless face. His eyebrows are scrunched down, as if he can’t fathom life anymore. Not the whole stinker, thing. No. Just me and Adam together. I laugh and it relaxes me into answering honestly.

“Adam's not a bad guy. He's just a little messed up.”

“Why? Did someone ask him to count past ten?”

I glare at him and turn back to the road and I'm fighting a smile so hard, it hurts. “He's smarter than he lets on but it doesn't matter. He's obviously gorgeous and he's actually a good guy or he was, once.” I make a sharp turn and again I feel calmer. “He was there when I needed him. That's all you need to know.”

“You know you shouldn't date someone out of pity.”

I know he's not wrong. I also know he's annoying me. “And you should mind your own business,” I scoff.

The tension is high again between us and even with the air turned on full blast, it feels hot. Jonah physically hauled me out of that place and while I'm not down with that, I can't help my surprise or how my breathing has become shallow.

“Where's the next shelter?” he asks, his voice an octave lower than usual.

I exhale again and slow the car to a stop. Of course, the road is empty so it doesn't matter. "A few miles down but if I'm guessing correctly then we're making another stop first." I pull a crumpled napkin from my pocket. I may have been over Jonah's shoulder and wailing like a harpy but I can still feel when someone slips something into my pocket.

I toss it to Jonah. "It's an address, isn't it?" I guess.

Jonah's hand reaches up to turn on his overhead light. Then I watch as his green eyes flit across the page, his fingers smoothing out the wrinkles gently. "An address and a name. 8124 Woodway Lane. Bran. We're going to help him?"

I take a minute to decide if I'm surprised who Adam has on the outside. No, just pissed as hell. It's funny, but I used to dream that if there was ever a crazy apocalypse, it would happen just so Bran could die horribly, like say, be eaten by a zombie.

Naturally the end of times was here and Bran was still fucking kicking. I hated him but right now he was my only lead to help people and find my mom. "If we play our cards right, he might help us."

CHAPTER 12

Spinach & Feta

I bang loudly on the door of a mansion in Spring Valley. That's right, a freaking mansion. The gaudy bastard would choose here to have a hide-out during a national emergency. The guy even had lights on at night, which told me he was either stupid or he had enough connections to get away with being here. Unfortunately, I wouldn't be surprised if he killed the occupants so he could move in whether they were stinkers or not.

We're actually close to home but right now it feels like we might as well be a million miles away. I just wanted to get this over with so we can get home, eat pizza, and sleep.

"Why do you look worried?" Jonah whispers in my ear. I look back at him and as suspected he's standing very close to me. I roll my eyes. I was fine. He looked worried. We'd made our plans and remade them about ten times before getting here. Jonah was obviously intelligent and a decent strategist but only I knew Bran.

I'd given Jonah a few details in the car of what we were walking into. I told him it was best if he stayed in the car until I gave him a signal but true to form, the kid followed me everywhere.

I wasn't big on sharing but I didn't want Jonah saying something to screw this up. Our plans were surprisingly decent and if he thought the stinkers were bad, he hadn't seen anything yet.

I bang again. “Bran! Open the stinking door, you big oaf.” I shout so loudly Jonah steps back from me, his laptop in its case, dangling from his hand. I sigh and roll my eyes heavenward.

The door opens and a girl in goth-style dress steps out. Her black hair is matte and dull, clearly dyed. She’s wearing all black but there’s no hiding the designer labels, and the eyeliner is out of control. She looks like she’s playing at being hardcore but probably goes shopping in her free time after taking bubble baths with strawberry-scented candles.

Jonah looks between us and I know what he’s viewing, the pipsqueak with the black hair and me with the white. “Where's Bran?” I ask.

“Don't know what you're talking about,” she says as she pulls out a cigarette. I notice her hand shaking infinitesimally.

“Let me guess, he told you to turn anyone away. He's probably looking out the window right now.” I look up and catch a movement out of the 5th window from the left on the 2nd floor, a curtain swaying on its own. I wave at the window then turn back to Wednesday Addams. She looks nervous now.

“So what if he did?” she pouts. “Get a clue, you can't come in. Now get off my property before the biters come out to play. I hear they'll bite just about anyone.”

Jonah laughs. “They're stinkers.”

I elbow him. Now is so not the time to play word games.

“You can come in,” Wednesday says suddenly, looking over

my head to Jonah. “Just ditch the girl.”

“Don't have to,” he replies.

“Why?” she asks with a pout, blowing her smoke in my face.

“Because H is about to break in.”

I can’t help my surprise and growing smile as I glance at Jonah. I tell the kid next to nothing about myself but even without that he sure knew me well. It was a little scary.

“What?” she cries but I'm already past her, her eyes are wide as I swipe her cigarette right from her mouth and stomp it out.

I keep stomping, easily pushing her aside and start yelling. “Bran!!! Come out, come out wherever you are. It's your favorite psycho!”

As suspected Bran comes out of the shadows from somewhere behind the massive staircase. I force myself not to jump as he touches my shoulder then pulls me into a crushing embrace that I so don't want to be in. “Well, if it isn't pretty, little H. I knew you couldn't resist me. Finally ditch our man Adam? He's a good guy but he never knew how to share,” he drawls slowly.

I know this is all a game to him. After our alliance was made, our dynamic changed and he decided the best way to put me in my place was to hit on me, repeatedly. It was his goal to make me feel as uncomfortable as possible and treat me like some whore that could be passed around. I was beyond disgusted by this change but I played along because it was better than being stabbed again.

I grace him with a half smirk and then glance around as more people come out of the shadows and crowd around Bran. Tall, ugly guys and girls, their ages ranging between their 20s and 30s, fill the room. They're not even trying to conceal their knives and guns. As I suspected the usual thug types are here, probably pissing themselves at the chance to live in a place like this. Little Wednesday might have been playing at badass but these others weren't.

I feel Jonah at my back again and I don't know why-because I'm not sure exactly how much help he'd be in a fight-but it makes me feel better. I slowly pull my arm out of Bran's grasp. "Yeah...Adam actually sent me here. He wants me to tell you that you need to get to a-" I pause as I step back and Bran follows and pulls out a knife, "-shelter."

"Lady, we'll give you shelter," a man with crooked front teeth yells from my left.

"Shut up," both Jonah and Bran yell.

"She's no lady and she's off limits," Bran says to them but only looks at me.

"So is he," I say about Jonah, my eyes making my stance on this very clear as they stare into Bran's. This was the way I had to be with him. I could never show fear.

Bran's eyes stare back and it's undeniably tense in the room. This is what I was worried about. Finally, Bran laughs and steps away, brandishing his knife on his duster jacket. "Do what she says, for now."

The group backs up slightly with a few grumbles.

"What makes you think I'm going to listen to you?" he drawls. He always spoke slowly, methodically, and in my opinion, it was creepy as hell but of course that's why he did it.

I pull my shoulders up and begin brandishing my own katana. That's right, buddy, mine is bigger than yours. I grace him with my full smirk now. "I'll tell you why...over dinner. Got any pizza in this...palace?" I ask. I know I've been craving it and Jonah seems to be craving it too if our conversations about it were any indication.

Bran snaps his fingers. "Erin. Make us pizza. Now." I watch smugly as Wednesday Addams pouts some more and she moves toward Bran. He pats her ass and she walks off, sending a nasty look my way. He's all yours, I want to say but don't. I still have things to accomplish and dear God do I want that pizza!

"The rest of you, leave us alone so we can become...reacquainted."

The room clears out with a few grumbles.

"Good. Now that that's settled," Jonah says as he leans against the curving banister with a broad smile on his face.

In a flash of movement Bran is suddenly at Jonah's side, his knife a shining gleam against Jonah's throat.

My stalker-extraordinaire turns as white as a sheet but suddenly he says in a calm voice that I have no idea how he manages, “Don't suppose you'd mind removing that.”

Bran stays where he is, assessing Jonah.

Shit was getting out of hand. “I know you'll hear me out, Bran,” I blurt out to distract him. I knew the chances of that were slim but I had to try. I slowly slink in closer to him.

“I know you'll listen because you wanted me to come in. You saw me in the window and you sent your little goth girl to open the door. If you didn't want me here, you would've sent one of your men,” I say confidently as I put my hand over his. Then I try not to flinch as I try to pull the knife back from Jonah's skin.

He lets me. Part of me wants to comfort Jonah but all my attention is on Bran. Besides I warned him what would happen if he tried to talk. “Or,” I continue, “because you know me and you know I would've gotten past your men, you would've come yourself. But you didn't.”

Bran finally turns to me. Then to my surprise, he laughs. “Maybe I just wanted you to come inside so I could kill you here myself. Show my followers what happens if they screw with me.”

“Well, sure,” I say with a fake smile, “but you wouldn't want to mess up your girlfriend’s digs with my blood. Besides you tried to kill me once before and it didn’t work. Adam wasn't too happy about that and I know you give a shit about what he thinks. So, I'm calling you out. Now, are you going to piss me off again or do you want to listen to why I'm here?”

“Follow,” he commands, and we do.

We enter a large dining room behind Bran, Jonah and I giving each other intense stares behind his back. Bran's friends are waiting there at the table eating from bags of chips and pretzels. I'm surprised they sat at all. I'd half expected them to eat off dog dishes on the floor.

I pull a bag from a guy that looks a little high on something because I know he'll be too slow to do anything about it. It's a bag of cheesy chips and I share it with Jonah and pull up a chair at the head of the table without saying a word.

"So obviously you've survived this long. Want to trade war stories?" Bran asks. I know this is his tactic to get information out of me but I decide it's best to share most of what I know in hopes that he'll help.

Jonah stays silent as I tell Bran everything I know about the stinkers, the bombing, the shelters, and even Senator Cookie. The people around us look confused but they still catcall at me and interrupt me constantly like I'm giving a strip tease and not talking about virus strains.

Bran doesn't say a word when I finish, damn him. This clearly wasn't going to be a tit for tat situation.

"So, what's your plan? This place is nice and all but it won't survive the bombing," I say finally. My patience is only so good these days.

He chuckles and replies, "You're assuming they'll bomb us? How cute."

"Bran, you need to listen," I try, barely able to hold back rolling my eyes. I had to tell him but I needed the right way to approach it.

"No, you listen, little girl. While you were passed out like a poor little princess during the outbreak some of us were actually fighting off these fuckers. You didn't see the city in chaos, you didn't see everyone getting turned, every-freaking-one," he says with an amused gleam in his eye that betrays his disgusted tone.

"That shit was serious and it lasted for hours. I wasn't in a fancy restaurant with idiots who let themselves get bitten. My neighborhood was in the ghetto and we're not known for taking things quietly. That shit went up in my flames. Those diseased biters got theirs. We got out."

This was immediately followed by cheering from the delinquents at the table around us.

"How do you know?" Jonah's voice asks steadily from beside me, and the cheering dies off. "How do you know that the stinkers are the only ones that died in that fire?"

The room goes silent as Bran turns his cold eyes on Jonah. "Some sacrifices have to be made for the good of the many. I watched it burn, yeah, some people went down, but not my people. I'll tell you that right now. We did what we had to do and we're still alive so I'm not explaining anything more to anyone else. Got me, asshole?"

Jonah raised an eyebrow and opened his mouth but I put a

hand out and spoke over him. “Well, that’s just dandy, Bran. I bet some more of your people got free and are out there. Don’t you want to make sure they don’t get bombed?” I asked.

“That's none of your business as of now. And like I said, the bombing is bullshit. Now shut up and wait for your food like the good girl you are.”

His friends laugh and leer some more. Jonah's face is tight. I stiffen and say nothing. Either I bite my tongue or I'll start a war in this house. The latter seems like a great idea but Jonah would be a liability. I sigh but sit tight. Pizza is coming. I'm slightly homicidal but I'm not an idiot.

“There’s more,” I say.

While we’re waiting, the huge chandeliers hanging from the ceiling start to flicker and the house goes silent. We all stare at the chandelier like it’s some science project about to explode. It turns off with a zap and the rest of the electricity in the house goes with it.

“What the fuck!” I hear Wednesday screaming from the kitchen. The first time I could’ve had pizza in a while and the damn power goes off. My hand automatically finds Jonah’s in the dark and he grabs it tightly. I try not to think about that so I look at everyone’s baffled faces and start to laugh.

“I guess the bombing is going to happen, Bran.” I can make out his form by the light of the moon from the window.

“Not my problem,” he replies with an arch of his brow.

I'd get no help here. Resigned, I pull my hand back, get up from the table and look at Jonah. His green eyes meet mine in the dark and I see trust in them that I hadn't seen before. He's letting me take the lead now.

“Let’s go,” I say as I walk away from the dining room into the foyer and good ol' me forgot to access my weapons before I opened the door.

I look at a figure in the distance and its white, glowing eyes zero in on me. Besides the moon, they are the only illumination on the street since the city lamps are out.

I close the door so fast it feels like I’m hallucinating. I turn to Jonah who is looking a little pale again. “What was that?” he asks, sounding a little confused but I can hear the fear in his voice.

“It was a super stinker and unless we want an epic battle we should stay until morning or at least try.” It’s easier to be attacked in the dark, and it was dark with the lights out. Bran sucks but this house is big enough for us to not have to deal with him.

I think hard on the saying that the devil you know is better than the devil you don’t. I breathe in deeply and walk into the dining room again. I see Bran laughing with the rest of his delinquent friends. I guess Wednesday is still in the kitchen making God knows what.

The moonlight bounces off my enemy’s ugly forehead. I hate him but I can use him. So, I will. “Bran, I need to talk to you in private.”

He glances toward me and stands without speaking and follows me to the door, which is a huge surprise.

"Look, we both know what's happening. Innocent people are going to die. I know that program messed us all up. We can't be the same anymore but we should at least help the people not in shelters. With your group, we can expand and cover more ground to get as many people in shelters as possible." I looked at him in the sincerest way I could.

"What's in it for me?"

"Well, for one thing we're the only ones with skills for this. Any civilian survivors are going to get themselves killed and official government soldiers are just going to let it happen. I'm thinking no one else can help them but us. As for you, I figure this is me saving you from the bombings so you owe me. Not to mention that Adam's in a shelter and 10 to 1 they won't let him leave. I know you don't give a shit about me but think of him. He told me to come to you. Plus," I say slowly, knowing this is what will hook him in, "I know you want out of this city as much as I do and Jonah here can hack into the government database to pinpoint the way out."

His eyes gleam with interest and I know I've got him so I add, "And while I'm in the moment we need to stay the night. I'm not in the mood to fight off a super stinker."

He stands silent for what seems like a millennium and says, "All right. Tomorrow as soon as the sun comes up we head out and cover as much ground as possible. I'll bust Adam out of that shelter.

That dumbass can help us out. I'll do this...just as long as you uphold your end and get me out of the bordered walls."

I nod my head in agreement, trying not to gloat, but seriously I'm awesome. "I've got maps. We'll split them as soon as the sun's up."

"Fine," Bran says. "Follow me."

CHAPTER 13

Tomato Pie

"Where?" Jonah asks.

"I'll take you to some rooms now. I can't leave those fuckers alone for long. They'll probably nick the crystals off the light fixtures while they're out," Bran says with a sneer.

This doesn't surprise me at all. I glance around the unfamiliar house and the ever-darkening shadows. "Got any candles?" I ask. I have my own supplies but I'm not letting him know that. He was the type of guy that would skin me for a piece of toast if he wanted it, after all.

Bran turns back around on me and his creepy slow voice is in my ear. "You're not afraid of the dark, little girl. Are you?"

Jonah snorts as if it's the funniest thing he's ever heard.

Bran ignores him but backs up off me quickly. "It doesn't matter. I'm telling everyone to get their asses to sleep too. Don't want this crew wandering around when I can't see them. Just in case I'd lock your door, princess," he says with a grind in his teeth as if he's loathed to warn me about anything. I know he only does so for Adam's sake.

Jonah stops walking before we hit the staircase and both Bran and I turn to face him. "Yeah, screw that. We'll take one room together or we're not staying," he states firmly.

I have no idea why he's making demands of the man who

had a knife to his throat not 40 minutes before but he doesn't seem to be kidding.

Bran eyes him coldly and the look melts into what I can only call grudging respect. "Fine," he says and keeps walking.

Jonah and I follow Bran to the second floor of the amazing house into a room by the end of the hall. Bran doesn't wait around to tuck us in, thank God. He just points to the door then walks right back up the hall the way he came. Jonah and I head inside and I open my book-bag to get a flashlight and look at the large room.

Whoever used to live here must've had a great life. The room is way too girly for my taste but there's no doubt that everything from the antique armoire to the weathered, teal vanity table to the massive, oversized sleigh bed are expensive. The intricately patterned bedding of geometric shapes and flowers was probably called something like shabby-chic and cost more than the first month's rent on the apartment downtown I was saving up to move into.

I find an en suite bathroom and sigh aloud; grateful we don't have to leave this room for anything tonight. "I'll be right back," I announce to Jonah then I head inside the bathroom. Once my face and teeth are clean and my contacts are out, I feel better but I try to avoid the mirror because the purple in my eyes still freaks me out a little. I walk back into the room with my flashlight and Jonah is standing, waiting for me. "You done?" he asks softly.

"Yeah," I say nodding. I don't know why but we're practically whispering. I figure it has something to do with the darkness. I shrug it off and Jonah passes by me as he enters the bathroom. I walk past the vanity table and run my fingers along a collection of glass perfume bottles. I play with them as I walk by and the clinking noises are the only sounds in the room.

Soon I hear the sink running in the distance though, and it calms me somewhat. On the mirror sits pictures haphazardly stuffed into the corners of the outer frame. A red-headed girl stars in all the pictures. Different people surround her in different settings; the mall, a school dance, the beach. Everyone looks so happy.

For the first time in a long time I don't begrudge the people of la-la land. I consider what it must've been like to have a normal teenage life. I stare at the picture of girls and guys lined up in a row in pretty dresses and suits and ties. I try to picture myself in the photo, my hair done-up, a corsage around my arm...but I can't.

I hear Jonah re-enter the room and walk past me but I'm still caught up in the photos. There's just something about seeing their smiles that gets to me, even now.

Eventually I do turn away from the mirror when I feel Jonah's eyes on me.

Jonah stares at me for the longest time and sits on the edge of the bed. I can sense the tension coming off him.

"What's wrong, now?" I say as I walk toward him and point the flashlight at his face.

"Are you trying to blind me? Give me that!" he says standing up and reaching for it.

"No!" I say, giggling for the first time in a while. He manages to get a hold of me and grabs one of my hands.

Jonah laughs and it's deep and masculine. Sexy. "You're going to surrender this flashlight," he promises with a smirk.

"Never!" I manage to get out of his grip and jump on the bed and he follows, somehow ending up on top of me. Our faces are inches apart. I notice a million details in a split second, like how long his eyelashes are, how shallow my breathing is, and the exact feel of his skin against mine.

We're so close I can feel his muscles shift on top of me and I move in, putting my lips on his.

Not to be outdone, he deepens the kiss and I swear I feel butterflies. I grasp at his shirt, trying to move it up and get to warm skin. I'm suddenly itching to reach beneath his sarcastic exterior.

Jonah groans and I'm not certain it wasn't just him. No, it was definitely both of us. Well, hello, six-pack abs. Who knew?

In a flash Jonah's lips fall away. I'm hoping he'll move them to more fun places but he pulls back and stares at me.

The moment passes and I stare back. "What?" I try to ask but without enough air it sounds wheezy. He is on top of me after all and he's kind of heavy. From the brief introduction I got with his muscles, now I know why.

"I'm sorry. I can't do this, H." He scrambles off me and stands up.

With a pitying face, he offers me his hand. I slap it away.

"Whatever," I say coolly as I sit up. I know my eyes are

shooting flames at him but I can't help that.

"Don't be mad. It's just that she might still be out there. This is wrong."

I blink rapidly, trying to process. "Excuse me. Who might be out there?"

"My girlfriend," he mumbles, looking anywhere but at me.

I wait, keeping my face blank. Jonah finally meets my eyes.

I keep staring.

"Please say something."

I laugh and my laughter bubbles up from somewhere deep inside me. I can't stop myself. "You carried me out of a shelter," I say.

"I know-" he begins.

I cut him off, the laughter still hijacking my voice. "You picked me up and carted me out of a shelter away from my ex-boyfriend."

"H-"

"You threw a hissy fit," I cry in between fits of hysteria. "You follow me around. You give me a hard time over someone who is an ex. You kiss me. And now you tell me you've had a girlfriend all along who may or may not be alive right now. Oh, God. This is too rich."

Tears spring to my eyes from laughing and I wipe them away. "You're a bigger idiot than I thought."

Jonah chucks a pillow at me. "Shut up," he says. "You're going to wake up the mad hatter and tea party people from hell."

"Screw you, Jonah. You are so lucky I don't kill you right now or at least break your arm or something."

"Look, I'm sorry I kissed you. It was a mistake. Can we let this go?"

"Damn right it was a mistake." I chuck the same pillow back to Jonah. "Here. You're sleeping on the floor tonight. Hope you have sweet dreams of your girlfriend."

Jonah groans and grabs the top blanket from the bed. "Fair enough. Goodnight," he says, resigned and a little petulant. I can't even explain how happy that made me to hear.

I lie back on the big fluffy bed and sigh happily. "Night!" I call back.

I toss and turn for a while and I wonder if Jonah was able to pass out easier on the hard floor. That would be so wrong. "Jonah," I whisper just to check.

"Yeah?" he asks with a rumbly sigh. His sleepy voice is really cute, damn him.

"Why did you act like you can't fight before? And how is it that you can fight at all?" I find myself asking. I hadn't known what I was going to ask but it's been bothering me and I realize it's been at the tip of my tongue for a while. I think I've just been too afraid of seeming like I care, but my curiosity is getting the best of me.

"It's not a good story," he says hesitantly.

"Trust me, my bedtime stories haven't had a happy ending since I was like six," I say as I stare up at the ceiling. My dad used to tell me stories of war growing up. They usually ended with a lesson, rather than a happily ever after. My mom read me the fairy tales and I vaguely remember liking those but my dad put a stop to that.

I'm not sure if my almost normal life made things worse for me. I know I'd be happier if I'd never been sent to the training camp but sometimes I think I'd also be happier if I'd never had a decent childhood. If all I'd known was war maybe I would be okay with that. It's the feeling of living in two worlds, of knowing both and not fitting into either one because the other pulls at me, that's what eats me up inside most days.

I turn again and notice there are little, neon glow-in-the-dark stars above me and for some reason it comforts me. "Tell me," I say, after some time.

"Ok," Jonah relents on a sigh. "You know World War III began when Russia attacked the United States."

"Yeah," I say slowly. Everyone knows that, especially me. I wait for him to continue.

"Well, my mom was in the military."

"Oh," I say. "I get it." His mom was in the military and taught him how to fight. I don't know why it was a secret but maybe his mom died in the war and he didn't like to talk about it. I can understand that.

"No. I don't think you do. Mom wasn't a part of our military."

I sit up. "Your mom was a...Russian spy?" I ask, disbelievingly.

"Yeah," Jonah says quietly. "It's not as cool as it sounds."

"Are you sure? Because it sounds pretty cool-"

"-She betrayed our country," Jonah says angrily, cutting me off. "She didn't care about me or my sister or my father. She chose her country over us and she died for it."

Slowly I lay back down. "That's why you don't like war or violence?" I surmise.

"She trained me, growing up. Even then I hated it. I just wanted to play on the computer and pull things apart before putting them back together. You pull a person apart? There's no going back. There's no making that better."

"I know," I whisper to the glowing, plastic stars on the ceiling.

"I know you do. So, you have to understand, I don't want to fight. Fighting is selfish. War is so damn selfish and everybody loses. There are other ways to live. Like using your brain."

"Brain is good," I agree. "When it's you or them though, you bet I'm going to fight and I'm going to win."

Jonah doesn't respond but it's like we've reached an understanding rather than some angst-filled impasse.

"I get why you don't like it but why did you act like you couldn't when I knocked down your door?" I ask.

"Honestly?" he begins. "The military had been in and out of the neighborhood, collecting the survivors. I made sure I didn't get caught because I don't trust them and I knew I had a better chance of getting out of D.C. on my own. I monitored them and knew when they'd be near me from their GPS trackers. When you showed up, you surprised me. I thought I'd play dumb for a while until I had more information. No offense but you scream military and I know all about spies. I wasn't taking any chances giving you more information. Then you began to walk away and I knew that you weren't there on the government's behalf so I decided I'd help you out.

My only response to that is a snort.

"You're strong, H, but I didn't know how much you knew. I had my computer and I figured I'd be able to hack the files sooner or later. I'd successfully hid from the military when they came around to collect me so I knew I could do it again. Force may be power but really, it's knowledge that has power."

I lay there, think over his admission, and come to one conclusion. "Then we'll outsmart them again and get out."

"Yeah," he replies quietly. My eyes start to drift close and I finally find a comfortable spot. "And H?"

"Hmm," I mumble into my pillow.

"If you and Bill are infected with the virus, I'm going to help find a cure. Okay?"

"Mmm," I reply sleepily and drift off.

The bright light of the sun streams in through the white windows. Relief washes over me because we get to leave here but dang, this bed is comfortable. I snuggle back in. Then Jonah's snoring comes into the picture.

"Shut up," I say as I throw a pillow at him. The next snore is cut off. I hear rustling and then he moves a little and sits up to look at me. “Well, good morning, Sunshine,” he says with a smirk.

I chuck another pillow at him as I get up. This bed had a lot of pillows, so why not. “Don’t call me Sunshine unless you want to lose your tongue.” I give him my best annoyed face and walk to the bathroom. Thankfully Jonah gets the hint and doesn't try to say anything else. I close the door behind me but it's suddenly dark.

I go for the light switch automatically, hoping the lights will turn on, but sadly, like I know what’s going to happen. The switch flips and no lights. Flashbacks of the Bitten Lock shelter slither through my mind and fighting the instinct to curl into a ball, I run to the bathroom window and open the blinds so light can flood the room.

Then when I can breathe again I walk to the sink and turn on the faucet, only to find freezing cold water running. I turn the knob a couple times but the temperature remains at a frigid thirty-three degrees, tops. “At least we have water,” I say to myself.

I splash the arctic water on my face and feel refreshed and reinvigorated. Then I quickly place my contacts back into my eyes. I think the brown looks more familiar to me now. I wonder if I’ll start to forget what my eyes used to look like if enough time goes by. I ignore that thought and focus on my tasks.

The internal countdown that’s been in my head since we found out about the bombing starts mentally beeping at me. It’s Saturday morning, we’ve got all of today and tomorrow and then the clock turns midnight Monday. However, we’re getting out tonight. I don't want to wait too long and risk getting held up and stuck here. I can do this. I can find my family. I can get us out of here. I have to.

We have to hit at least 30 more shelters today and if we split up the work with Bran's people we can probably get to all of them in D.C. It's honestly way more than I could've imagined. It's kind of amazing.

Plus, there's always hope that out in the field Bran will get turned into a stinker. A dumb one. A dumb one that gets hit by a manure truck. Power failure aside, the day was already looking up.

I go back to the room to grab my toothbrush from my bag to find Jonah in the same spot he was in 2 minutes ago, just staring at me and watching my every move. I feel his eyes on me and it's making me tense and a whole bunch of other things I don't want to feel.

Most of all I'm pissed off because I know I won't be kissing him again, and his kiss was something I most definitely wanted to repeat. When he was kissing me, I was lost in it, thrilled by it. It felt so right. No one had ever made me feel like that. Not even Adam made me feel like I was alive.

I ignore him as I head back to the bathroom and start brushing my teeth. I splash my face with the cold water one more time and look up to see Jonah standing at the doorway shirtless and just staring at me. Okay, this was torture. He needed to put a shirt on, like yesterday. Jerk.

"You're beautiful," he says in a gruff voice.

I turn around and stare at him. “I know,” I say, smirking hard to cover my anger as I walk past him.

He grabs me around the waist and pulls me closer to him. “Why do you need to have such a smart mouth?” he says, getting closer to my face. I suck in air.

Maybe I wasn't the only one pissed that the whole kissing thing had been taken off the table. But it was, so he had to deal with it. We both did.

“You should back off a little. Your girlfriend might get jealous,” I say acidly. He just shakes his head at me, his face softening and his eyes never leaving mine.

I decide I need to break his hold since telling him off isn't working. Before I can follow through, his mouth is on mine and he’s kissing me like he’s desperate. His lips taste better than I remember and I give in. Before I can pull back or sink further, I’m not sure which, he pulls back but his arms stay tight around me.

“I needed to do that. It seemed right.”

“Right?” I burst out. He was the one with the girlfriend.

“There’s something you should know...” he begins. There's a deep look in his eyes that's darkened the green and it's all I can do not to pull his mouth back to mine.

Instead, I shake off his hold and walk back. This was messed up. “Save it, Jonah. Now is not the time to be a douche, especially after last night. You had me then. You just can’t stop wanting me and come back to me in the morning like nothing ever happened.” I had tried to keep my voice angry but it was coming out kind of sad.

I blow out a breath and try again. “It’s not fair and I'm not that type of girl,” I add, straightening my clothes out and wishing I could take a shower. I glance back up but he won't meet my eyes. This makes it easier and harder at the same time.

“I’m doing this wrong. I know it. The worst damn part is that even if I tell you now, you won’t believe me,” he forces out, his voice cracking. The raw emotion coming off him catches me off guard and then suddenly his eyes dart to mine, and my brain blanks out on me.

After all that I’ve seen and done in my messed-up existence, the look he has can just take it all away from me. I feel shaky, like I’ll suddenly fall over at any minute but I can’t move. I’m reduced to a deer in the freaking headlights and all because of the look in his eyes? It’s owning me.

“Jonah?” I question breathlessly. His jaw is ticking like the words on the tip of his tongue are paining him. Maybe they are. I don’t want to care and I don’t want to hear. I need to.

The realization slaps me hard across the face that I can’t need anything. Not anymore. There’s unbearable pain down that rabbit hole. Just like that I shut down. In survival mode, I go into my head, out of this moment and into my body. I methodically focus on my movements, starting with each of my toes, forcing the feeling of movement to go up through my feet and shoot up my legs. My world has suddenly shifted to putting one foot in front of the other.

“Look, I’ll see you downstairs. We have a lot of shelters to get through. Maybe your girlfriend will be in one. If you want to stay with her in it, then do it, okay? I've got Bran and hopefully we can spring Adam. We'll be just fine," I hear myself say dryly as if from far away. We'd find a way past the gates without him, I think to myself.

Jonah says nothing. He's just there, arms crossed. I barely register that he's angry and since I'm no longer processing emotions, I absently assess that he must be seriously pissed off. I just don't care.

I shake my head and walk out and down the hall. When I make it to the top of the stairs, I stop and sit. I just breathe for a while.

I'm not sure how long I've been sitting here when something red catches my eye. I turn to see a splatter of blood on the hardwood floors of the landing. I wonder whose it is and how it got there and I have no idea why, but this brings me back to myself.

Forgetting the blood, I wonder what's wrong with me. I want to literally do naughty things to Jonah one minute but I want to murder him the next. Girlfriend? Seriously? Of course, he has a girlfriend.

"Aww all alone, princess?" a high-pitched voice coos in a derisive tone. I whip around to see Wednesday Addams behind me on the stairs. I remain seated and ignore her. "What? Trouble in paradise? Tall boy hasn't left your ugly self, has he? Can't say I blame him, Bran told me all about your reputation. Is there anyone you won't sleep with?" she continues.

"Don't you have an Evanescence wannabe convention to

get to?" I say as I pull out the map from my backpack. I need to start splitting up the shelters. All I hear in reply is an angry huff. Then I hear nails tapping on the railing.

I take out the pen and start marking things down.

Suddenly, a pair of ripped stockings are standing in front of me. I look up to see Wednesday staring down at me. Poor thing wasn't very subtle. I've had pets that needed less attention. "Oh, dear God. What?"

"You slept in my old room; you know. You should be grateful to me."

"This is actually your house?"

"Yes! Jealous?" she retorts proudly.

I do another assessment of her. Freckles peek out from underneath a too-light shade of foundation but the copper red-tinted eyebrows give it away now. She's the red-headed girl in the pictures. With my training, I should've caught onto that sooner but she wasn't exactly a priority.

"How'd you end up with Bran?" I ask, looking around the opulent mansion. It was probably called an estate. I bet she had butlers and cooks and maids once. "Let me guess. You wanted to piss off your mom and newest stepfather?"

Wednesday stepped down a step, her black stained lips forming an O shape. "How did you know? I mean, it was more about my asshole dad but what's it to you?"

"Just a guess," I say. I almost felt bad for her. She tried to be hard but it just wasn't in her. She was broken. I got that. I looked back to my map hoping she'd go away.

"Well, it doesn't matter now, does it? My parents are biters, not that they've been home in weeks. I found them at my stepdad's office three days ago. The whole building was infected until my man burned it down. Bran's been living here with me for a while now because my parents weren't around and didn't give a shit. He's all I need," she says defiantly, as if I were going to fight her on it. "Bran saved me," she continued, "And he's mine so you better stay away from him."

I look up again. I didn't have time for this. "I don't want Bran. All I want is to get this map marked up and split up the shelters. Then I want to get the hell out of D.C. and I want to do all of that alone, but since I can't, I'm doing what I can and then I'm gone. Okay, Wednesday?"

"My name is Erin," she huffs but I can feel her earlier indignation deflating. She looks like a wounded puppy, the thick eyeliner helping her eyes look even more pronounced.

"Ok," I say slowly. "I promise not to go anywhere near Bran unless it's to push him off a bridge or something. You get it?"

She stands there as if she's waiting for more. I have no idea what she wants. "Look, I'll tell you something then I'm going downstairs so I can get the heck out of here."

"What?" she says.

"You should know that Bran's not a good guy. In fact, he's probably one of the worst but from what I've seen he's loyal to those he likes, and it looks like he likes you, so you don't need to worry about stupid things like other girls getting his attention. Personally, I think you should let him take you to a shelter and you should stay there. It'll be safe there and once this is over you can move on. You don't need to let the guy you went out with define the rest of your life. You can actually have a life after this, okay? Just think about it."

"I don't know," she says.

"Just think about it, Erin. I'm going downstairs now," I say as I zip up my bag and grab my katana from beside me as I take the stairs two at a time.

CHAPTER 14

Chicken, Bacon, & Ranch

"I want it," Bran says again as he slams his fist into the table.

I chew on another spoonful of cereal, the satisfying crunching noises echoing throughout the room. "No, you get to do recon on the White House even though Jonah needs access to their computer system in order to figure out a way out of the quarantine borders. You called that even though it makes more sense for me to go but since you're demanding that, I get this. Besides, it makes no sense that you get it when it's directly in my path."

"I don't care. I still want it."

"You want to steal from it, Bran," I say loudly, not buying his helper act for a second. I spare a glance to the men and women around the table, hoping they continue to stay quiet during our impromptu negotiation.

"Oh, and you don't?" he says.

"I don't want to steal anything. Besides, I think there are plenty of other places to steal from and I think since our lovely government has been on top of this that you'll get caught. Our end goal is to get out of here, not end up behind bars."

"I won't get caught."

"Yes, you will and we don't have time to argue. All you need to worry about is staying alive. We need to get going." I grab one of the many walkie-talkies Bran just had lying around this house-go figure-and shove it in my bag. I'd asked him how he had these but of course I got no reply. I didn't need one though. I could guess. In fact, I was ready to guess some more. "Weapons?" I ask.

Bran opens his mouth again but Jonah comes around the corner, entering the dining room for the first time. My heart starts pounding wildly but I try my best to make it stop. From some stupid reason, I hold my breath.

It doesn't help. "H, I checked the perimeter from the upstairs windows. The super stinker is gone," he says, looking only at me.

I ignore Jonah and gesture to Bran with my spoon. "See, it's time to go." I thrust his hand drawn map with his route on it along with the other six maps for his cronies with their routes toward him. "Why don't you go jack a sweet ride. You'll get over it, you'll see."

With that, I toss the spoon and sip the milk right out of the bowl. I didn't know if I'd be eating again anytime soon and besides, this milk was going to go bad very soon now that the electricity was out. It would be a shame to let it go to waste. I wipe my mouth with one very fancy cloth napkin and stand up.

Bran signals for me to follow him and I do, Jonah right on my heels. "Where are you taking us, Bran?" I ask, trying not to sound shaky or piss him off.

"To get wine, princess," he says with a smirk as we go down a flight of stairs to the basement, where, just a guess, there's a wine cellar. I gag and just shake my head. I hope he means fire power, which is good, but he's still gross when he says it like that.

The stairs seem to go on forever and all we have are flashlights to illuminate our way.

"Hear that? It sounds like a heartbeat...coming through the walls," Jonah whispers in my ear, his lips barely brushing the lobe, giving me shivers.

Bran laughs darkly, probably sensing my shiver and mistaking the reason for it. I flick Jonah away with one hand and keep my flashlight steady in the other.

I hate that there's no windows...and that there's a 50/50 chance Bran will murder us and leave our bodies in what may or may not be a wine cellar where we'll never be found.

Then I remember that I've taken Bran down before and I could do it again. Suddenly the stairs seem to end and we all turn our flashlights to a big medieval-looking wooden door surrounded by a brick arch. The door itself is covered in locks.

"Why is it locked?" Jonah asks, questioning him.

"Couldn't let the hoodlums get into high-end military weapons," he says, pulling out a lanyard of keys and unlocking the door.

"Weapons?" Jonah queries and I swear he's breathing down my neck. I inch forward for space but Jonah's footsteps mimic mine until he's right at my back again. I glare at him.

His eyebrows lift and he stares right back in challenge but doesn't move.

I hear the creak of the double doors opening, so I turn away from Jonah and come face to face with what Bran has revealed.

Have you ever been so happy that your stomach gets butterflies and you feel like doing the happy dance? Yep, that's me. I walk into the small room with the biggest smile on my face.

"Pick your poison," Bran says with a smirk, his beefy arms crossed on his chest. I survey the room in awe. There are rows and rows of my favorite weapons on wooden shelves lining nearly every inch of wall space. Guns, a glorious number of guns and ammo, knives, daggers, grenades, crossbows, hell, I think I even spy a pitch fork mounted on the far wall.

"Whoa! I've never seen half this stuff before," Jonah says in amazement.

"Why am I not surprised?" I say and snort when Jonah crinkles his eyes at me. Then he chuckles and I shut up because he's annoying me with his undeterred hotness.

"Well, get used to it and let's stock up. We don't have much time before the others notice we're gone and come looking for us," Bran says, grabbing a PSS pistol. I quickly go for a beautiful short barrel AK and put it on my back. I look at Jonah and throw a small pistol towards him. He catches it with a frown. "What the heck? Why do I get the girl gun?" he asks sarcastically.

"You want me to trust you with a gun? I thought you were a pacifist," I say laughing.

He puts the pistol on his belt like he's done it a million times then grabs a Soviet Rifle and puts it on his back. Bran scoffs in the back.

I move farther into the room and pop a couple of grenades into my backpack with a smile. These hand grenades are perfect. From their slick look to their minimum weight, these babies were pure destruction.

“Let's go,” Bran commands, heading for the door.

“Just a minute,” I say as I spot a machete on my left. It's so shiny.

“I said let's go,” he grumbles. “You've got 2 seconds before I lock the doors. Don't care which side you're on.”

I grit my teeth but follow Bran out the door.

“Where'd you find this guy? Isn't there a bridge he should be patrolling somewhere?” Jonah mock-whispers to me, and I can't help it, I crack up.

“What was that?” Bran barks as he locks up the prettiest room I've ever seen.

“That it pretty much sucks we can’t take the whole room with us.” My words are a way to lie to Bran with the truth. I tack on a pouty face for good measure as we head for the stairs.

Bran grumbles and leads the way up. Equipped with weapons or not, I don't want him where I can’t see him.

I silently follow. I want to ask Jonah what weapons he took but I’m not about to since I’m still pissed at him and also because he seems to have more mood swings than a pregnant woman craving pickles and caviar.

We get upstairs with eyes following our every move. I fake a smile and look at Bran. "We'll meet up at the Washington Monument at 7pm just before sundown. Don't be late and for the love of guacamole, don't get bitten."

Jonah chuckles and follows me to the door. I keep ignoring him and open the door to feel the warm rays on my skin. I have a whole new appreciation for the sunshine now that I have freaking super stinkers creeping around at night like it's their mission in undeath.

"Ignoring me, I see," he says. I keep walking.

"Maybe if you weren't such a jerk, things like this wouldn't happen," I say, annoyed with his presence, mostly because I was annoyed at my reaction to it. I climb into Daredevil and feel up the steering wheel. I was in need of some speed to forget everything that's happened these past couple of days.

Jonah climbs in and stares at me, baffled. I put the key in the ignition and the glorious engine comes to life. That sound was slowly becoming my drug. I start to reverse then quickly slam on the brakes because I almost ran over Wanna-be Wednesday Addams.

"What the fuck, you jerk!" I hear her annoying way-too-whiny-voice say over the engine. God, this chick was everywhere. Bran taps the hood of my car and laughs. I lower the window and glower at him till he stops laughing.

"Just want to remind you that your loser computer geek better have the coordinates to the entry and exit point of the border walls or you'll no longer be of use to me," Bran threatens.

This was the deal we made but it's not like I'd forget it. He was such an asshole wasting precious time trying to intimidate us when we could be on the road by now.

I sit up and glare because I may not like Jonah right now but he needs more pressure to get the coordinates like I need a hole in my head. "Make a damn good effort to search the shelters or you can kiss the coordinates that Jonah *will be getting* goodbye," I shoot back.

"Don't worry, whore-mony. I won't forget about your sweet little mother or his," he nods to Jonah, "sweet little girlfriend. In fact, I can't wait to meet them." I flinch and nod. I hated his stupid nickname, the twisted version of Harmony. The last time he called me that I lunged at him from my desk at the training camp and it took Adam and two others to get me off him. I had to grit my teeth hard now but I also hated that I had to tell him and everyone else to check the lists for my mom and brother. Jonah did the same about his girlfriend. I excused myself from that conversation so I didn't have to hear it.

Of course, I didn't tell Bran who the woman and little boy were to me but it was easy to figure out since I was claiming them and describing them. Fortunately, we had a tentative understanding and I needed him to check out the shelters I couldn't get to so we could focus on finding a way out of the city.

The main idea was to meet up at the end of the night, hopefully be reunited with my brother and mother and then get the hell out of dodge before the bombing. That's what I needed to happen. So, if I had to suffer Bran's teasing, which would likely give me nightmares about my mom having to be near him, then I would.

"Washington Monument at sundown. Don't die," I say with a smirk on my face because we both know I never cared if he died or not before. He bows his head and walks toward the line of huge pickup trucks parked on the driveway of this huge house.

"I'm sorry for whatever I did, okay?" Jonah says, sounding sincere.

For whatever he did? Like he didn't know. I was no longer annoyed. I was mad. Livid. Seriously pissed off. Don't punch him, I remind myself. Don't punch him. "What's your girlfriend like so I can reunite her with you?" I say through clenched teeth.

He sighs heavily then moves a little trying to get to his back pocket. Then he pulls out a dark brown leather wallet. He flips it open and takes out a small picture and hands it to me. I yank it from his hold so his hand never touches mine and then I flip it over. Then I freeze. It's of him with his arm around a fucking plastic chick. As in the Plastic Chick. Her perfect blonde hair, big boobs, and acidic smile. It's the one from the pizza place. The one on the date. This is...this is unreal.

"Why do you look like that?" he asks, starting to get annoyed.

The quiet voice in the back of my mind tells me to lock this down, to not say anything but I haven't listened to that particular voice in too long to start now. "Is this a Joke? Because she was cheating on you," I burst out before I can stop myself.

Jonah's eyes widen like I've lost my mind. "What are you talking about?"

"The day of the outbreak she was in the pizzeria with a hot guy. He had the dreamiest eyes," I say, knowing I sound cold.

"No, she wasn't. Quit fuckin' around."

"Oh yeah? Where was she?"

"Not that it's any of your business but she was studying with her best friend," he says, his voice getting louder. "Don't make up shit because you're jealous and pissed at me."

I slam on the brakes and the car screeches. It gives me no small amount of satisfaction to watch him jerk in his seat with the car. Then I turn to stare at him. "You're seriously calling me a liar? I saw it with my own eyes, Jonah! Like damn I want a best friend who will let me shove my tongue down his throat in public," I say raising my voice.

"I'm not calling you a liar. A psycho, maybe, and one that holds a grudge and sees whatever the hell she wants to see, but not a liar."

"What did you just say?" I shout. My anger rising so swiftly, I can barely breathe.

"So, you see a blonde chick eating pizza once and suddenly you know it's Bethany. Get your head out of your ass. Did it occur to you that it could be someone else? Why would you immediately assume that my girlfriend is some cheater? Is it because it would be convenient for you? I hurt you. I said I was sorry. I'm not saying it again."

Black swamps my vision and I lift a hand and one finger. Unfortunately, it wasn't the one I wanted to flip up. "Number one, I have military training. I remember shit, Jonah. I remember people, and I sure as hell remember that day. Number two, there's nothing convenient about it. It's a fact and I couldn't care less how you feel about it. Get over yourself."

"It wasn't Beth," he says staunchly.

He's hurt. Really hurt. I can see it behind the anger in his eyes. It does something to me. Something I can't explain and it angers me more. To spite myself and him, I keep going. I just can't stop. "She was wearing a low-cut blue dress with rhinestones on the straps and eating ridiculously small portions of cheese pizza. Does any of that ring a bell?"

Jonah stays silent and then he's getting out of the car.

I look around the empty street to make sure it's okay to leave Daredevil on then I bolt out after him. His stupid long legs have him halfway down the street and I have to jog to catch up. He's standing in the shade of an awning next to a row of offices.

"Get in the car."

"Really, H? Are you kidding me?"

"Get in the car, Jonah. You're causing a scene for a chick that's dead. We don't have time for this."

He stops cold, stares at me. "Did you just say dead? Are you fucking kidding me?"

Shit. I stomp closer to him. There's no time to break this to him gently or give him false hope. "Listen to me. After I woke up she was already a stinker. It was self-defense. I wasn't trying to kill her but she attacked me."

I can see his face turning red. "H, this isn't something to joke around about! Screw you. I loved her...I loved her," he repeats.

His voice cracks and I feel like it's cracking something inside of me when it does, something I can't afford to open. I stop dead in my tracks and stare at him feeling all sorts of jealous and freaked out and sorry, so damn sorry to be telling him this. I realize how cold and insensitive I've been. I killed his girlfriend...and I just told him so. No, I practically threw it at him. Things have gone from bad to worse between us.

"I'm sorry," I say, trying to make him understand. "I didn't know she was your girlfriend then. All I knew was that she was trying to bite me and she wouldn't stop." I can't tell him how I killed her. I've said enough.

He starts to tear up and hits the wall. Then his body slides down until he's on the ground, his head falling back helplessly against the side of the building.

"Jonah, sometimes we have to put these things in the past. She's gone and she was a horrible person anyways. She didn't deserve you."

Jonah lets out a breath and surprises me by standing back up in anger. "She didn't deserve that," he says through what I can tell is a fight to choke back tears. "Don't talk about Bethany as if you knew her. I loved her and we were together for 2 years. She was human and we've all made mistakes. Just like the one I made this morning," he says acidly. I feel my heart shatter into pieces.

I nod and force myself to keep it together. "Then you're as good as dead too if you don't get into the car. We have a job to do," I say, completely disregarding my feelings for him. I go back to being the unemotional girl I was when I met him. I turn my back on him and my mind is blank as I climb back into Daredevil.

I get back in the car, the engine purrs and for the first time not even this can make me feel better. I drive slowly, giving Jonah time to decide if he wants to join me since he's still standing by the abandoned building. Things are pretty much the worst they've ever been.

I take a mental recount of the past few days since this virus has been unloaded and destroyed my city. My dad was a super stinker and I wasted him. My mom and brother are still missing. My only ally hates me because I killed his cheating, stinker girlfriend, and my worst enemy is the only hope I have of helping anyone and getting out of my country's esteemed capital before our government blows the entire city away.

Time's running out too quickly and the one thing I can cling onto is that the kid fuming at me from outside my passenger side window might be the only one able to help me get out of here. That, and with Bran's help, I might actually get to fulfill the promises I've made before I get out.

I slow to a stop and we stare each other down. We both know he has no choice here but he's going to make me sweat it out and wait for him. He knows I won't leave him behind and somehow,

I've become the vulnerable one.

"Get in the car," I mouth. I'm not bothering to roll down the window.

He stares back then flings the car door open before storming in and slamming it shut. I turn the volume all the way up on my radio and "She's Long Gone" by the Black Keys blasts out of the speakers. I want to change it to the next song on the C.D. when I realize the irony but then I think that'll just make it worse.

We're stuck in this tension-filled car until finally we arrive at our next shelter. I park and without making eye contact, I turn to Jonah.

"You should stay here, focus on getting into the mainframe and cracking the code or whatever it is you're doing," I say, throwing out random computer words that I saw on a cop show.

"I've got that under control. So, get over it, I'm coming," he says tersely, in a tone that brooks no argument. Then he hands me my katana and a shiny handgun. "Let's make this quick."

I nod, resigned and we walk up to the entrance of the bunker like we usually do. I'm feeling confident with my brown-colored contacts while Jonah follows me like my own personal bodyguard, except he's more like an actor who plays one on TV or something. He sure as hell doesn't care what happens to my body anymore. Then, like always, we're greeted by the wonderful guards.

I pass a glance to all five of the men as if they're unimportant. "Hi. I believe you all know my father, General Booker? He assigned me to this bunker and if you could move I can do my job without a disturbance and you won't lose yours. How does that sound?" I say, sounding cold and efficient.

The officer directly in front of me looks at me in attention and smirks. "Yes, ma'am, after we've done the eye scan and fingerprints test. It's standard government policy," he says.

I'm already annoyed and this is just the cherry on top. "One, wipe that smirk off your face. Two, you have 10 seconds to let me through before you lose your job and a couple of fingers," I reply. I've totally lost my cool and possibly the upper hand.

Jonah stiffens beside me but says nothing. "I'm sorry but we've received orders. Not even the president can get through without getting scanned, so if you could please stand right here before I scan you," the same soldier says, pointing to the small black carpet on his right.

I freeze for a minute, panic setting in, then my voice gets louder. "I demand to talk to whoever is in charge. You're disobeying my orders and I can assure you that my orders override yours."

The officer nods and talks through a walkie, paging over a name I prayed I'd never hear again.

I hope I'm hallucinating but I know I'm not as Colonel Croft walks over from the shadows and smirks at me. I don't know if I should run away or hide. I think I want to do both.

"If it isn't one of my proteges Cadet Booker. What's the problem here?" he says, looking me up and down.

I see the other officers trade worried glances when they hear my last name and status. I start to wonder if maybe this might work out in my favor, after all. I puff up my chest, feeling more confident as I say, “Your imbecilic officers don’t know who I am or who my father is and I demand to get through.”

He looks over at the cadet. “Is this true?” he screams at the officer, fear now obvious in his eyes. Or maybe it’s only obvious to me because I know that look personally. I know what it’s like to be yelled at by Satan himself.

“Yes sir! The lady won’t get scanned. It’s protocol!” he says.

I scoff and look at Colonel Croft. “So, can I go through?” I smile, about to pass and he stops me.

“You need to go through protocol, unless you’re hiding something...” he says suspiciously.

“I’m not hiding anything but I don’t need the scanner. I’ve been through about 50 of these shelters already and I don’t have time for this. We all know I’m not stupid enough to get bitten,” I say trying to keep my cool.

“Then get scanned,” he says.

“No,” I spit back, holding my ground. “Now, I’m insulted. Touch me and you’ll regret this.”

“Then as you wish, Cadet,” he says. He turns to the men behind him. “Hold her down and scan her now!” Colonel Croft shouts and three of the officers are on me. “And bring the hand-held scanner,” he continues.

One soldier watches passively while the last soldier stands in front of Jonah like he’s daring him to make a move.

I knew it. I was screwed. I was done for and these contacts

could hide my eyes but they couldn't do anything to stop what was about to happen.

My eyes find Jonah's and I shake my head slightly, silently warning him to stay back. I half expect him to grab some popcorn as he watches this go down.

"Please stop this. Just let me through," I say with pity, hoping this bastard will let me go, yet knowing he won't. This man wouldn't know pity if it spit on and shined his shoes.

He leans over me and whispers in my ear, "Cadet Booker, you got nowhere with pleading at the camp. What do you think pleading will get you here?" he asks.

A growl emerges from my throat and all the pain and suffering I endured in that camp comes back to me. I want nothing more than to slit this man's throat. What he did to me, to Adam, to all of us was despicable. He beat us, starved us, tried to strip us of our humanity, and turned us into soulless killers without remorse. He deserved nothing less than being ripped to shreds.

"We were just kids," I yell at him. I'm certain he'll know exactly what I mean.

His sharp eyes, so dark they're nearly black, stare into mine. "You maggots are still alive during this outbreak because of me. You should be thanking me. I made you strong. I gave you that. Now do as you're told."

"We made it despite you. You ruined us. You never cared if we lived or died. Rot in hell, you miserable old man," I cry until he places his nasty hand over my mouth and nose, preventing my speaking and breathing. Then a loud call comes over the walkies.

Colonel Croft picks his walkie up and listens intently before speaking, all the while his hand remains over my face like it's no big deal. I'm fighting hard to get any air in but no matter how much I struggle, it does me no good. Darkness starts to consume my vision before the Colonel pulls his hand away. I gasp hard for air, so grateful for my lung capacity, it's unreal.

"If she fights," Colonel Croft continues to the men holding me down, "shoot her." Then he stands up and walks away.

I close my eyes and breathe in the new air I'd been deprived of as I try to plan an escape. I open my eyes to see Jonah watching me from beyond the other soldiers with a smirk. What the heck was he up to? I know he hates me but this is colder than I expected.

"Look, I get that you're military dudes and violence is your thing but can we just talk about this?" he says, his tone light and jovial as he makes his presence known once more.

I laugh and so do the guards as they turn to face him, still clutching me tightly. I wonder if Jonah is relying on me to get us out of this like I always do. I wish I could warn him that I'm not faking being held down. I really am stuck. "I guess it will be my way then," he says. He walks towards me and the guard stops him at gunpoint.

"One more step and I blow your brains out," the soldier in front of him says. I hear myself screaming at Jonah to stop. He may know how to defend himself from some time long ago but I doubt he could face down the barrel of a gun or the five trained military men on his ass.

Jonah's eyes change suddenly along with his whole posture. He's standing...like a fighter. "How about you don't do that," he says and then Jonah kicks the gun out of the soldier's hand so quickly my eyes almost miss it.

A squeak escapes my throat but Jonah keeps moving, quickly putting him in a choke hold while grabbing the gun in one swift motion. All hell breaks loose and the men around me are scrambling to get to Jonah but two remain on me. I can probably break their holds but not yet. I need the right moment.

"Now," Jonah begins once more, and even his tone of voice is new to me. It's like he's an entirely different person. "You're going to have to trust me here. I don't want to do this...but I will. Let her go or you all go down." The guards laugh, and the two not holding me down, point their guns at him.

"Nice move, kid but we've got you and the girl surrounded," the soldier who's in Jonah's chokehold spits out.

Jonah smiles and just goes for it. He swiftly shoots three guards at their legs not killing them but injuring them until they let me go. I punch the guard above me while he's distracted by Jonah's awesomeness.

I get up and look at my unlikely hero. "Let's go before the backup comes," I say as I take hold of his hand and whisk him away. We don't have time to spare.

We run out of the building like it's on fire. Finally slowing down once we are out of sight, I look at Jonah to thank him, to tell him I'm sorry. I fully intend to grovel but instead I'm distracted by a bright light.

He's scanning me.

"Where did you get that?" My mouth drops open and the scanner beeps and turns red. Jonah stares at the screen. "You're infected, H."

Shit. "We knew that, Jonah," I say defensively.

"No, I suspected and you never said a word. I brought it up over and over and you ignored me. That's not the same thing. You should've just told me what was going on with you. After this, you need to trust me, damn it. I could've left you there to die," he says, looking sincere. "How many times do I have to keep proving that I've got your back?"

I'm surprised he did but I'm not going to mention that. "I know. You're right," I say and start to walk away but some part of me wants to open up for once. I want to explain myself and I want Jonah to trust me too. I can't even believe it but I do trust Jonah and he deserves better than how I've treated him.

"But it wasn't like that," I say, "I mean, I knew something was up but I couldn't admit it to myself. When that little girl, Tessa, told us about the people getting scanned and taken away, I figured it had something to do with the virus. I just didn't know what. Then I remembered you said there were three outcomes of the research. We've seen the stinkers and the super stinkers. I don't know for sure but I think I might be the third type.

"I think I survived the virus. On the day of the outbreak I went down fighting, maybe I was...bitten. When I woke up I had three-day-old cuts and bruises everywhere so one of them could've been a bite. I wasn't sure and I didn't want to know. When I found Bill, he was under a pile of stinkers. I guess he survived the bite too."

"And you couldn't just tell me that?" he replies, anger and disappointment coloring his tone in equal parts.

"I still don't know what it means but you didn't know me. There's no way I could ask you to trust that I wasn't going to try and eat your brains in the middle of the night. I didn't want you to think I was a freak, okay?"

"I figured it out a long time ago, H."

"That I'm a freak? Real nice, Jonah!" I say with mock anger, trying to lighten the mood.

Jonah ignores my joke and puts his hand over mine, asking for my full attention. "I was just waiting for you to tell me your suspicions. You never did."

I hold my breath. I know this is a turning point but I can tell he's still angry and I just don't know how I feel. "You knew and I knew that you did too. I figured that was enough."

"Does it feel like enough to you?" he asks me, pulling his hand away.

I think it over. I want to ask him if his mom taught him how to fight and shoot like that too. It makes me wish I could've met her, even though she was a traitor. She made him. It's just too weird and I realize my don't-get-too-close-and-discuss-personal-information-with-Jonah-rule wasn't working out as well as I'd hoped. I want to know Jonah.

I care about him. I haven't felt any of this in so long. I've already messed up beyond repair and I know why. I'm cruel, unkind, selfish.

I don't know how to change that so I push people away. If I can't be a decent human being, the least I can do is keep those that are far away from me.

I'm torn, not knowing which way to go here.

I take a breath before I begin but then my exhale comes out as a wheeze as we walk towards the car. I try to ignore the pain and instead feel glad I'm able to walk away with nothing worse than a bruised lip and the cardio of a lifetime.

Once we get back in the car, I speed off and start to ramble. "So, we need to regroup. I don't think I can go back into a shelter just yet. If they're scanning people and all..." I stop talking as I realize Jonah is ignoring me. His body posture is rigid and he's as far away from me as he can get in the passenger seat. "You're still pissed at me," I say aloud. I know it's true and I feel the pain of it worse than my injuries.

"Just do us both a favor and stop talking, H. You saved my life, I saved yours. We're getting out of here and then we're done." He pulls up his laptop and his angry keyboard tapping commences. "Just drive."

Knowing there's nothing else I can do, I nod. I become robot H again. My parts are pretty much broken and they should probably take me off the shelves and shut me down but here I am. I have a job to do and the only thing getting me through this is remembering that despite everything, I have someone waiting at home and counting on me.

I'm almost to the street that leads to where Jonah and I both live, since apparently, he's lived in the community next to mine for years and I never knew, before Jonah's head whips sharply to me.

"Bill?" he questions. I blink at him in confusion. He doesn't ask where we're headed or why. He just assumes, and he's partly right.

"Yeah. We need to pack up the house and bunker and grab him. The meetup is at the National Mall and the way things are going, I'm guessing we won't have time to come back here before then."

Jonah turns back in his seat to face the front seat as he puts his laptop back into his bag. "Fine," he returns, his voice empty.

"Fine," I reply.

Getting-the-last-word-in master, thy name is H.

CHAPTER 15

Carnavale

We're only about 20 minutes from home but with the way I drive, the lack of any other cars on the road, and the sheer awkwardness of breathing in the smoke and fire that Jonah is breathing out from the seat beside me, I make it back to my place in 14 minutes flat.

I hop out and I'm bolting through the door, running through the hall, and undoing the bunker locks as fast as I can. "Biiiillll, you old man, where are you?" I yell out as I round the corner, entering the darkened bunker.

"H! Thank God you're home! And I'm not that old, okay? Have some respect," Bill replies as he meets me out in the hallway with a huge smile on his face. He's illuminated by what I recognize as the emergency candles. I'm glad he found them and I feel bad for not telling him where the bunker's solar powered generator was before I left just in case this happened.

I see the short, old man with grey hair and crinkles around his purple eyes and I smirk. It's strange but I missed him.

"Listen. There's something I need to tell you," he begins but then he pauses. "Where is Jonah?"

I squint my eyes at him and shrug. "I don't know, maybe a stinker got him on his way to the house. Pity. Back to that other thing though. What do you need to tell me? Is it about my pizza?"

My voice begins to rise as dread fills me.

I push past Bill and speed toward the kitchen. A million thoughts run through my mind. I need this pizza. I don't know what I'll do if he ruined it. I'm literally just getting by. I need my damn pizza. I know it's crazy but I don't care.

"No," Bill wheezes from behind me. "The pizza is fine. It's in the fridge, though it stopped being cold a few hours ago. If you tell me something happened to Jonah I won't believe it. He was with you. You wouldn't let anything happen," he says with a ridiculous confidence in his voice. He's so damn wrong about me.

I rush to the fridge and fling the door aside. There it is in all its glory. Pizza. My pizza. It smells so good, the individual scents of the peppers, cheese, and pepperoni are making my mouth water. All I can do is breathe it in and stare like I'm possessed.

"Oh yeah. H is a superhero, all right," Jonah's voice rings out clearly from behind me and the sound of his voice is enough to distract me momentarily from my moment with the nectar of the gods.

"What do you mean?" Bill asks.

The kitchen goes quiet but I don't turn around. My arm shakes infinitesimally as I reach for a slice, as if I'm afraid any sudden movement will draw attention to me. I don't need this. Especially because Jonah is right. I'm no superhero. I passed out during the outbreak. I've killed. I've killed a lot. I made a deal with the devil and I still haven't found what's left of my family.

I didn't ask for this but I expected more from myself. I can't help but feel like I'm letting everyone down. My stomach roils and even as I touch the pizza I know I don't have the appetite to eat it.

"I'm fine, Bill," Jonah says and suddenly his voice is right behind me, as in his breath is on the back of my neck. I freeze and can only wonder how he managed to sneak up on me.

Then his arm brushes mine and he nabs the giant slice of pizza from out of my hand. I still don't move. His face is mere inches from mine and he's staring me down, daring me to do something. I may feel like I've swallowed a gallon of sawdust but I'm no coward.

I turn my head to the right and toward him. Our faces are now a breath apart. He brings the slice up and bites into it.

The crunch of the crust is the only sound. The finality in it is something both of us are painfully aware of. His eyes are sharp on me, assessing. In them I see burning anger, pain, and something that looks a little like fear. "Problem?" he questions defiantly.

"No," my voice comes out quietly. "You can have it." If he wants to burn this last bridge I'm going to let him. I give him one last withering look then make my retreat.

"Bill, you have 20 minutes to pack whatever you need, including food and provisions but pack light. We're getting the hell out of this zombie wasteland."

"But I have to tell you something!" he calls after me.

I spin around and I no longer have the energy to hide my emotions. I let all my weariness and regret consume my face. "Can it wait until after I shower?" I plead.

Bill stares at me slack-jawed, his mouth gaping like a fish

out of water. “Yes. Sure,” he finally manages. “I'll make sure to save you some food.”

I don’t respond and moments later I'm pulling out my flashlight and entering the darkness of my room. Again, I think about the generator. Now it's too late to bother turning it on. Soon I'll be leaving this place, my home, for good.

I find my way to the bathroom with only my flashlight to illuminate my way and I turn on the shower. Knowing this will be freezing and unpleasant, I brace myself. Then I place the flashlight on the sink counter, strip off my grimy clothes and hop in.

Soon I'm clean and just leaning hard against the tile wall as the cold water stings my skin. I climb out and attempt to dry off. I collapse onto the closed toilet seat. Head in my hands, I let my mind fall blank and let it all go.

I don't know how much time has passed. I’m still wet but I’m no longer ice cold. I'm finally resolved to one truth. The things I've done are unspeakably horrible and I can't take them back. The lives I've taken, my father's and Jonah's girlfriend's especially, will forever remain on my soul. I’m not religious but this kind of thing feels like a basic truth.

There is no absolution for this and the sooner I realize it, the better. I also have to accept that I've lost the tentative friendship I'd made with Jonah. While it sucks, I can't linger on that either.

The only thing I can do now is try to earn retribution, try to find my family, save as many innocents as I can, and then once I know my family is safe, I'll leave them. Their lives will be better without me reminding them every day of what I've done. I'll disappear. It sounds selfless but the truth is I can't face them. So, there it is, my plan.

I re-wrap myself in my fluffy towel and sigh. I leave my flashlight on top of the TV so I can leave my hands free to change.

I dig through some clothes on the floor and nearly drop everything when I see a giant man lying on my bed. In a rare moment of surprise, I squeal like a girl and frantically grab my towel.

"Relax, H. Shh. It's just me," a very shirtless Adam says as he sits up.

I try to slow my breathing as I glare at him. "Adam? What the heck?"

"H, baby. Didn't the old dude tell you? I'm...here."

I bite my lip as a smile tries to form. "No! He hadn't gotten around to mentioning that," I mutter. Not that I'd given him a chance but whatever. Adam just nods sheepishly in the darkness and is making his way toward me.

Like he always used to, he wraps his strong arms around me and I'm cocooned in his heat, his bulk, and his amazing abs. "Miss me?" he whispers as he lifts me off my feet with the force of his hug.

I smirk and then the door bursts open and a glaring white light is shining in our eyes.

"H! H!" Jonah yells as he runs toward me. "I'm coming."

I pull out of Adam's arms and open my mouth as everything comes to a standstill. “No, Jonah. I'm fine,” I manage.

Jonah stops suddenly and stumbles back before he reaches me, his flashlight going back and forth between Adam and me.

“I'm fine,” I repeat calmly. “Adam just surprised me is all.” I clutch my towel and back out of Adam's embrace, my wet hair hitting my shoulders with the movement, giving me chills.

“This kid's still alive?” Adam asks with a nod, indicating Jonah.

I roll my eyes at my ex.

Then Adam bounces back on the bed and leans back like it's just another day at the beach.

“I don't like what G.I. Joe is implying and where’s his shirt? Does he think he’s modeling for Hollister or something?” Jonah says to me, walking toward me again, eyes only on me.

Adam snorts. “Wasn't this the dude who manhandled you, H? Is he giving you a problem? And what? You have a little crush on me, can’t handle seeing me shirtless?” Adam asks.

Before I can answer, Jonah's at my side. “What the hell is he even doing here?” Jonah asks me, completely disregarding everything Adam said. He reaches out and touches my arm but doesn't try to do anything with it. It's not a touch for movement or possession. It's like he's just checking on me.

I know this can't be right because I'm fairly certain he hates me. I'm trying to process the change and that he actually came in here to save me. My eyes find his for a moment and then he pulls his arm away.

"I don't know," I begin. "He just suddenly popped up right now," I continue calmly. "I was just asking but you barged in before he could explain." I turn to Adam since Jonah and Adam wouldn't be addressing each other like they were 6-year-olds. "What are you doing here?" I ask drolly, my disgust for the task of go-between dripping in my tone.

Adam smiles at me and says, "Bran broke me out of my shelter. Figured I'd come here and wait you out. Fell asleep on your bed. Just woke up now. Anyway, I guess I was right that you'd come back here. Pretty smart, right?" Adam holds his palm out for a high five.

I give him one. "Nice."

Jonah snorts now. I shoot Jonah a side eye that I'm sure he can sense even with so little light in the room.

"Super. Glad to have you on board. Now let me get dressed. I'll be right out to explain the plan." I turn to Jonah. "As you can see there's no stinkers here. Everything's good so..."

I look back and forth between Adam and Jonah. "Get out."

Jonah's green eyes connect with Adam's blue ones and I don't know what to make of this except I'm about to start throwing punches unless they move their little staring contest outside my door.

"I'm not going anywhere until he goes," Jonah says.

Adam barks out a laugh. "What do you care?"

My head snaps back and forth between them.

"I think H made it clear that she cares, bro," Jonah says, clearly making fun of Adam with his tone and that last word.

"Hey," I begin.

"She hasn't got anything I haven't seen before, bro, many times before."

"Um what?" I sputter, disbelievingly. He did not just say that.

"As in the past," Jonah says with a smirk. "She just asked you to get out now."

"I heard her," Adam says gruffly, standing up from the bed.

"Yeah, but can you understand her? All those syllables to contend with must be confusing."

"Hey!" I shout.

Suddenly the door swings open again and more light floods the room. I shield my eyes against the glare of yet another flashlight and see Bill walk through the door.

Bill freezes too and it's all I can do not to laugh. Everyone starts to notice then that I'm the only female in the room and I'm wearing nothing but a towel. Bill is the first one to sputter as he moves his flashlight off me and across the room like I'd burned him. "Oh, I'm sorry. I came to make sure everything was all right. Jonah never came back and I..." He's backing out of the room in utter embarrassment.

I grind my teeth before replying. "It's fine, Bill. Besides I figured out what you had to tell me," I say as I gesture toward the hulking shirtless figure that is Adam. "Now all of you need to listen to me. I'm tired, hungry, annoyed, and my hair is wet and dripping icy cold down my back. So get your flashlights out of my eyes, your egos back in your giant heads, and get the hell out of my room." I say this calmly but firmly.

Bill moves his flashlight around and out to the hall as if it's a signal to the exit. "Boys, follow me and let H get dressed in peace." There's a cool edge to his voice that I've never heard from Bill. It's kind of sweet that he's pulling it out to protect me. I can kind of see why Jonah thought he was my grandfather now. I want to give him a smile but I'm too pissed off at the cavemen in front of me. Between my glare and Bill's, both guys storm out.

Once dressed, I walk out into the small makeshift dining room to find Jonah and Adam staring at each other while waiting for the next move. Screw world war III, Jonah and Adam were going to make a bigger war all thanks to testosterone.

Bill is in the corner staring at them intensely, ready to break up the fight. With what strength or skill, I haven't the slightest idea but his look alone is pulling it off.

As soon as I step into view they both stare at me like I'm a piece of steak and they haven't eaten in a while. "Okay, boneheads. Let's get something straight. Never walk in on me again if you guys don't want to lose both your eyes and maybe even your heads," I say as I'm pulling out my chair.

My hand trembles slightly as I realize this chair, all these chairs and the table, are the set that my father and I built together as a gift for my mom when Justin was born. When my dad started making more money we bought a new set and this one got relegated here to the bunker. This naturally fills me with rage, because I just can't handle it so I sit down and throw my shaking hands in my lap, hoping no one notices.

I look over at Adam and he's smirking. Bastard number one was not taking me seriously. "Adam, wipe that smirk off your face before I slap it off."

Jonah chuckles.

Adam looks at me and smirks even bigger. "Well, it's kind of pointless not to walk in on you when I've already seen everything you were hiding under that towel."

I freeze and Jonah stiffens, his jaw clenching hard enough that it looks painful. Adam was overconfident and acting more stupid than usual.

"Shut up before I punch the smirk off your face," Jonah says in a cold, hard voice.

"Oh really? Little Jonah is going to punch me? I want to see you try," Adam says, getting up from the table, pushing his chair so hard it falls with a loud bang. My chair. He just pushed my chair to the floor like it meant nothing.

Jonah gets up too and puffs out his chest. He takes a stance I know all too well. He's ready to take a swing at Adam. I stare at them, then back at the chair, then back at them. That's when my vision goes black at the edges.

"STOP! The both of you just stop!" I scream, breaking down.

They both stare at me and I absently notice Bill jump back

and knock his elbow on the windowsill.

My throat is raw from that one shout but I don't care. "I just want to get out of here, maybe see my family, at least the members that I've not yet had to brutally murder because they threw me down and tried to do the same to me, but you know what? Screw that." I wrench a few strands of my white hair out of my face and stand up.

"Let's have wrestling matches, hold a pissing contest or two, that seems to be more important. I thought maybe we could save anyone left from being nuked like a day-old pizza but I see that's not going to be possible. Instead I'm dealing with two idiots who can't get over their egos and won't stop arguing like children," I shout.

"Now I'm going to leave it to the both of you, either you two get your shit together and you help me or you get the hell out of this house and never come back." I start bolting for the door.

"Wait, H. Where are you going?" Jonah sputters.

"Target practice. Follow and I'll assume you're volunteering," I rasp out and then the door is slamming behind me. I storm out of the bunker and run through the house, hoping for some peace and quiet or maybe some fresh air.

I wanted things to be normal again. I wish I was at Georgia's Pizzeria waiting on my anchovy pie and some fresh garlic rolls and rolling my eyes as Justin begs Mom for more quarters to play video games.

I needed to be strong but sometimes even the strongest

people break down when the world around them is crumbling. I thought I'd never go through something worse than soldier training, but I've finally reached my limit. It wasn't about the guys and their bickering. It was reality finally setting in.

CHAPTER 16

New York Style

I know time is running out but I can't spend the rest of the day with all of them if I don't get my shit under control. Besides hopefully while I take this time out Jonah will explain the plan to Bill and Adam. This way I can do this one last thing alone.

I finally reach the front door of my house and walk out to a nice breeze and a bright sun above me.

I briefly consider taking Daredevil but I need to save what little gasoline it has left. Besides, I need to clear my head so I'm running, plain and simple.

I pass by the decomposing teens on the corner and they're so rotted that they barely make a grab for me. Even so, the one that manages to roar its rotten breath in my face gets way too close.

I throat punch it, my fist sliding through the gunk of its neck like butter. It falls back and knocks the others down like bowling pins. I'm disgusted but also kind of exhilarated. I wipe my hand on a tree nearby, get back to running, and start to feel better.

I'm about 7 miles in and running on adrenaline and luck. I stop to scarf down an energy bar from my pack. I bite into it, the very-much-not-pizza. That's when I spot a car worth stealing. It's a 1970 Plymouth Hemi 'Cuda and what a beauty it was. It's locked, of course.

I rip off a tree branch and smash through the back-driver's side window because I don't want to be sitting on any remnants of it. Then the car alarm sounds. It's loud and annoying but between the smashing and the alarms it feels like training drills and it gets me moving.

I dive into the back then carefully and skillfully crawl into the front seat, avoiding any glass shards. 6.4 seconds later the alarm has stopped and the engine is hot wired and roaring. It's a personal best and I'm pumped.

I'm flying through the streets. With no radio or other noises, I shout a war cry into the air. I may die today or maybe tomorrow but right now I'm living. All my thoughts are blessedly gone. I've had a total breakdown and God damn it; I need this. All too soon I pull up short in front of the gas station.

I check the clock on the dash and know I've really got to speed things up. Mind blissfully turned off, I get out of the car and just go for it. I locate a nice spot of earth next to the store. The grass is green and the sun seems to be shining the most right here. I think Dad would like it but I guess it doesn't matter now.

I start digging and throw myself into it. As the sweat rolls down my back, I can feel my breath beginning to hitch and all at once it comes pouring out. Sobs wrack my body as I dig. I cry hard enough that I can barely see through my own tears but it's a release and it's awful but I need it. I know the exact moment when I'm done. Given the dimensions of my father's body, I know just how big the hole needs to be. This isn't the first grave I've ever had to dig.

When I'm done I wipe off my tears and as much dirt as I can, and head to the store.

The smell hits me first. The decomposing stinkers of Bill's attackers and of course my father's body lay scattered on the floor. I need to pick up my father and bury him. Just pick him up and bury him. That's all. I can do this.

Ok, it smells awful and I need to be in this room for too long of a time. I find that newspaper stand and prop the door open so I can breathe in fresh air.

Now to my dad. So yeah.

I need some food first. No big deal. I need strength to pick up his body. I'll need some food. Screw Jonah and his stupid pizza stealing revenge.

I scavenge around the overturned shelves that once held food. They're still barren like before and that sucks.

My eyes lock on my gunk and blood-stained note of shelter. No one read it and no one came to my house. I'd been three days too late and mostly everyone was already in real shelters. I lift it up and crumble it in my hands. Underneath the note lies the raisins. I pick them up.

Well, I guess it has come to this. I'm that desperate. I rip open the package and down the raisins. I don't know if it's because I'm starving or my self-preservation skills have dulled my sense of taste to protect my sense of smell but they don't taste bad.

Ok, I dug the grave, I've eaten, I've opened the door, and

I've stalled enough. I peer down at my father's body, focusing on the outline and not on any details. This needs to be as painless as possible. I reach down to hopefully prop him up and into a fireman's carry when I hear footsteps behind me.

It's then that I realize I'm unarmed and not ready for a stinker. I slowly get up to see both Adam and Jonah behind me. I think I would've preferred a stinker.

Jonah slowly walks close to me, hands out front, like he's a lion tamer and I'm ready to strike. I take a step back and regret it. "You should be home waiting for me," I bark out through a lump in my throat. "How did you even find me?" I continue, unable to look away from Jonah.

"Old dude told us about the man you fought in here and his suspicions. After what you said, we put the pieces together, babe," Adam said, diverting my attention.

I blink, coming out of my work trance and back into myself. "Well, you shouldn't have come but since you're out and we all know where I am, you should be checking our assigned shelters. We left Bran's over an hour ago. We're falling behind. Where's Bill?"

"No more splitting up," Adam replies. "We're in this together. Bill's in the car."

My head swings back to Jonah but he's not saying a word. "Yeah?" I ask. "And why are you here?"

Jonah just stares back, hands now tucked into his pockets. He's wearing a green lantern shirt and I wonder if he went back to his home to change and say goodbye. I feel like he'd do something like that. He doesn't answer me though. His face is unreadable and I don't have time to play games.

I turn back to Adam. "Look I need to bury my...I need to...bury him. Mind helping me lift it?" I ask.

"You got it. You make a dig site?" Adam inquires, easily lifting the body from the floor.

I'm sure he knows I did since I'm covered in dirt but I answer anyway. "I made the full hole. It's behind the store. I'll be right out there. I just need to rinse off in the bathroom."

I can't watch as Adam walks out the door. I head for the hallway leading to the bathroom, leaving Señor Stoic behind. The door is open from the last time Bill used it to get dressed. It seems like so long ago. Somehow, it's only been a few days.

I run the sink and only a few drops of water drip out. Great. I grab a bunch of paper towels and hold it under the drops to wet them. I strip off my shirt and lay it over the closed toilet seat. Then I run the dampened paper towels over my face, neck, and chest.

"Pink bra, huh? I would've guessed black all the way. I like the lace though."

I ignore the voice behind me and try to re-wet the towels. "The rest of your clothes should probably come off too," Jonah continues joking from the doorway. I look up to see Jonah's reflection in the mirror, his usual smile firmly in place.

This had to be a trick. "So, you're talking to me now?"

"Yes."

I size Jonah up and wrack my brain for any possible motive. "Wow, you must really be intimidated by Adam, huh?" I tell his reflection as I attempt to cool off the back of my neck.

"No, it's not about Adam, H. It's about you."

"Oh yeah, sure. I'll believe that. One minute you hate my guts and eat the only thing that's been keeping me going the past few days in front of my face. Next Adam shows up and you're suddenly a ball of sunshine. But those two instances are not related. My bad."

Jonah's hand clenches and unclenches on the doorframe like I'm zapping away every ounce of patience he has. Seeing it makes me smile. "No. See, you're forgetting the part when you were in the shower. Bill explained some things to me and I had time to reassess. Decided to cut you some slack. I did this before I knew muscle mania had entered the building. Then he just got under my skin and I messed up, again."

The smile immediately drops from my face as I feel my stomach plummet. I'd admitted to killing Jonah's girlfriend and threw it in his face that she'd been cheating on him. Why in the hell would he forgive that? I drop the paper towels in the sink and turn around to face him. "What exactly did Bill explain?" I ask, my voice breathy and mortifyingly cracking with anxiety.

"He mentioned his suspicions about your dad. He told me about everything you did for him, reminded me of everything you've done for me...I'm pissed at what you did, H but after I had time to think about it I realized some things," he said, remaining rooted to the spot just outside the doorway.

"Like what?" I ask, almost aching with the need to move closer to him but my fear keeps me in place.

"First you didn't know any more than the rest of us did about what's been happening when you woke up in that pizza place. I know you, fought beside you, and I know you wouldn't kill an innocent girl. You saved Bill and you tried to save me or at least warn me. You had to have been fighting for your life. Second," his long-tapered finger points up to meet the first as he counts. I begrudgingly notice how nice his hands are and remember the feel of them on my skin.

My head whips up immediately as he continues speaking. "While your communication skills seriously suck, you came clean about what you saw and what you did. You could've lied and let me believe she was still out there. While part of me wishes like hell that you had I know that never knowing would be worse. I can't afford to be idealistic anymore. My mother was the ultimate liar. Half of my life was built on that shit. You hold back but far as I know you've never lied to me."

I nod in agreement and wait for him to continue.

He brings a third finger to join the other two as he counts. "Lastly, like it or not, we're in this together. I can prioritize and I know we have to get out, you and Bill especially. We have to trust each other to do that. So, you can accept that I've let the past go so I can save my own ass, or seeing how you don't trust anyone or anything, you don't. I'm not going to spite myself here. We don't get along, then there's only one reason, and that reason won't be me."

Jonah crosses his arms in front of his chest but it's his words that send me reeling and I'm speechless. When my gears stop spinning I notice the silence is stifling and I at last meet Jonah's gaze. It's never left me this entire time and it dawns on me, belatedly, that he is stronger than I ever gave him credit for.

I swallow hard and try to match his quiet strength. "Jonah, I am sorry about Beth. I'm sorrier about the way it all came out. While you're right that I don't lie to you, I also can use some...tact. I was angry and I let that push me. You didn't deserve that. I'm willing to learn to pull some punches, okay? I'm hoping you'll stick around long enough for me to get it."

There. That had to be enough. It was woefully inadequate compared to what I'd done, even I knew that and I was socially deficient, but still. It was all I had.

Jonah nodded, not giving anything away but finally, finally stepping forward and into the small room. "I already said I'd forgiven you."

I stay where I am and wait as he purposefully comes closer. "I still had to apologize."

"Yes," he says, as he moves right into me and his chest brushes mine, "you did. And I need you to know I'm sorry about how I acted. And I'm really sorry about your dad. I didn't know."

My nerves are jangling but I'm trying not to let it show. I'm not used to any of this emotional stuff. I'm half-naked and more vulnerable than I ever wanted to be. I'm desperately wishing for a punching bag or a stinker to take it out on. "So, truce?" Damn my stupid girly voice for cracking again.

Finally, Jonah's handsome face shifts back to normal and I'm so relieved to see it, I want to cry. "Truce," he replies as his arms slip under mine. I think he's going to wrap them around me but instead he reaches behind me.

He pulls one arm back and he's holding one of the damp towels. He reaches up and begins patting the towel gently over my eyebrow, supposedly wiping away a smudge of dirt. Then his other hand does wrap around my naked waist.

"I have something to tell you before we leave. Just in case after we get out and I never see you, I want you to know," he states.

I swallow hard and my stomach starts to turn. "Is something wrong?" I ask with concern in my voice. I inch even closer to him, hoping he won't leave.

"H... I'm in love with you," he breathes.

My body jerks at the words because I'm in total shock but Jonah doesn't let me go. His hands are steady at my hip and face.

"It's driving me crazy. I can't stop thinking about you." He slowly brings the towel down to my neck. I instinctively oblige and tilt my head to the side, arching my neck. I don't want him to stop. Not his touch and not his words.

"I don't know what you're doing to me, H," he continues, his eyes focused on the place he's cleaning.

"The moment I laid eyes on you I knew there was no going back. I didn't want to tell you, but Beth and me? We were just pretending to be together for our parents. It was stupid and I couldn't admit it to you."

"What..." I begin because that is seriously far-fetched but Jonah cuts me off.

"-Just listen. We grew up together and our families ran in the same circles. We were close. Our parents had certain expectations for us, especially hers. I knew she was seeing other guys so I couldn't understand why she would lie about it that day. It made me think she wanted to keep me as a backup. I liked to think we were both in on the play but hearing that she lied to me? It made me feel like she was playing me too. I did care about her, love her, but not like that. I couldn't tell you."

"Jonah-" I tried again, having no clue what I'd say but it didn't matter, he didn't stop talking.

"Worse, I was freaked. I used the idea of Beth to keep you at a distance so you wouldn't get too close. I didn't know if I could trust you. You were so damn secretive. Meeting Adam didn't help things. I don't know if you feel the same way but I need you to know. I need you to know because you frustrate me, confuse me, even scare me sometimes but you're brilliant and beautiful in every way I can think of. You're like this one bright light in a world upside down."

I can't breathe, can't move, can't think and I need time to process but Jonah keeps on talking.

"Please, just be safe." The paper towel slides down to the top of my bra, his eyes following, but then stops moving. "I don't know what I would do if anything happened to you."

He finishes talking and his eyes leave my chest to meet mine. I'm speechless.

This guy just confessed his love for me. My head is everywhere and I start to think maybe my mouth is open or something so I snap out of it. "Is all of that true?" I ask, my voice a whisper.

"Yes," he replies with enough emotion for me to know it in my bones.

I smile and grab his face and kiss him softly.

He tugs me closer, deepening the kiss with no hesitation, and instantly I'm breathless. My legs wrap around his waist and I tug his shirt up as we topple over to the sink. He stops kissing me long enough to throw his shirt over his head and kick the door closed behind him. While he does this, I reach behind my back and manage to turn the occasionally dripping faucet off.

Our mouths are sealed again. He shudders deliciously and there's a sound coming from the back of his throat, a half-moan half-growl, that sends little shivers of pleasure through me. He deepens the kiss and slides his hands down my body. His fingers, skimming so perfectly over my skin, send the blood rushing through me.

Then one of his fingers lightly circles the scar on my stomach, the one Bran gave me when he put a knife through me.

Jonah's hand is so gentle there as he kisses me softly on the lips just once and it's filled with meaning. Then before I can process it, he renews our frantic pace and his hands move over me again.

I stop thinking completely. There's only this, skin to skin. Jonah's skin and mine. I'm running my fingers through his hair and down his chest till I reach the top of his jeans. I'm struggling to pop the button free. My body is aching for him and I just want more. I manage to unbutton his pants then I rush to get out of my shorts. I want him closer.

He pulls from the kiss and looks at me. "Are you sure you want to do this?"

I grab his face and go in for another intoxicating kiss. "Yes. I want you, Jonah."

One of his hands slips between my legs and I'm flying on blissful sensations even as I feel an overpowering craving for more. "You're beautiful," he groans against my lips. The kiss changes and I can feel how hungry he is for me, and me only. I'm melting under him.

His other hand skims up my spine, leaving shivers in its wake as it goes for my bra clasp. Just as his fingers take hold, I hear the door creak open.

"Oh!" Bill shouts.

Jonah spins around, knocking his shin hard into the ceramic toilet, and I quickly reach down to tug my shorts back up.

"Jesus, Bill. Have you never heard of knocking?" I ask, panting.

Bill mumbles something incoherent and flees for the hallway.

Jonah lets go of his shin, which must be stinging in pain, and he grabs my face with both of his hands. “We’re going to give that guy a heart attack for real.”

I laugh and trace the outside of his hand on my cheek. “He’s actually pretty strong. He’ll be fine. So, I guess we should get out of here, huh?”

Jonah steps back and nods. “Your dad, H. We should go and say goodbye. It’s time.”

I nod and just looking into his eyes, I know I’m going to get through this. “Ok,” I exhale heavily, trying to get my breath back. “Ok. I’ll hotwire the car I brought. I think it’s time to leave Daredevil behind.”

I hop off the sink before Jonah can think of assisting me and I grab our shirts. I hand Jonah’s green lantern shirt to him with a snicker and a whispered, “Nerd.”

He winks back. Then he pulls his shirt on and grabs hold of my hand. “You sure about the car?” he asks with a lazy grin.

“Yeah. We’ll just transfer over the stuff you guys brought,” I reply as we walk out of the washroom hand in hand. “It’s annoying to have to hotwire and there’s a broken window but it’s got more fuel.”

Once we get to the makeshift grave, we break apart, but not before a pointed glance from Adam and an embarrassed nod from Bill. I look down at the patch of dirt.

Adam covered the grave back up so I wouldn't have to see him like that anymore.

I sit down beside the dirt and place my hand over it. I say goodbye in my head over and over. I say I love you and I'm sorry but the words are stuck on my tongue and never leave my lips.

When I've repeated my mantras enough that I feel dizzy, I sit back on my heels.

It's then that Adam walks over to me, plops down and pulls me into one of his infamous bear hugs. "I'm sorry, H, about this and about before. We both are."

I look around and see Jonah and Bill already down the road, heading to the cars. I huddle deeper into Adam's warmth and listen to the familiar, deep rumble of his voice. "I think it's safe to say that things have been tense for all of us but that's not an excuse. We didn't mean to upset you before. You were right, we need to stick together. We will stand by you to the end and we will get to the bottom of this problem. We'll get out of Washington D.C. and we'll find your family, that's a promise," he says, looking down at me with genuine hope in his eyes.

"Even if I'm with him?" I whisper in his ear. I don't have to point to Jonah. He knows.

"Jesus, H. You even have to ask? I've got your back always. Besides, you'll probably come back to me. I give it a week. You never could stay away long."

I push him away. "Cocky bastard."

"Damn right. Now get your pretty butt up and let's make a

plan to kick ass because, baby, I'm ready," Adam says with a killer smile on his face. I look at him and can't help but smile back.

"Oh, and there's something you should know," he says as we meet up with Jonah and Bill who are trying to lug their stuff, two katanas and 9 bags, into our new vehicle. "I don't want to freak you out but..."

I wait and put my hands on my hips. "Spit it out."

"Just that there was this metal gunk crawling out of your dad's body. It was like a bunch of tiny, metallic spiders."

"What?" is all I can manage to say.

"The buggers were fast but I managed to smash one. I swear it zapped me, then it stopped moving. Old guy saw them too. I thought you should see," Adam replies before pulling a shiny object the size of a dime from his pocket. It was kind of shaped like a spider with its circular center and little crooked pieces sticking out on either side of it. I gaze at it in confusion as Adam wipes some of the gunk that still clung to its edges with his thumb.

I take it and hold it up to the light of the sun, assessing it quickly and thoroughly like my training taught me. It looked like it would be smooth but it has miniscule ridges. It feels like the metal end of my cell phone charger. Actually, it feels like something I've felt before but can't put my finger on. It reminds me of a chip of some kind.

Things began to click together in my mind. "It zapped you?" I ask to confirm.

"Yeah. No big deal but definitely electrically charged. That shit wasn't natural. It reminds me of some of the stuff we used to mess with back in training."

"I was thinking along similar lines." I place the object in my pocket and run my fingers around it as I turn to Jonah, who's watching us with interest. "What do you make of this?" I ask.

"I'm not sure. Let me mess with it in the car."

I nod as I slide into the driver's seat of the new car. "Ok. Let's get ready to rock n' roll, boys. We got a long couple of days ahead of us," I say, taking one last look at the grave out the window. Everything will be better and I know that for a fact.

"Can I drive?" Adam asks and both Jonah and I manage a, "No," at the same time.

I slip my hand into my pocket and pull out the odd piece of metal and wires and goo and add, "Look for any similar technology in Milano's files."

Jonah already has his laptop up and running and he's typing in his manic way that I'm coming to recognize.

Adam surprises me by speaking up from the back seat. "You mean the senator?"

"Yeah, didn't Jonah fill you and Bill in? She's been the spokesperson for this since the beginning. She acts like some sort of hero because she stuck around even when the president ditched us to die. She's the one who decided to drop the bombs."

"We didn't have TV's in the shelter. I was rounded up in the first wave of rescue missions and stuck in the shelter within hours after the outbreak. Superboy over here well, yeah, he explained that but he was talking about some evil cookie lady."

I turn to Jonah and he's looking sheepish. I can't help but laugh. Adam didn't even question that there was an evil cookie lady. He was so street smart sometimes and then something like that slips right by him. "That's just a nickname we use for her. What do you know about her?" I ask as I zip through the streets.

I watch Adam in my rearview mirror as he runs a hand over his head. "I've got a nickname for her too. It's Moneybags Milano."

I snort. "Why?"

"She funded Operation Aries."

I cringe at the words I so desperately tried and failed to forget and slam my foot on the brakes, causing the whole car to rush forward around me. I hear Bill's wheezy squeak above the din. I also feel Jonah's hand come in front to protect me from falling too far forward but I don't have time to acknowledge it. I twist my body around and stare at Adam.

"She funded our World War III training? Tell me you're joking," I shout.

"You need to stop doing things like this!" Bill yells to me.

"Swear to God, baby, and you didn't have to stop the car like that, think of the brakes."

"Adam focus!" I yell and I notice Jonah half-turned in his seat and quietly checking on Bill, who has a hand to his chest. I roll my eyes and get back to the point. "How do you know?"

"Bran always had me as a lookout when he snuck around the camp at night. He had eyes all over that place and was selling some information on the black market. In exchange for the help, I'd get a cut."

"What the hell? You're an-"

"Idiot...yeah, I know but what else was I going to do?" Adam said, cutting me off. "I wasn't sleeping at night and Bran was a good ally. We snuck into the office during conference calls a couple of times, heard a lot. We were a trial program that Milano just kept throwing money at, even after they knew the war was ending and soldiers were coming home. Eventually we got shut down because she said her money was being tracked and questioned after the war ended but she was pissed."

"You're sure she was the backer?" I ask again, my mind racing.

"Oh, yeah. Moneybags was a bitch too. Word has it she married an old man and killed him for his money. They couldn't prove it because she was too rich. She ended up as a senator a few years later. Still it was funny to watch her and the Colonel go at it. I swear it was the only time I got to see that bastard sweat."

"What does this mean?" Jonah asks from beside me. I nearly jump out of my skin at his light touch on my arm and face him.

"Not sure just yet. You say the Milano files are encrypted, right?"

"Yeah, I've been trying forever but I can't crack them all. When I figure out a code word, I unlock just a little more."

"Ok," I say as I look back and forth between the guys in the car. “Look in the files for a government file called Project Aries or maybe Operation Aries. It should be the highest-level security clearance. Can you get those?”

Jonah smiles and his green eyes glitter at me. “Piece of cake,” he says and immediately the typing resumes.

Adam is working his jaw with his hand. “You think they’re related to all this?” he asks, just a few steps behind.

“I don’t know what to think anymore but this is the only lead we’ve got.”

“Does that mean this Bran character knows about the connection between the two?” Bill asks.

I smack my forehead and cover my eyes. I suddenly feel like the biggest idiot in the world. “Yeah, Bill,” I say, looking through my fingers. “He knew about the connection...and he didn’t say a word. He wants to get out of here just as badly as we do. Not sure if this information is vital or not but I’m sure it would’ve helped us to know what we’re dealing with. He’s such an asshole.”

“Holy shit,” Jonah mumbles. His voice holds so much disbelief that my eyes fly to his face. His own eyes are glued to the screen of his laptop.

“What?” I ask. This question is quickly echoed by Adam too.

“Holy shit,” Jonah says again, the hysteria in his tone rising. His fingers are flying and he doesn’t even look up.

“What?” I shout at him. I try to look over his shoulder but suddenly his shining emerald eyes meet mine.

“Guys!” Jonah says excitedly. His words come out as fast as

his moving fingers. "Hell yeah. I did it. I got the access points."

The rest of us begin talking all at once. My heart is jumping out of my chest and I'm so relieved I can barely breathe. Luckily my voice is still the loudest and I'm the one that's heard as I yell, "Are you sure? How?"

Jonah throws his hands up to silence us and he grins at me. "Project Aries led me down one path, which led to another. Suddenly I've got access to a lot of files, and I mean a lot. Including Milano's floorplans to the wall." He turns his laptop screen to face me and my eyes feast upon page after page of floorplans. Adam's hand falls on my shoulder as he pulls his body forward to stare at the screen too.

"Well, I'll be damned," Adam says with a quick smack to Jonah's shoulder. "We might actually get out of here."

My smile is so wide, it's hurting the corners of my mouth. "Did you have any doubt?" I ask, haughtily. I did, of course, but I love being cocky when the opportunity arises. I feel my face flush at the look of satisfaction in Jonah's eyes, and he only has eyes for me.

"Then it's more than probable that your past seems to be connected to this, H," Bill says, breaking Jonah and me from our moment.

I swallow hard, feeling certain that this connection is not a good thing. I've decided I'm going to maim Bran for leaving me in the dark. See if I share the plans with him now! Maybe he didn't even need them, though I figure if he didn't then he'd be long gone before the biters sprang up. I couldn't figure out his angle in all of this.

I reach down and rummage through the bag at Jonah's feet until I find what I'm looking for. I pull out the walkie-talkie and turn it on but all I get is static. I throw it back into the bag and swear like a sailor. "We're too far from anyone to make the connection yet. When I find him, I'm going to kill him."

"Don't worry about that now, H. We've got somewhere to be and now we've got our way out. We've just got to find your family," Bill replies.

I blink and take a deep breath. "You're right. We'll hit the last few shelters and then I'll maim him." My pronouncement is met with silence so I quickly restart the car and begin speeding again. Before I can even ask, Jonah is loading a CD into the player and soon a heavy bass drowns out the rest.

CHAPTER 17

Supreme

"Listen, H, about the shelters," Jonah says after a moment.

"I thought we took that plan off the table," Adam replies.

I turn to look at Adam because focusing on the empty road just isn't all that necessary. "No, this is the plan. We've got a list of 29 more shelters we have to hit before we meet Bran and his goons at the Washington Monument tonight. Didn't you guys talk at all while I was gone?"

The men stay silent for a moment and I'm not sure why but I know I'm going to dislike this immensely. Jonah turns to face me. "We did talk and after I told them what happened this morning we decided that we'd work on strategy, hit up the Smithsonian for any intel I might need, then wait until Bran shows up so we can get out of here."

"You guys just decided to blow off our end of the bargain. I doubt even Bran is doing that. It's only a few shelters. We need to do this," I say firmly.

Jonah doesn't even blink at my tone. "We can't risk them scanning you, not when we know what it means now."

"We have to, Jonah. When I found out about the bombing deadline I never thought I'd be able to get to all of the shelters in time. I need to know if my mom and brother are out there. If they're safe. Somehow, we got the help we needed and I'm not going to waste that by not hitting up less than 30 shelters. We could help people who might still be out there. Maybe we'll find my family."

"I get that but it's not safe. I'm not risking your life for a maybe."

"Me either," Adam says gruffly.

"You know where I stand, Angel," Bill adds.

I hold in my scream because I'm trying to work on that and instead I grit out, "Well, that's just too bad. I'm driving and I say we're going."

"We're not, baby," Adam says.

"She's not your baby," Jonah states matter-of-factly before turning to me, "and if you won't listen to reason then how about we compromise. How about you drive us to the shelters. Adam and I switch off going in. We'll check for your family and offer help to find missing civilians. The work gets done but you and Bill stay in the car where they can't scan you."

"I don't like that plan," I grumble. In fact, I hate it but again I'm trying to be nice and all that.

Bill whistles out an exasperated breath. "I didn't want to do this already but I think it's best if we lay out all our cards on the table, boys."

I turn to see Adam with a sly smile. I turn back when Jonah chuckles. My hackles rise.

"What?" I moan.

"If you take Jonah's deal there is...pizza here for you. You can sit and you can eat with me while the boys finish the job. Will you do that for me, H?" Bill asks all sweetly. Then he reaches into a bag and after some crinkling sounds the scent of heaven hits my nostrils. I barely manage a swallow around the saliva collecting in my mouth but I refuse to give up so easily. I try not to turn around, to see what I already know will look like everything my dreams are made of.

I have one more try of being strong but then hit the gas pedal hard. "You guys suck," I shout in defeat.

I turn to Bill and I can't stop my Cheshire Cat smile pulling at my cheeks. He's up in the front in Jonah's seat. He's passing me the pizza. It's got everything on it and God, it smells good. This moment feels religious to me and I bring out both hands to hold it.

The moment I bring it to my mouth I freeze. I can't stop the blast of images from the last time I held pizza this close to my lips. I can almost hear the bomb sirens as if it's happening all over again.

The tears in my mom's eyes are streaming down in slow motion. The screams are muffled but the glass is shattering all around me. We have to run. I have to get them away from here. Why didn't I grab Justin's hand? Why didn't I protect them?

"H? Is it not good? I'm sorry, the boys seemed to enjoy it. I knew I should've brought something to keep it warm. I'm sorry," Bill says.

"Huh?" I ask bewildered. I shake away my memories, my mom, my dad, my little brother. Now all I can see is Bill's worried face.

Can this really mean so much to him? The stern crease between his white, fluffy brows tell me it does. "Um no, it's fine."

He doesn't seem convinced, probably because I haven't actually eaten it yet. I take a big bite. It's good, no, it's fantastic. It's pizza. I smile to show my pleasure and take an even bigger bite. "You lied. You can cook, old man."

Bill huffs. "Yes, well, I'm glad you like it. I had a lot of time to myself while you were away. Your house's kitchen had plenty of cookbooks."

"I thought you didn't cook," I say.

Bill looks sheepish and I don't think he's going to respond but he does. "I wanted to make good food. I figured it out. Makes me appreciate my wife even more."

I gobble up the last sliver of sauce and cheese before I hit the crust. It's my favorite part of the pizza. "How long were you married?" I ask, genuinely curious. This surprises me but I am. I lean back against the door and stretch out the best I can in the seat.

"Forty-six wonderful years. Now Maggie, she could cook. I never had to lift a finger in the kitchen with her around. I knew she was too good for me so I did everything I could to make her happy. Never felt that it was enough," he adds forlornly.

"You should've made her this pizza," I quip and grab for another slice.

His contact-covered eyes light up as he watches me and it warms me. "Maybe," he says with a twitch of his lips. "I would've done anything for her. I'm glad she's not around to see this but then again..." he trails off with a little laugh.

"What?" I ask around my mouthful of food.

"She would've liked you, H. She was smart like you. She kept me on my toes, kept me feeling alive. I think...she sent you to me."

I straighten up. "Don't think that. I'm sorry, Bill but I'm not a hero. Not an angel." I'm a broken war machine with an attitude problem. I don't know what I'm doing half the time except hurting people, I think to myself. "If your wife could help you in some way, she would've sent you far away from me."

I look down at my hands. I can't even look at him but I can't live this lie anymore. He's the only person who believes in me but I don't deserve it. Suddenly a warm, shaky hand is covering mine. He pats my hand once and pulls away.

"H, as you so love to remind me, over and over, I am old." I look up at him, confused. "I am old but I'm not senile yet. No one knows what to do here. The world seems to be ending. You could've stayed in your bunker and lived your life without bothering to help anyone else. I did that once."

"Bill-" I begin but he stops me.

"When I had to put my Maggie in the ground after her death I hid away. I drank all day and all night. I lost my job then lost the only family I had left. When I felt that pain and understood deep in my soul that life was unfair, I turned my back on everyone. I didn't think it mattered, nothing mattered. Years went by, too many years."

"What happened?" I asked. I knew he had a job at the gas station. I didn't know much else.

"By the time I sobered up, it was too late. My kids grew up, had families of their own. They moved away. I don't blame them. At least...at least I know they're safe."

"You didn't make up with them?"

"No, H. Some damage, abandoning your children in their hour of need, it can't be undone."

I nod. This was the kind of stuff I understood well.

"At least that's what I used to think," he adds.

I swallow loudly. "And now?" I ask.

"Now I know that even if they reject me, I have to try. They deserve my every effort. I've been weak and I've been scared and I've been stubborn. Now it's time for me to be strong. When I get out of here, that's what I'm going to do. At the very least they should know that they are loved. Maybe I'll get to meet my grandkids. Maybe I'll get lucky and one of them will be like you."

I just shake my head. "I keep trying to tell you, I'm not a good person. I'm just looking for my family. I'm selfish."

"Harmony, may I call you Harmony?"

I jump back in shock. "Hell no," I yell out with a questioning gaze. I can't help it, my eyes dart around the area. I know there's no one around to hear but still.

Bill just laughs. “I figured. I found a lot of paperwork in your home. Birth records, things of that nature. I brought it with me in case you or your family need it. I put it in your backpack.”

I nod in thanks but don’t say anything more. I should’ve thought of that. I should’ve thought of a lot of things. Bill grabs a slice and begins to eat.

I think that’s the end of things but Bill keeps on surprising me when he says, “I could remind you that you did save my life and gave me shelter, a complete stranger. I could point out that you have two young men out there right now who are willing to do anything to save you. They’ll follow you anywhere. I could remind you of those things but I know you’ll probably find more excuses for them. You’ll ignore me.”

I bite my lip and nod once. He’s not wrong.

“I will just say this. No matter what you’ve been through you’ve done your best. You want to do better? Then keep going. There’s no one else I rather be with and there’s nothing you can say to make me believe otherwise. So, stop trying.”

I check the rearview mirror to see the boys running back to the car. I think they’re racing and I chuckle. Bill turns to watch them too then he opens his door and slowly gets into the backseat.

I turn back to stare at Bill and he stares back. “We will get us out of here. We’ve got this. Do we have anything besides pizza?”

Bill smiles that old man smile. “We do. There’s plenty.”

After a long day of being a chauffeur who gets to eat delicious food and anxiously await the boys, I’ve somehow bored myself into exhaustion. As Jonah and Adam finally approach the car they shake their heads at me, just like they've done for the last 27 shelters.

In response, I slam my head back into the headrest behind me and cry out. My hope that they'd actually find my mom or brother or even something for me to do like find a civilian has dwindled to the size of a dust mite. I try to take solace in the fact that at least we can officially leave now and maybe Bran has found my family.

As I watch Jonah head to the passenger side door, I swing mine open and cart around the front of the car. I reach out and tag his arm and pull him behind me in one smooth move. I keep pulling him until we're behind some trees. I turn and walk into him until we're face to face.

Then because I feel like it, I grab his face and decide to make out with him. I pour every emotion I have in me into him and it feels so good. I'm grateful he found the coordinates. I'm freaked out that we haven't found my family. I'm relieved that the rest of the search is almost done and I can focus on getting us out of here. Before he can pull me in closer and take control of the kiss, I back off.

"I'm joining you in the Smithsonian," I say, and then inwardly congratulate myself on my stroke of genius.

Jonah sputters and then comes out with some nonsensical sounds before his ability to speak returns to him. I almost have time to feel flattered but then his words aren't what I want to hear.

"No, H." His hands slowly stroke up and down the outside of my arms. "We're almost done here. I've nearly got the files I want unlocked and I finally know where the access point is on the gate. Just let us get through the last shelter and we can go."

I don't know what files he's talking about this time so I ignore that. I lean in slowly and then nip at his bottom lip. "I have a counter offer for you. I think it's only fair that you hear me out. I have five points you'll want to hear."

Jonah practically growls which does nice things for me and this time he does hold me close. "I'm listening."

I smile up at him and I'm surprised to find that it's easy to do. I can't remember the last time I was genuinely happy. I try to hold back that shock and stick to the plan I've just devised in my head.

"You see, number one we're out of pizza which means you're out of things to bribe me with. Number two, it is the last shelter and it's important that we use a distraction to make sure we get what we need. Nobody is better at distractions than me. Number three, we both know none of you can stop me if I decide I'm going in. Number four, I'm bored to tears and so I have decided I'm going in."

I smile again and Jonah kisses me back hard and wild. "And number five?" he asks, slowly pulling away.

"Be good with this. Help make this easier for Adam and Bill to handle and I'll let you drive."

I just can't keep the grin off my face as I throw him the keys.

He catches them with ease. Damn, how did I not catch his quick reflexes earlier? Now that I know of them I can't unsee them. Maybe he just finally stopped pretending he didn't have them. I'm still smiling as we settle into our new seating arrangement.

"What the hell, guys?" Adam gripes.

Suddenly I feel kind of bad. I'm being rude and insensitive, again. Adam could probably guess what we were doing behind that tree. I'm about to awkwardly apologize but I'm cut off before I can. "I totally called being the driver. So not cool," he adds with a pout.

I laugh in relief and Jonah and I just smile at each other.

"By the way, I'm going into the Smithsonian. Jonah already agrees and you two can get over it," I announce.

Both Adam and Bill grumble but somehow both know me well enough to know that I'm not likely to back down this time.

"Ok so let's get this straight. We're going to the Smithsonian for what?" Adam asks Jonah from the back seat. I'm glad for the subject change.

"It's a shelter, believe it or not. I'm guessing it's got the best security, considering the priceless exhibits. If any shelter has any computer access, it'll be this one. I need to try to get to it if I can. Any help to know what I'm dealing with when I get to the gate will be invaluable.

"We may know where the access points are but we can't just stroll through them without being noticed. We also need to check that shelter for H's family and I need an in on their security program. I'm going to try and reprogram it and connect to some of the government's servers."

"Why do you need to do that?" Bill asks.

"Like I said, if we are going to get out of this city we're going to have to go through the one and only gate. To do that we need to get everyone into and through the building undetected. That's going to be especially tricky for you and H," Jonah says. "I don't know what the deal is but they're checking for purple eyes and we've got four of those in this car alone."

"That's messed up," Adam replies.

"Right," I say while checking the map on my lap and stretching out my legs. "So, it's up to Adam and me to sneak into the shelter to try to find my family while you search for any computer to hack?" I say reaffirming his madness.

"Yeah pretty much. I've already got one of the hand-held scanners, and I have a plan for that. If somehow, I can access one of their computers I'll be able to access the system and get us through the gate undetected, but we are only going to have minutes, maybe even seconds for you and Bill to get through to the outside. We'll just need Adam to switch off the devices before any of the guards notice, which hopefully will be easy," Jonah says.

"Okay got it and what about Bill?" I ask with concern.

"What about me?" Bill asks.

"I think you should stay in the car, Bill," Jonah says to Bill sitting behind him. "We'll give you a hand gun so you'll be able to defend yourself, if needed. You'll be safer here."

"Yeah, we can't really assure that the Smithsonian will be

safe for any of us, but it'll be worse if you've got H's purple eyes without her mad skills. Sorry, my man," Adam adds on from the backseat.

"I completely agree," says Jonah, shocking the hell out of me. I almost figured he'd change his mind just to go against Adam.

"I don't," Bill says in a huff.

"Well, it's three against one so we'll go with the plan," I reply. "Now we have some time before we get there. Jonah, since you're driving, talk me through the details of the technological aspects. Bill, maybe start thinking of how you can link up with your kids once we're out of D.C. It's important to have a plan in place. Adam double check on weapons, ammo, and make sure we have everything because we are getting out of here," I say with a reassuring smile.

"Damn right we are," Adam returns.

Now that Jonah is driving, my mind has time to race. All I can wonder is whether my mother and brother are out there. I tried every minute I could to see if our walkie got any signal with Bran or his cronies throughout the entire ride but there was nothing.

When a muffled sound comes out of the speakers I almost don't believe it but I still grab the walkie up quickly and listen closely. Jonah turns the music down but nothing else happens.

"Bran? Can you repeat that? Do you copy?" I beg, looking at the walkie-talkie. My heart is pounding and I'm staring at the thing like it's going to make all my troubles go away.

"Pay attention, damn it," Bran's voice says. I've never been so happy to hear his voice. I wait for him to continue. "We searched the remaining facilities and no one matching your descriptions has been found. We are currently on the way to the White House. 5 more shelters left to visit in total. No injuries. No tail. No further updates. We have approximately 3 hours until sundown. What's your 20?"

I sigh in disappointment and respond, "Got it, beefhead. No luck our way either." I pause and contemplate telling him about the Colonel and demand that he explains what he knows but my internal warning bells are telling me to wait and sit on the information a little longer. "We are almost at our final destination. See you at 7. Over and out."

I put the walkie-talkie back in my bookbag and Adam breaks the silence. "Why didn't you ask him about Croft?" he asks. "He was actually being decent, for him."

I scoff and reply. "We both know he can't be trusted. He'll find out soon enough that we have the floorplan to the wall. Let's just finish what we have to do."

Adam shakes his head and looks out the window.

As we drive past all the white buildings, I become uncomfortable with the empty streets. The sheer lack of stinkers in the area is odd but I try to be grateful instead of suspicious. In the distance, I see our very last shelter, the Smithsonian National Museum of Natural history.

I used to love coming here before the war. It always amazed

me how huge this place was, how breathtaking it was. Artifacts from all different times and all different places kept in one spot, displayed side by side. I thought there was power in that. Maybe that power will protect the people inside it once the bombs drop but I doubted it.

Jonah puts the car in park a couple of blocks past the front of the infamous steps just in case any guards are watching. We all sit in silence for a couple of seconds. Deep down inside I'm praying to see the familiar faces I love. I'm ready for what's coming but I know we all fear what's going to happen if I can't get by the scanners or if we don't get what Jonah needs to get us out. It doesn't matter because I know I can't think like that.

I open the door and step out into the cool Washington D.C. breeze. I peer into the car and throw my bag on my shoulder along with my katana. "Ready?" I ask, my voice devoid of the fear I'm feeling.

Jonah turns off the ignition and hands the keys to Bills along with a small pistol.

"Ready. Everyone know the plan? I already have one of the scanners but I need a few more things. They are probably on the lookout for H so Adam you'll have to go in and check the shelter for H's family. I'll log into their system and get the remaining information I need to get through the gates." He pauses and looks at Bill.

"Bill, stay on the downlow. If anyone approaches the car, shoot them. If a stinker comes your way and it's rabid, shoot it. You have 12 rounds on that pistol and there's extra ammo in the glove compartment. If you run out then drive away. Don't think twice about leaving us because we'll be fine. We'll meet at the monument tonight if we get separated. Got it?" he asks sternly.

Bill nods and replies. "Just be safe in there, kids. I wish you the best of luck even though I know you'll all be okay." He gives each of us a reassuring smile. I raise an eyebrow to Jonah, who apparently thinks he's captain now. I knew letting him drive would go straight to his head.

He clears his throat when he catches my eye.

"H, I need you to snag another scanner if you can. I think that might help me. I have another plan for once we're out and the more evidence I have, the better."

"Piece of cake," I reply.

"After that, you stay with me. I know you're a big girl and everything but at the moment you're the golden rabbit and it's hunting season," Jonah says, raising his eyebrow right back at me and giving me that sexy smirk that drives me insane.

I sigh theatrically. "I mean I guess," I say sarcastically with a salute.

Adam throws his bag over his shoulder and looks at us. "Let's ride out," he says with a smile and starts walking towards the direction of the breathtaking museum.

It's strange walking through the buildings with no movement or sound apart from random birds chirping. Finally, I see a cluster of dumb, statue-like stinkers on street corners. I laugh to myself that it makes me feel better. How sad. Still I don't let my guard down for a minute. Jonah looks nervous but not Adam. My unflappable ex-boyfriend has got an ongoing conversation with no one about what he's going to do once he gets out of this place. I try hard to ignore the thing about the party drugs and the strippers.

It's just another reason I become hyper-focused on our surroundings. This place used to be filled with tourists from all over the world and there was always joy and amazement on their faces as they walked through here. Now it's a total wasteland with nothing but memories. For no other reason than the fact that I'm sick of being a Debbie Downer I grab, squeeze, and release Jonah's hand. Like I thought it would, it gives me strength. I'm not sure if I'll ever be able to express that to him but I'm grateful for it.

After walking for about half a mile we all come to a halt in front of the famous flight of stairs leading up to the Natural History Museum. I open my bag and grab the walkie-talkie. "Bran, we are at the final shelter. See you soon. Copy?" I say and wait for a response.

Some static and then Bran comes on. "10-4. What are you wearing?" he whispers over the line.

I cringe so hard I get a crick in my neck. There's the gross Bran I remembered and loathed. I double check the channel on the walkie-talkie and pull out another one from my bag.

I hand it to Adam. "You deal with the pervert. Since I'm forced to be with Tech-head over here you can intercept on my behalf. We all need a way to communicate in case things take a wrong turn."

Adam grabs the walkie from my hand and starts walking up the flight of stairs and we follow him to the main entrance. "Well, at least we get to go in for free," Adam says, opening the big doors to the building with his flashlight in hand.

I consider telling him that this museum is free, or at least it was when it was open but decide against it. I walk in right after him with Jonah so close behind me, I can feel his body heat.

I can't remember ever feeling this comfortable with someone at my back. It's unnerving.

The inside of the museum is dim. The only light is coming from the emergency lights and all I can smell is a hint of rotting flesh. Not sure if it's better or worse that no guards greet us. My skin is tingling and my ears are ringing with warning bells. I know what this means. "Guys, keep your guard up. I've got a Bittenlock type of feeling about this place."

Adam gives me a look and then I remember I have to explain that reference to him. I just shake my head and say, "bad news."

We walk through the random exhibits with weapons in hand and our guards up, until we finally reach the stairs to the underground part of the building turned bunker. Adam doesn't hesitate on walking down the stairs.

We follow, stopping at the end of the stairs, waiting for Adam's signal to keep going.

We wait for what seems like an eternity but I look at

Jonah's watch and it's only been 10 minutes. I start getting impatient and worried and Jonah seems to have the same look on his face when we hear someone or something's rapid footsteps.

I quickly shift into a fighting stance, ready for whatever is running in our direction. I look at Jonah once more and am surprised to find his tall frame and stern face make for an imposing figure.

Still, I hope he's ready for whatever comes his way.

The footsteps slow down and Adam appears, his face worried.

"This place is empty. There are no guards. No one in the bomb shelter. This place was evacuated. There's something wrong here."

My heart drops. I want to speak, say something, but I can't find it in me. Luckily Jonah doesn't seem to have this problem.

"The last time we saw something like this, it was because the biters had taken over," he begins. "The whole building was infected. This may not be like that but now I'm worried that we walked straight into a trap or maybe there's nothing here at all. Either way we should retreat. I can figure everything else out with my own gadgets on the fly at the wall. It would've just been easier if I had more information."

Adam nods his head in agreement.

"Let's go," he says as he starts walking up the long flight of stairs back into the museum.

CHAPTER 18

Stuffed Crust

We reach the top of the stairs and walk past the abandoned exhibits. Something really doesn't seem right. The faint smell of rotting flesh is everywhere but there aren't that many stinkers around and the ones I can spot are just standing motionless. This is strange. I have to wonder if there were more around and if so, what happened to them?

We keep walking in the same direction we came and everything is clear but for some reason I can't shake my uneasy feelings. I don't know if it's from the situation or the fact I keep feeling like something is watching us.

It's just then I hear the strange growling echoing through the museum accompanied by the sounds of jaws clicking. The sounds of my nightmares. The sounds of super stinkers and it seems like it's coming from everywhere.

We all stop and grab our weapons ready for anything. "I can't see them, let's make a run for it. The exit shouldn't be that far off," Adam whispers holding his stance and ready to bolt.

"No, if we make any fast movements they'll attack," Jonah whispers back. We stand in the middle of an exhibit with no plan on what to do.

Finally, my brain comes back online and I open my mouth to

speak. “Let’s just move slowly in silence and they won’t attack. I don’t think they know where we are either,” I say confidently.

We all lock eyes and nod in agreement as we slowly start moving. Then I feel something wet drip on my face. The smell of it makes me cringe. I halt abruptly and wipe my face. I look at Jonah and Adam before I get the feeling to look up.

I see blank, white eyes staring straight at me. Not one, but at least a dozen of them. They’re clustered on the spiral staircase above us. I feel fear all right and it’s real for once. “Fuck, guys. On the count of three we run,” I whisper, barely putting the words out there.

Still I know they’ll do it anyway. They know we can’t take them all, even with our training. There are too many. “One...Two...” I pause, “Three!” I bolt, running for the direction of the exit, hoping I won’t get lost. Jonah and Adam are flanking me on either side.

We don’t make it far before they start coming for us, the super stinkers, by the dozens or it seems. We have a head start but it won’t be long until they catch up to us. I feel my legs wanting to give up but the adrenaline is also pumping through my veins. “In here,” Adam shouts, pulling us into a room and swiftly slamming the door shut.

We hear the bodies thumping against the closed door in the next moment, telling us just how close on our heels they were. Jonah and Adam scurry to move random things in front of the door to prevent them from coming in as I hold it shut and try to catch my breath. I'm praying and hoping we make it out of here before becoming a stinker snack.

I didn't know what would happen if I was bitten, possibly for the second time, but I wasn't ready to find out. I finally catch my breath and the strong odor hits me again. I grab my katana ready to strike with one hand with my pistol ready in the other and I walk forward, stepping in a puddle of gunk.

The awful growling starts and the thumping from the doors stop. I feel Adam and Jonah following me, in what seems like a death wish on all our parts, further into the darkening room. There are less windows in here and the sun is steadily getting lower in the sky.

I sheath my katana in its holder across my back and exchange my pistol for the flashlight on my utility belt. "Spread out," Adam whispers. We do this but I try to keep an eye on the boys as we do.

The further I walk into this exhibit the growling fades but the stench is still present. They were here, a lot of them.

I keep walking slowly, keeping an eye and light on all angles, including above us this time. I'm making sure nothing gets past me. I catch a movement in my periphery and shine my light in that direction when I hear Jonah's voice screaming my name.

I spin toward his voice but suddenly I'm grabbed by my middle with fierce momentum and I'm shoved hard to the floor. The force of the landing slams my head hard to the ground and my flashlight goes flying.

I quickly regain consciousness and manage to kick one of the stinkers off me. I don't know how many there are but I hear gunshots and the sound of metal going through flesh in the chaos. I feel nails clawing at me and I keep throwing punches without knowing what I'm punching. I manage to get my pistol off my waist and I start shooting at the rotting bodies on top of me until I'm able to get up and regain my balance.

I look around to see Jonah surrounded by four stinkers. Adam is trying to get to him, fighting off stinkers himself. I point up my pistol and start shooting the rotting bodies coming towards me. I run out of ammo and quickly take my katana off my back and start swinging, feeling the familiar rush as I do it. I'm not proud of killing things, even abominations, but each step that brings my friends and I closer to safety is a step I relish.

I finally break free and start running towards an exit sign, knowing Adam and Jonah are going to follow. I bust through the doors of the emergency stairs and quickly try to come up with a plan as I'm wheezing and trying to regain my strength.

Jonah busts through the door and looks at me. "Adam went the other way," he says through heavy pants of breath. "We have to get him but there's too many stinkers out there." I can tell he's trying not to panic but he can't hide the fear in his voice.

"Follow me," I say and turn to run up the stairs as I grab the walkie and start speaking into it. "Adam if you can hear me you need to find stairs and go up. I repeat, find an emergency exit and go up. Jonah and I are fine but we don't know how we're going to get out just yet. We'll meet you there."

There's no reply but Jonah and I keep running up. "Let me think," I say. On autopilot, I run through scenarios in my head, succinctly discarding everything I can think of as quick as it comes.

I pick up my walkie, ready to try and reach him again when the door swings open and a bulky figure falls through. I'm so relieved that Adam made it that I want to cry but my relief is swallowed whole when I catch the man's face.

"Bran?" I yell out, irrationally angry that he's not Adam, stomping up to him ready to tear him limb from limb. "What the hell are you doing here?"

Without saying a word, Bran reaches into his jacket pocket. Jonah quickly hauls me back away from Bran and behind him before I can blink. I peek under Jonah's extended arm to see a gun aimed toward Bran on the end of it. "Well damn," I breathe.

Meanwhile Bran, frozen with his hands in his pocket, begins to move slowly and open his mouth. "Slow down, computer nerd. Not pulling a weapon." He slowly brings out a blindingly bright and shiny object with a long sparkling chain hanging from between his fingers.

No matter that I'm running to escape a super stinker infested museum, my mind goes blank and my mouth drops open. "You didn't!" I hear myself shriek past the shock of being dazzled.

Again, Jonah is hauling me back because this time I might actually kill Bran.

Then because the world is not fair and I can't kill Bran when I want to, more super stinkers fly through the doors below us, filling the emergency stairs with their stench. "Run!" Bran yells and Jonah and I are way ahead of him.

I hear gunshots as Jonah and Bran shoot while we run but I'm not going to let this distract me. As much as I wanted to drop-kick Bran to the floor and let him be devoured by the stinkers, I find my last shred of patience. "Bran! I told you this was our shelter and I told you we'd meet you later," I growl, "and I told you not to steal the infinitely priceless, possibly cursed freaking Hope Diamond." A super stinker catches up to us and I punch it in the face before slicing it through with my katana.

"Quit bitchin'. This doesn't concern you," Bran spits back. "My people are on the other jobs, going through the shelters. What I do is none of your damned business. I heard you were here on the walkie and I figured now was the time to make my move. I did it. It's done."

"Yeah, well, if you risk this mission in any way or I find out you skipped your actual assigned shelter to come here I will make you pay," I roar back, finishing off the last of the stragglers of super stinkers.

We start running up again and I don't stop till we make it to the top. I crack open the heavy emergency door as slowly as I can and peek inside. My eyes fall onto one hell of a giant elephant and relief washes through me.

"We made it to the first floor," I whisper to the guys behind me. I keep watch and notice stinkers, jaws clicking as they prowl around the floor. I count as many as I can see then give up when I realize it's no use. Again, there are too many and this room is too big to account for what I can't see, not to mention all the rooms it opens up to and all the floors above it that look down on it.

I turn around and find Bran and Jonah in an intense stare down behind me so I straighten and step between them. "Ok, first we may have found the exit but it's crawling with super stinkers. Something weird is happening here. None of the other shelters were like this," I gesture wildly around us, "organized like this. The thing is we don't have time to figure out why so we need to focus on just getting out. Secondly, Adam is still MIA."

I turn to face the douchebag that most definitely wants my head on a stick. The feeling was totally mutual. I give him a cold stare hoping that he realizes that he messed with the wrong girl because this girl doesn't get defeated.

"Bran you better hope like hell you can find him and get him to safety or I can guarantee you that you will not be getting anywhere near the quarantine border with that diamond necklace. You feel me?" I say with a hand over my gun.

"Don't think you can threaten me, princess," he says like he really couldn't care less.

"You know what? Never mind. All you do is blow shit up and make things worse."

And it's then I remember the grenades in my bag. I quickly take one and look at Jonah. He's already got one eyebrow raised like he knows I'm thinking something. I nod to him. "Open the door slowly and make sure Adam isn't out there.

He opens the door slowly and gives me the all clear. I peek through the door to see the rotting bodies looking for flesh, alert and ready to destroy anything that breathes in their direction. I pull out my walkie again for good measure. "Adam if you can hear me, stay off the first floor. We're coming in hot with grenades. I repeat, grenades on the first floor near the tourist entrance. Stay clear until further notice. Do you copy?"

I wait about a full minute but there's no reply, the only sounds are of our combined heavy breathing as we wait. Needing to take the chance I quickly pull off the latch and throw the grenade as far as I can and close the door.

Jonah, Bran, and I start bolting down the flight of stairs to the landing to seek shelter when all the sudden Bran's beefy hand hauls me up and forces me ahead of him. Then when we hit the landing he covers my body with his. "What the fu-" I begin when I'm cut off by an ear-shattering explosion.

After a breath, I push hard at Bran's giant body and wiggle out from beneath him. "Have you lost your mind?" I scream thrusting one finger into his chest because this seriously freaked me out.

"You're welcome, princess. Now shut up, we've got to get back up there," Bran says before shoving me away and jogging up the stairs. Jonah catches me before I can regain my balance and all I can do is stare.

"I don't think so," I retort finally, following him up to the door. "What are you playing at, Bran? There's no way you would try to protect me and by the way don't think I don't know about Milano and Crofts connection to this and to Project Aries. You're going to start explaining soon or I'll slit your throat myself," I growl, my suspicions growing more pronounced in my mind.

"I said shut up already! I want out of D.C. and I need you alive to do it. Don't think I'll be protecting your ass again, you ungrateful little-"

"Don't finish that sentence," Jonah says in a scary voice I've never heard from him. "Now all of us, let's go."

After a very tense moment Bran opens the door, filling our dank stairwell with the smell of rotting, burnt flesh. Bran walks out the door making sure it's all clear to move. There are no signs of life, not even the undead kind.

When Bran signals us, we disperse into the vast, now empty room. I stare hard at the elephant that managed to make it through but is now missing a tusk while I pick up my walkie and try again. "Adam come to the entrance when you can. We're all clear. I repeat, all clear and ready for our exit. Do you copy?"

I wait with the walkie close to my ear but there's no reply, only blank static. I look to Jonah but his face tells me he doesn't believe Adam will be coming. I turn away and wait. I just know Adam is going to saunter in any minute now.

"This hellhole is nuclear. We need to bolt unless you want to get bitten or infected from the blast. We can't get out if you're dead," Bran repeats again oddly.

I throw my hands up in frustration. "We're not leaving him. So help me, Bran. I will shoot both your legs and leave you to suffer as the biters eat your flesh if you even think of moving to the door."

Bran looks like he's ready to do just that when in the distance I hear a loud engine approaching us. A cherry red motorcycle comes flying through the building from another room.

Its rider is in head to toe black leather with killer black stiletto boots. The woman is heading right toward us and I hear her voice shout, "A man named Bill sent me. Follow me," over the sound of the engine. I look at Jonah in alarm and we start running behind the motorcycle without looking back.

"Is he all right?" I ask but my voice is drowned out by the engine. The female on the bike comes to a screeching halt. "Wait we have one more of us in the building!" I say.

She just nods. "Is Bill okay?" I ask again desperately, trying to decide if I should go to Bill or Adam.

The girl stares at me for a second and then yells, "Go through those doors and keep running. I'll meet you outside," before she speeds off.

My head is full of the million scenarios in which Bill is hurt and in need of me, I surge through the doors and through a long hallway. The boys' footsteps pound loudly alongside mine and echo throughout the halls.

We finally reach the end and burst through the door into the cool air and the sun beating down on us. I spy a waving Bill a few feet ahead, leaning against a column and holding a wrapped bandage around his leg. He looks otherwise unharmed though.

Once my brain fully comprehends this I immediately fall onto the floor to try and catch my breath. Then I look at Jonah with no words because I feel my heart about to leap out of my chest and I'm shaking from the adrenaline rushing through me.

I've also still got more to worry about. Bill is fine but we left Adam behind. "Jonah, we have to go back for him," I cry. I don't bother appealing to Bran. I spy him out of the corner of my eye speaking into the walkie.

Since I can't hear his words through my walkie, I know he's on a different channel, probably speaking to his crew. I honestly don't care enough to scroll the channels like a stalker. I roll my eyes and Jonah helps me to stand up.

Bill slowly walks over, favoring one leg. I want to greet him and make sure he's okay but all I can see is the fear in Jonah's green eyes. "H, we can't go back there. We don't know if we'll make it out alive," he says, sorrow lacing his deepened voice. I'm ready to tell him he's wrong and doesn't know Adam like I do and that I never, ever leave a man behind but the sounds of an engine approach us in the distance.

I turn to the mystery chick, ready with a million questions, but this time there's two people on the bike. A breath I hadn't known I'd been holding releases with a heavy sigh of relief. I see the familiar face of Adam, his eyes already firmly on me. When the bike comes to a halt, he jumps right off. I absently notice the bike revving up once more and then shooting down the stairs.

This is some daring shit, even for me but I don't have time to admire it. I turn to run to Adam, ready to hug him like it was the last time I'd ever see him. I stop when I notice his mouth is moving and his hands are gesticulating wildly in panic mode. I've seen these signals before and it all becomes clear when he yells, "Run! Now! Bombs in the building! Run!"

I grab for Bill but Adam gets to him first and pulls him into a fireman's carry. Relieved, I turn and run alongside them. Bran, needing no further encouragement is already 10 steps ahead in the distance but he keeps looking back to check on us, which shocks the hell out of me again.

I'm running down after him when suddenly Jonah is running beside me and his hand grabs for mine.

Then I'm flying down about a million stairs, scared to death that I'll trip and break my neck or end up blown to bits or worse that I'll drag Jonah down with me.

When my feet hit solid ground, we keep on running and I'm practically being dragged by Jonah but we don't stop. I turn to look at him just as the explosions begin.

CHAPTER 19

Thin Crust

I roll and keep rolling. Asphalt and dirt must be tearing up my exposed skin but I don't feel it yet. All I feel is immense heat at my back and the remaining dregs of my energy. I roll a few more times then slowly get to my feet. With a sick ringing in my ears and smoke in my lungs, I begin coughing like a maniac.

My eyes seek out Bill first, not because I don't care about Jonah or Adam or this unlikely savior but very cool chick, but because Bill needs me. Out of all of us he's the weakest. And okay, yeah, I need him too.

So the second I clock him, I'm already sprinting towards him. Unfortunately, I pass the cockroach that is Bran, seriously will that dude ever bite it, and his girl Wednesday Addams, plus a couple of his other goons who have suddenly shown up but I don't have time or energy to sneer at them. We'll be rendezvousing with their dumb asses soon enough.

"Bill," I yell out through my abused throat passageway as I attempt to haul him up toward me.

Just as I get my arms around his coughing frame, which luckily tells me he's breathing, the load is lightened and I see I've got extra support from Adam. I notice the motorcycle chick is standing behind him, alive but holding one bleeding arm.

She leans forward to help us with Bill but I shake my head once but with a small smile that I somehow manage. We got this, thanks to her.

Together Adam and I prop a shuddering Bill up and I pat the old man's back as I move us slowly but surely further away from the destruction. It is far away, it has to be for us to have survived that blast but it's still in my sights, roaring smoke and flames, so it's still too close for comfort.

I only stop when Bill's seriously-strong-for-an-old-dude's-arms lock around me. I know we need to keep going in case there are any residual explosions but I can't seem to move.

Instead, for once I allow myself this embrace. “Your leg?” I ask, holding tight to Bill as he holds tight to me, his tremors becoming softer and tamer.

“It'll be fine. I'm just fine.” I sigh and sink my forehead into his shoulder. "Angel," he breathes into my hair. The sound of the word makes me smile slightly. I'm just thankful he's okay.

I take a deep breath. "Never," I reply. We hold each other for what seems like forever but still not long enough. The only sound that manages to break through this moment is other hacking coughs from behind me and I'm relieved that they are coming from Jonah.

"Jonah," I gasp out, also like a 6-pack-a-day-smoker, which I'm sure is very attractive. He just looks at me and I see everything I'm feeling in his eyes. Then Jonah and I collide into each other.

"Is everyone okay?" he asks, hugging me back tightly. I nod my head trying to fight back the tears while Adam approaches us. "Yeah, I hope so," I say. Then feeling like this whole sentimental thing is getting to be a bit too much I let go. I try to nod to Adam, but him being Adam he scoops me up and spins me around.

"Okay, okay. Put me down. I'm fine!" I yell to him. When I'm placed on my feet Adam steps away. Then he pulls out something from his bag. I blink twice just staring at the object. "How did you get a scanner?" I ask in excitement. Jonah's arm reaches out and takes it from Adam's hand.

Adam just smiles. "When we got separated I found a room with our type of shit, military packs, cots, and supplies. I spotted a computer but it was smashed to pieces. I also found papers with lists of names on it so I threw that in my bag. There were weapons too and I was tempted but I only had time to grab one more thing when the super stinkers caught up to me again and I thought this would be more valuable," he says, pointing to the scanner.

Jonah smiles at me and then at Adam. "You did good," he says simply.

Then I'm facing the girl on the motorcycle and it's a nice one at that. She swings one leg over and stands up. Her small frame is offset with a massive black helmet, which she slowly takes off to shake out her masses of red locks.

I hear a gruff, "God, you're hot." I roll my eyes and elbow Adam in the ribs. Still I can't help but stare at her in surprise. We all stare at this small woman with auburn hair and a soft, delicate face dusted with freckles. She looks like a super-hot version of Mary Jane for God's sake.

I snap out of it and realize we are all being weirdos by staring at this girl who can't be that much older than me.

Bill limps over to the girl and shakes her hand vigorously, saying, "I can't thank you enough."

"You got it, Mr. Bill," the girl says with a strong, southern twang.

I tilt my head and blink slowly. Mr. Bill? What? "Who are you?" I ask with my voice slightly cracking.

She brightens and says, "The name's Roxanne, though everyone calls me Roxie. You're welcome for saving your lives." The words sound cocky, and I would know, but she says them with a warm smile. This girl kind of just sassed me but I don't care. "Who are you guys?" she asks.

Adam steps forward with a smirk and says, "Well, Foxy Roxie," he begins. I slap the palm of my hand to cover my face but he keeps going. "My name's Adam. That unattractive wimp over there is Jonah and the girl over here is H. Seems like you know Bill. Nice to meet you."

Jonah scoffs in the background. "I seriously thought we were over this, Adam," he says annoyed.

Roxie laughs and shakes her head, her eyes falling on me. "I knew it!" she squeals. "I knew you had to be H. I mean the glowing white hair is a dead giveaway, though I'd say it's more of a platinum blonde color than white and golly the fact that you're probably the only other actual humans out and about but still."

I snicker at the glowing white hair part. "You've heard of me?" I ask.

"Hard not to, there are rumors everywhere about the daughter of some big shot walking all over the shelter guards like they're her personal stomping grounds. Heard rumors that you saved people that the soldiers gave up looking for. Some of the guards are mighty chatty, they gossip like you wouldn't believe and all you've got to do is flash them a smile."

"Right," I say, kind of loving but also hating that I'm some sort of a legend.

"Anyway, thought I'd run into you sooner or later. You guys were lucky to get out of the museum. This place is a mess. I came back to salvage some valuable exhibits before they got destroyed by Lord knows what, some crazy virus, so they're saying. Then lo and behold I've got the dashing Mr. Bill yelling for help, fighting off three leg draggers, mind you. I couldn't believe my eyes that another living, breathing human was calling out to me that I had to stop and help. Then he told me about y'all and well, you know the rest. Not for nothing but why are y'all here?" she asks.

I step up and look at her finally getting my senses back. "We came for the shelter but it was evacuated or attacked, obviously. I'm shocked they didn't have security."

"I suppose they didn't think they'd need it, what with the virus victims running around the place. These are strange times."

"Yeah," I add, my mind whirring. I glance back at the bursts of flames surrounding the buildings and frown, still not believing any of the crazy things that just happened. "Look I'm sorry but we need to keep moving. Can we talk on the way to our car?"

Roxie shrugs and shakes her red hair out of her face. "Sure, Sugar. I'll walk my bike so long as we go slow. Plus, I think Mr. Bill here could use a slower pace."

"Slow is fine as long as we're moving. Adam do you mind helping Bill walk?" I ask him.

"Oh no, I don't need," Bill begins but is cut off by Adam, who supports him easily. Then we all begin to move.

"So, Adam," I begin casually, as the steady weight of Jonah's arm slides around my shoulders and settles on me, "did you just?" I ask, nodding back towards it all. I stop to let out another cough then continue. "Blow up the National Museum of American History?"

"Yes," Roxie answers emphatically from over her shoulder as she walks with Bill and Adam ahead of us. "I'd say you could bet the farm on that."

Jonah gives me a sideways glance but Adam adds, "Heard you over the walkie the whole time, H but couldn't get a free hand to reply because I was fighting those suckers off. Still I heard you and I thought firepower was just what I needed too. They were piling up on me like crazy. I had the stuff in my bag but I just needed a way to do it where I could get away and not get caught in it. When this hottie came riding in, I knew just how we could make our exit."

Roxie winks at my ex but looks back to me. "So," she continues, "I don't know about y'all but I'm ready to go paint the town and the front porch! And just sayin' I always wanted to blow up a building of leg draggers. Surprisingly, this never happens in Texas," she adds excitedly.

I blink slowly at Roxie then I feel the corners of my mouth pulling high. "Finally!" I shout in triumph. "Another girl I can relate to. You," I say pointing to her, "You're my new favorite."

Jonah squeezes me in protest but I just laugh at him with my eyes.

"Thanks, darlin'," Roxie replies. "I dig you too. Long as I got a biscuit, you got half. Now seriously it was nice meeting y'all but I've got my Harley and I'm raring to go."

Adam suddenly bends down in front of Roxie, leaving Bill to stumble a little without his hold but he manages all right. Then my ex-boyfriend is clearly proposing. There's no ring in sight but he's holding his hands in a pleading prayer position. "Foxy Roxie, I think you need to marry me."

Roxie, completely unfazed by this barely gives Adam a glance. "Is he serious?" she asks, looking at me.

I just shrug. "He has a type, apparently. Feisty."

Then to my shock Bill smacks Adam across the back of the head and is pulling him from the collar of his shirt to standing. “For the love of Pete, can you young people please try to hold your hormones together until we get out of this forsaken city?” he asks disapprovingly, making me so glad I was not on the receiving end of that set down. Upsetting Bill was just plain wrong.

“Yeah, Adam. Get it together,” I add because, well, it was hilarious.

“So disappointing, man,” Jonah chimes in.

Adam rolls his eyes but moves him and Bill closer to Roxie as we continue our path away from the burning pieces of history.

I know I should be sadder for all that we've lost but there's only so much mourning a person can let in and obviously I don't have room for that now. Later, though, I know this is going to eat at me big time.

“Roxie, thank you for helping us. We are trying to leave D.C. before it’s bombed. You should come with us,” I say unable to keep the concern out of my voice.

“How are you planning on doing that? There are guards everywhere. I’ve tried and I know just how to persuade them.” Roxie raises her eyebrow at me. “I may not be from around here but I sure know how to slip by authority. It’s kind of my specialty.”

I laugh. “We’ve got our ways. Now listen, not sure if you know this but it’s not a good idea to be out here. We can bring you to a shelter but you don’t seem the type who’d want to stay cooped up in one. You saved our lives and now we'll return the favor," I say, looking her right in the eye. "We've got to get some food and restock our supplies before we head to the wall." I decided I'd let Bran know he could meet us there since there was no point in meeting here now.

"What about that other hulk of a man?" she inquires as if reading my mind. "He sure ran off fast, and where'd he get off to? Is he with y'all?"

"That was Bran. You may have heard of him too. He was responsible for most of the fires right after the virus spread. He also just stole the Hope Diamond. Flat out? He sucks, but for now we have to work with him as a part of the escape plan. You don't have to trust him but you can trust us, Roxie."

She takes a minute to inspect all of us. Then she says, "I think that'll work out just fine. I know you guys got the Hemi parked up front where I met Mr. Bill but I need to ride so I'll follow on my Harley. Also, just to say, I'll trust you, but cross me and we'll have a problem," she adds, giving us a stern look that seems at odds with her sweet face.

"And just to say, cross us and I'll have to pull your pretty red hair out of your head strand by strand and make you watch as I feed it to the stinkers," I say with a smile. She smiles in response then puts on her helmet and her bike roars to life.

Adam nods to me once and lets me know he's got Bill with just that dip of his chin. I nod back and then turn to look into

Jonah's eyes. I've got this deep sense of knowing that we're on the same page, and maybe that sense has been there a while.

"Your mom and brother...we'll find them, H. Don't give up hope," he whispers to me, proving me right that he does know what I'm thinking about. I close my eyes for a brief moment then I lay my weight into him like I want to. Then he's steadying the both of us as we travel farther and farther away from the flames.

CHAPTER 20

Neapolitan

I jump into the driver's seat and once everyone is settled, I reach my arm back, basically sticking my walkie in Adam's face. "You deal with Bran."

"Babe, do I have to?" Adam whines.

"Unfortunately for you, watching Roxie out of the back window is not actually helpful. I'm driving. Jonah needs to study the floorplan and figure out which computer he can access when we get close since this place was a bust. Bill needs to tend to his leg." I pause for a second. "Oh, and Bill made the pizza."

Jonah turns to me, his green eyes glittering but he manages not to laugh. "Yeah. Makes sense," Adam replies congenially.

"There's also that Bran is your friend," Bill adds with a clear of his throat.

"Yes, that!" I say. I catch a glimpse of Roxie in the rearview mirror and throw her a quick wave. We had different styles but badass is badass, and I respect that.

"Hold on," I add and shake Jonah's arm. "Jonah, can you find a place that's close to the border entry point where we can all meet but not be seen?"

Jonah hits a bunch of keys really fast which is ridiculous because it sounds fake but it actually works because soon he's turning the screen and pointing. "Here's good. It's under a cliff.

They have patrols so we can't stay there long but it'll work for now." If I didn't love this nerd before I would fall again now but I'm keeping that in. Besides Adam being two feet away, no one needs Bill to say the word hormones again.

"Adam, tell them the coordinates and some landmarks to help them find the meet place. Also get a head count for his cronies. We'll need the number to get a real plan in place. We're going in pretty blind so we need to account for every detail that we can get our hands on."

When we pull up under the cliff I'm surprised how dark it is. It seems like the sun has just gone down but I guess it's really been an hour or so drive. I feel like we're about to go into the final showdown and a strange, tense quiet has settled on all of us as we mentally prepare.

I try to pull into the ditch quietly but it's a challenge with the roaring of Roxie's engine right behind us. Soon enough I'm finally able to park the car and turn off the ignition. In the distance I see figures moving, their shapes being outlined by the moonlight.

"Is that you guys?" Adam asks into the walkie, hoping for good news.

"Yeah, we are setting up camp for the night," Bran replies a breath later. I step out of the car with my boots hitting the gravel, realizing I'm beyond exhausted. All I want is to be free of this nightmare but as I look around at Jonah, Adam, Roxie, and Bill and the wall that is just within reach I have to believe that everything is going to be okay.

We walk towards the shadows moving in the distance. I shiver slightly, not realizing how chilly it was and the lack of clothing I was wearing. Jonah notices and puts his arm around me, surrounding me with his body heat. This immediately makes my body go warm and my heart slightly skip a beat. When in the hell did I become this girl? Blaming the biters makes no sense but it sure makes me feel better.

We finally make the short walk to the makeshift camp the hooligans set up. They have a small fire and multiple tents set up surrounding the fire in a U shape. We approach Wednesday Addams who's by the fire giving everyone a plate. I grab one from her to have an all too familiar goo slapped onto the paper plate by Adam. I look up at him with a smirk. "Just like old times."

"What in the fiery pits of hades is this?" screeches Roxie.

Bran emerges from the shadows and turns to her with what seems like disbelief. "It's slop, sweetheart. This ain't no five-star restaurant. We make what we can. So, eat it or starve."

Roxie looks at him in utter shock. I honestly thought I was going to see Bran go down in flames, as in literally get pushed into the fire pit, and I was ready to help.

"Well, it damn sure seems like you have no respect to talk to a lady like that."

We all laugh until Bran stops me with his beefy hand slapping hard on top of my shoulder. "Your tent is over there. There's a first aid kit we found so you can take care of the old man.

It would be a shame to lose him so close to leaving."

His words send chills through my spine and all I can do is keep my head high. I never trusted him but I could always count on him being a jerk. Somehow this new side of him made me hate him even more. "Thanks, I guess," I toss out.

I walk forward, not looking back towards the tent, my slop in hand. I sure as hell didn't miss this cold mush of mystery foods. My particular plate seemed like it was going to jump alive at any moment and infect us all.

I take the first bite as everyone stares at me, realizing it honestly didn't taste bad, or maybe I was kidding myself and I was starving.

"Oh God this is amazing," Adam says in the background kind of making me want to puke.

We sit in silence devouring our slop until Roxie speaks up. "So, what's the plan for the morning? Why aren't we just sneaking in tonight? How are y'all planning on escaping? We're cutting it mighty close; don't you think?"

I start to open my mouth to speak only to have Jonah jump up, his long fingers swiftly pulling out a device from his bag. "Well, the original plan was for me to hack into their computer system from within the Smithsonian, override their security system and cameras then have us all sneak through tonight."

He frowns and a muscle ticks in his jaw. "Unfortunately, that didn't happen so we have to be stealthy and try to get them to invite us in, only they won't know we're us, they'll think we're supposed to be there. That at least I think I can manage since they're external files and not controlled from within the wall. Anyways, now all we can focus on is getting everyone inside. From there, there should be less security and we can make our way out."

"We'll make it work," I add confidently.

"You see this?" Jonah asks, finally pointing to the object he'd gotten out of his bag. It's the eye scanner.

He rigged it so when it scans Bill or I, it says we're not infected. He told us all about it in the car. We'd decided as a group that we shouldn't reveal that Bill and I were infected somehow. We didn't trust Bran and when it came down to it, we didn't know Roxie. We needed the scanner to work for us but we made up a story about its real purpose.

"This will help change our identities into new ones. It'll tell them we belong there," Jonah lied smoothly.

Jonah and I look at each other and laugh before he continues.

"The only downside is we can only trip the scanner once every 3 minutes. Bill will go first with everyone including Adam, you, and Bran and his goons. They have to make sure to switch the scanner they'll encounter without getting caught, which they are great at, and it will be a lot easier since we are going in different groups. Once you all are through safely, H and I will go in next."

Roxie does not look entirely pleased with this plan. "And if the scanners still go off. What then?" she asks.

Jonah responds with his usual cool demeanor. "Then we

switch to Plan B. H and I will find a way to rescue you guys if there's trouble, but we're hoping it won't come to that. Like I mentioned earlier, I can get us new identities so they won't immediately try to kill us since some of us have a bounty on our heads. If we claim to be authorized to be there, they'd see that we're in the database as authorized and that might buy us some time."

Roxie's red eyebrows lift. "What will time give us, exactly, if we're trapped in there? Plus aren't the bombs going off tomorrow? Doesn't seem like time is really on our side. That sounds like a big hole in your fence."

Jonah looks at her. "I realize we're down to the wire but if the bombs do go off, the best place to be will be in the wall. Like I said, we just need to make sure everything goes as planned. That reminds me, let me grab my laptop and we'll get your fingerprints and your iris to change your identity on the program. We can't leave anyone behind. We can't forget any detail. We've got this one chance to outsmart them and we can't miss it," Jonah remarks, then gets up from the ground and scurries over to the tent to grab his stuff.

Roxie looks up into the sky and scoffs.

"What's wrong?" I ask. In my opinion, she should be relieved we found her.

"I'm fine. I was just thinking how everything changed so fast. One moment this country girl is on a plane to Washington D.C. for her dream job at the museum and then this happens," she scoffs again in disbelief and stands up to go to the tent that Jonah's already in without another word.

We all sit in silence, not knowing what to say. We were really getting out of here.

Eventually, I walk to my tent and open a water bottle in order to splash my face with the lukewarm liquid. I manage to rub off as much of the dried blood and debris from my face and hands as I can before I head to sleep. I look out to where the moon bounces off the top of the border wall. No, I would not be staying another day in this hell.

I wake up feeling the sunlight and the humidity in the air. I fix my messy hair and hear chatter outside the tent, making me realize that I'm alone and everyone is clearly awake and preparing without letting me know. I throw on my boots, infuriated, and walk out to find everyone else getting ready. My eyes land on Jonah and I decide not to notice how attractive he looks because I feel betrayed. I walk over to him in disbelief. Why would he let me sleep in? He knows this is big for me.

"Um excuse me, why was I not woken up? In case you haven't noticed, nothing goes on here without me knowing," I practically snarl. I'm running this whole operation, screwed up as it is. It's already Sunday morning. I check my watch and it's 6:40 am. The bombs go off in 17 hours and 21 minutes. Does no one else realize time is of the essence?

Jonah doesn't even try to hide his smile. He thinks I'm being cute because I'm mad and it makes me want to punch and kiss him at the same time. “H, calm down,” he begins. “I just wanted you to get your rest while we cleaned up. I knew everyone had the plan down and you looked so peaceful,” he brings a hand out and caresses my cheek with it, which I thought was pretty brave considering my glare. “I was going to wake you up soon,” he adds.

I look back at him and shake off the anger. “Whatever. Where are we at? When are we moving in?”

His big green eyes narrow in concentration and I can’t help but smile. “Well, we are ready to go in about 30 minutes. Bran has the scanner, he’ll switch it out and will get Bill, Roxie, and Adam in first. You, Erin, the rest of Bran’s goons, and I will be the second group.”

I bite the inside of my cheek and think about how once we’re inside, Jonah and I will have to quickly and efficiently lead the way to the other side of the walls and eliminate any obstacle in our path. I’m also surprised to realize that I’m not as worried about that as I thought I would be. Jonah has proven himself to be a leader. I just blink up at him as he keeps talking. “Bill is as ready as he’ll ever be, I think. At least he has Adam to keep Bran in check.”

I nod my head and notice the concern in his eyes. I really hope we didn’t mess up in trusting Bran. “Adam will definitely protect Bill. So once Bill is safely through, Bran will create the distraction, and the rest of us will sneak through, right?” I confirm.

“Right,” he says. “Piece of cake.” I laugh at him with my eyes as he repeats my earlier words to him.

I walk over to find Bill. When I make it to him he looks like a nervous wreck. "Hey there, are you ready to get the hell out of here?" Bill laughs and throws his arms around me in an unexpected hug, then whispers in my ear, "I'm so glad you came in the store that day and didn't leave me to die. You're an amazing person, H. Never let anyone tell you otherwise. Thank you for taking me this far."

I can't do anything but hold back the tears that are clogging my throat and reply, "I'm glad I found you too. I don't know what I would've done without you."

He lets go of the embrace and I smile at him. "I'll see you on the other side, old man. We did it." I walk away knowing it's all going to be all over soon. We were all going to freedom. Hopefully this mess hadn't spread beyond the walls.

Bran gathers with his minions and calls Adam, Roxie, and Bill over. I stay where I am but still listen intently. "Okay. We are coming in from the east. If you're feeling nervous then don't bother coming. Just do as you're told. You know the story, say we got cleared from the shelter for evacuation. We need them to think everything is cool until all of us are inside. Got it?" Everyone nods in agreement, including Bill.

Then everyone's eyes are on Jonah as his fingers fly across the keys in an odd staccato rhythm. Time seems to slow as we wait and wait.

Then Jonah's eyes lift to meet mine and his hand lifts too. It's the signal we've all been waiting for. I manage a quick, genuine smile at Jonah then turn to watch Adam, Bran, Roxie, and Bill move in toward the giant gate keeping our city closed off.

I keep watching from a distance as they walk with confidence and when they start to get too small to spot, I pull out my binoculars. My eyes fly to the front doors and I'm nearly chomping at the bit waiting for my turn to go through them.

They finally reach the guards and I watch as a conversation ensues. Everything appears to be tense and I can't help holding my breath as I watch. Then like we'd practiced it a million times Bran smoothly and efficiently switches out the scanner right from a guard's hip. That particular guard was staring into Roxie's chest. She really was good at this and I was relieved because she came in clutch.

I watch as the red lights of Jonah's scanner flicker and then return to normal. I peer over at Jonah through the corner of my eye, hoping this works. A couple more of these tense moments tick by, followed by the guards lifting their walkies and talking into them.

Soon they're nodding and the tense postures start to loosen. My own spirits start to lift and I get into a runner's stance.

My eyes lock on Bill as he walks through and is held still under the lights of the main scanner but even I can hear the sirens going off. I want to cry as I see the lights flashing like they did when Jonah first scanned me. It didn't go as planned, it failed. I failed. I freeze in some primal response I can't shake no matter how hard I try.

Not a moment later and the double doors are flinging wide

as more guards burst out. Bill's face is terrified but Adam is already in front of him, fighting off the guards. Chaos ensues as an endless stream of guards run out into the fray, taking on Adam, Roxie, Bran, and some of Bran's ragtag crew. All I can see is Bill being jostled around as he stupidly tries to move forward toward the doors. He should be running the other way. This wasn't happening. It couldn't be.

I grab at Jonah, my limbs finally moving of their own accord. "We have to get down there and get him now!" I yell and then I get up to start running towards the gate. That's when I see Bran pull out a gun, face it towards Bill, and without hesitation he pulls the trigger. I watch in horror as Bill's lifeless body hits the ground abruptly. I nearly double over from the massive pain shooting from my chest but I can do nothing but scream a shattered cry, sob uncontrollably, and run.

I hear Jonah yell after me but I can't stop. My heart is aching as if every piece of it was being ripped apart from the inside and my legs really want to buckle underneath me and give up but I can't let them. Bill was going to be all right. He had to be. Also, Bran was going to die and I was going to be the one to make him pay.

I see some guards look at me as I approach. One is immediately pointing a taser gun at me and telling me to stop. And I just can't. I look down, unable to stop as my heart shatters over and over again. Bill is lying there in a pool of his own blood. The mass of it draining from the gunshot wound in the center of his chest. His glassy eyes, open in death. I pull out my gun with a clean shot at Bran. “You son of a bitch,” I say. I’m ready to pull the trigger but something stops me.

I fall to the floor in agony, landing half over Bill’s prone body. It’s too late though. I can’t protect him anymore. As everything goes black all I hear is Bran’s cold words ring out. “What did I tell you? I brought the bitch to you, just as promised.”

CHAPTER 21

Sicilian

The first thing I notice is pain right behind my eyes. It's staggering and I immediately try to hide from it, to force myself back into unconsciousness but it's a no-go. Thanks a lot, self-preservation skills.

Slowly I open my eyes and feel like I've been slammed in the back of the head with a shovel. I reach back and feel a giant lump forming on my skull.

On second thought, maybe I'd been hit by a bulldozer. Once the main source of pain has been assessed my instincts kick in and I look around. I mean I just woke up and I have no idea where I am.

I start to stand up when the pain of witnessing Bill's death hits me all over again. I suck in a sharp breath. Everything hurts and I sink onto my ass, barely feeling the sting of that fall.

I think of my friends that were still alive when I was brought down. Did the government agents capture Adam and Roxie? Kill them? Did Jonah get away? Are any of them still alive?

Bran sold me out to the government. Best I could figure, he conspired with someone, maybe Croft, to get me here. Did he find out the bombing was real and think it was a good idea to serve me up on a platter in exchange for his freedom out of here? I knew he was acting strangely at the museum. I should've known. Now Bill was dead and I didn't know what happened to the rest of my friends.

A strong urge hits me to get in the fetal position and rock back and forth. In my mind, I see myself doing it but some part of me realizes I can't wallow like I want to. If the others are somehow alive, they could be in danger. Heck, I'm probably in danger. I don't have the time or luxury to lose my shit.

I take several deep breaths and wipe at my eyes and nose on my sleeve, trying to block out all the blood already staining my shirt.

When I can, I look up and around me again, actually seeing things this time. All I find is glass sheeting in a circular cone around me. I'm in some sort of tube? What the actual hell?

I peer through the glass in front of me. There are rows of similar tubes with dark figures in them, I can barely make out the shapes of other bodies, but I can tell that they are bodies. My eyes swivel the room from left to right, the ceiling to the floor, leaving no view unseen.

There's no other human that I can see in the room, just the figures of bodies in the other tubes. There are white walls, grey tables with vials and beakers on them, and freakishly high ceilings too high to climb up to reach an air vent, that's when I realize I must be in a room inside the border wall.

My head continues to swivel. White coats on the wall, computer screens filling just about every available space on the wall next to...a flash of red.

I sag in relief when I realize it's an exit door. Okay, so...I'm in a tube in some sort of laboratory inside the border wall. There's one exit, that is, if I can get out of this tube.

I start to climb up but just as fast I slide down.

I check my watch for the time but realize it’s missing. My weapons are gone too.

There's nothing to grip and the walls are just a little too wide for me to touch each side. I want to panic but I swallow it down.

I start to bang against the glass, knowing immediately it's a stupid idea. The glass is thick. I can't break it by banging into it alone.

I look behind me and decide I have enough room to run and then push into the glass wall to try to break it.

With as much effort as I can muster I slam hard, feeling what will definitely turn into a bruise along the entire left side of my body.

Tears leak from my eyes again, blurring my vision but I wipe them away on my bloody shirt and try again.

I think of Jonah and slam again, barely jarring the glass tube from its spot. Is he safe? I pull back before I can think too hard and slam again and again, thinking of Adam, my mom, and my brother. The glass doesn't even crack.

I assess it, looking for weak points and my heart is pounding as I accept that there is nothing. I feel the panic start to want to take hold of me and I push it back, banging a furious fist onto the floor. The sheer pain of it, the noise it makes gives me the smallest bit of satisfaction.

I bang it again. The floor creaks and my eyes fly to the floor as my breath freezes up in my chest.

I bang my fist once more and the floor creaks even harder, splintering a little.

I check the floor I'm standing on and realize it's elevated off of the floor in the room, by maybe four inches at the most.

If I can break the floorboards I can try to slide out from beneath the glass tube. Then again, I worry that ruining the foundation will just trap me inside and the glass will tear me to shreds.

I visualize it piercing my organs and eyeballs as it all crashes down but honestly this is my only shot out. It's a risk I have to take, I just have to be smart about how I plan to break the floor.

Slowing my breathing I concentrate on the floorboards at the edge and closest to the center of the laboratory. I have to make a hole large enough to fit through but small enough that the entire tube doesn't collapse.

I slam my fist straight into the floor and use double the force by pulling back like my fist is bouncing. It works and I slide through about an inch of wood like it's butter.

I look down in shock, ignoring the blood around my knuckles. I have to blink twice at what I find. This shit is hollow!

These lab people were seriously dumb. And I am seriously awesome.

Once I make the hole big enough to crawl through I'll go down and then make an exit hole in the circular platform. Then I'll be free and I can make my next plan. Whatever it is, it will involve the slow and painful torture and demise of Bran Demanski.

I beat my fists into a bloody mess and manage to make the tiniest hole possible that I can try to slide through. Once my feet are through they start a bouncing kick to break through a new hole to crawl out of.

In what seems like 8 months later but is probably only a few minutes cool air meets my bare ankles. I know I've made a hole that reaches into the room.

I have to slither to fit and try to blindly avoid any wood shards from stabbing my body.

The further I reach, the more I have to kick to make more room. Finally, my head is the only part still in the glass tube. The rest of my body is sitting with my knees crunched into my chest inside the platform.

I know the hardest part will be trying to squeeze my head through but with a final huff I push my feet hard and extend them out into the outside as I suck my head under. I make the hole bigger and after wiping the slickness of my blood off on my pants, I grip the underside of the hole and swiftly slide out.

Cool air hits me and I breathe in the acrid smell of

antiseptic. I hear the soft beeping of machines and the humming of all of the electronics. Yep, total evil lab vibes all around. I look towards the exit and then back towards the other tubes.

Decision made, I get up and run to the nearest glass tube. There is a panel of buttons outside of it and I want to figure out which one will open the tubes. I pull my hand back swiftly when I realize it's all fingerprint controlled.

Guaranteed if I touch this without the proper access, an alarm will sound. It's honestly a miracle I haven't set any off yet so I need to be smart. I press my face to the glass and peer inside.

A girl peers back at me, her stare is completely devoid of emotion. I don't even read fear. She looks young, maybe 13. Her pupils are purple, just like mine underneath the contacts.

Thinking of that I reach up, and realize my contacts are gone. Did someone remove them? I get completely creeped out that someone did that to me in my sleep and I shut down the thoughts about what else may have been done to me.

I focus on the girl. "I'm here to help you," I shout at the glass in as loud of a voice as I dare. "Do you know if there is an override button or another way to get out?" I ask.

I decide if all else fails I can break through her platform from the outside but I don't know if I'll have enough time. There won't be enough time to do that for every tube and possible person in here.

The girl just stares back, she looks so sad and she looks

familiar, I realize. I met her little sister! What was her name? Theresa? Tessa? Yes, Tessa. This must be Tara. Holy shit!

"Tara," I yell to her. "Your sister sent me. Tessa sent me. I'm here to rescue you!"

That's when the girl looks up and if I'm not mistaken I see the glimmer of hope. Then her lips part and her mouth opens. I lean close.

"Now how did you manage to get out of your cell?"

The words send a shiver down my spine because they didn't come from Tara. They came from behind me.

CHAPTER 22

Marinara

I turn, my mind recalling the exit in this room, deciding I need to make a run for it.

All of that thought stops when I see who is speaking to me, a smirk clear on her pinched face. I recover quickly though.

"Senator Cookie, what a surprise. Not."

"Ah, Harmony. I see you live up to your reputation. The Colonel spoke of you often. None of it good, you understand, but he is a misogynist prick and I can read between the lines."

"Don't call me that," I say as I silently inspect her for weapons. She looks unarmed and weak. I can take her down, break through the wooden floor of Tara's tube and get us out. I knew I could.

"I wouldn't try to run if I were you. It would be utterly disappointing, not to mention useless."

I am about to pounce, conjuring up about six different ways to incapacitate her but something about her has me pausing. I'm covered in blood and I must look half-crazed. Why does she look so calm? She is defenseless against me and she knows where I was trained in combat.

"You think so?" I ask.

"I know so. I have complete control over every specimen in this room, you included."

“I’m not a specimen, you sick freak. Neither are they,” I say as I wave a hand toward the other tubes.

She ignores my jab, not allowing it to ruffle her Botoxed expression.

“Freeing yourself was clever, a trait I find necessary in your strain of virus but if you try to run I’ll be forced to exert my control. Ultimately, for this war I need you to have functioning brain cells, need you to blend in with humans seamlessly while also having you within my power with a simple flick of a switch.”

“Hate to break it to you but I am human and you have no power over me. Your cage can’t hold me and neither can you.”

Milano tsks at me, actually tsks like a school teacher to a naughty child. I’ve had enough of this. I decide I’ll show her just how naughty I can be. I’m about to charge her when she extends one thin arm to Tara’s tube. Her fingers barely graze what looks like a light switch there.

The guttural growls hit me like a fastball. I spin toward the sounds and find the young girl within her tube utterly transformed. She is, without a doubt, a super stinker but there’s an odd intelligence shining behind her eyes. Her young face is twisted with the look of cold rage and she is beating violently and intently against the glass.

I’m shocked to find the glass is truly cracking under her fists. I’d felt that glass around me and knew I couldn’t damage it even if I’d tried a thousand times. I skid to a halt in front of her, appalled. “What have you done to her?” I yell.

Milano says nothing and the glass begins to splinter and crack but not break.

"Stop it," I continue. "She's just a child. Stop!" I'm ready to strangle Senator Cookie to get her to obey me but she's already fiddling with the buttons on the keypad in front of Tara's tube.

"Fascinating, isn't it? The strength and precision of her blows," Milano says and then hits a red switch.

Tara's whole body relaxes, head drooping and hair hanging low before she collapses to the floor.

I run at her tube but my hands slam and slide pointlessly against the glass. I can't reach her, can't help her. I look up at Milano and I want to hurt her but she has the answers to make this stop. I wonder about Jonah again. I worry if he's safe. I need to get out. I need to save him if I can.

"Happy, Harmony? Of course, I did it for the sake of the lab equipment but we women can pretend, can't we?"

I turn to her fully at a loss for words for this type of crazy. Milano only clasps her hands in front of her, some mock-pious gesture that is more sickening to me than if she'd stabbed me.

"She can do anything I program her to do. She can run faster than 230 miles per hour, jump higher than a twenty-story building, and leap longer than the length across Kingman Lake. I've programmed her so that her skin won't tear and her bones won't break. She is my perfect creation. An ideal match to my serum, as are you."

She turns back to me, eying me as if I really am just a

specimen in her lab and my whole-body shivers involuntarily. "What do you mean?" I ask, fearing for my life in a way I mistakenly believed I was no longer capable of. However, what she'd just shown me was a fate worse than death.

"We knew going in that the odds were against us. Less than .001 percent of the population of the United States would react the way I needed them too, would become my bionic soldiers but we couldn't be sure until we tested it on a mass scale. I knew my own city would make lovely test subjects but I never dreamed it would turn out so well."

I begin inching toward the exit.

"This whole thing? It was a planned experiment? You infected the whole city to find the few of us that would react to your stupid serum?" I spit out in rage and disbelief.

"Few of you? I would've taken just a few. It would still be worth it. We allowed certain people to live. We sadly couldn't infect everyone. We had to set up a semblance of humanity within the shelters. We needed some survivors to tell the story. I only expected 40, maybe 50 of you but 73 of you reacted positively to the bionic serum, 73! I've got my hands on all of you thanks to the rounding up and scanning of the survivors. I've got my entire army here in this wall."

Seventy-four, my brain silently whispered, thinking of Bill. I wonder if she'd known that Bran had killed Bill to get me here. Hell, he didn't have to kill Bill at all. I was already on my way. He did it because it would hurt me. Bran must've found out from Colonel

Croft that I was infected but he didn't know about the old man. Did she know she could've had 74? It didn't matter now.

Maybe it was better Bill was dead than have him live as an experiment, as this demented woman's weapon.

"Fate is a funny thing, Harmony. Don't you agree?"

"There is no fate," I say, my eyes burning into this horrible woman's.

"There's only people and their choices. Yours for instance, are desperate and sick and if you're looking for someone to blame? Check a mirror."

"And how would you rate your choices? Was it those choices that led you right back to me? You'll be surprised then to learn that you were meant to be my soldier back then. We were almost finished with the serum when the war ended. My project, Aries, was brilliant but before its time. You were all going to be my test subjects because you were chosen, you were strong and young. We thought most of you would survive the injection but don't you see? It was meant to be done on a larger scale and at a different time. It was fate, and apparently you were fated to be my soldier."

"Lady, I won't be a part of your psycho army. I'd rather die. Now I'm only going to offer this once, free the others now and I'll let you keep one of your limbs. You can even choose which one, I'm magnanimous like that."

Milano laughs. "You're truly not getting this. It's a shame because I had high hopes for you too. Listen to me, little girl, you do not have a choice. You are mine but I'll keep your death wishes and threats in mind later when we are reprogramming you. For now, we'll continue our tests and when we're satisfied we'll ship you all out to infiltrate our enemies and restart the fight."

I balk at her words. "You want to restart the war? You really are insane. We finally have peace. The world is starting to rebuild. Why? What good could come of it?"

"No, not a war. It'll be a revolution. A true takeover from the days of old. When the mighty conquered lands and took them as their own, shaped them into something new. We'll be international heroes, and you'll get to be a part of it. As a former and failed soldier, I'm sure you can appreciate the gifts I've given you."

I could feel vomit rising in my throat, the acrid taste of it spilling into my mouth. I push it back down. I need answers.

"What about the rest of the city? The people in shelters? The kind of stinkers that attack and the kind that don't? What will happen to them?"

"All test subjects, but the ones with purple eyes, are failed test subjects. They've served their purpose. Your colonel wanted to keep the attack subjects as you call them around a little longer, use them fully until they decompose naturally but the bombings are more important to the cause. The attack subjects have done a good job at infecting others where we placed them in the streets and in certain shelters but eventually the serum is too much for them. They fall apart just as the inert ones do, if at a slower rate. The only ones to survive the virus do so immediately."

I blanch at her explanation. There was no saving the stinkers or the super stinkers, even if I'd wanted to. My dad, Bethany, and the other stinkers I killed would've died anyway. That didn't make me feel better. It was still senseless murder.

And for what? To sort out the different reactions to a bionic serum to murder more people. My mind is left reeling in the face of this evil and hatred.

Ultimately no one in this city had stood a chance. It was death and destruction in order to create more death and destruction. It was either don't get bitten at all or become like Bill and I to survive. Bill was dead though so it didn't do him any good.

"Their brains, magnificent brains like yours become one with the virus, changing your DNA make-up and forming something entirely my own to wield. Sadly, with all my money, I found that true loyalty cannot be bought or bred but it can be created. I've created the perfect soldier and with the survivors, the remaining humans of this city, I will create a blinding loyalty to me, the woman who saved them."

"You expect people to live in those shelters forever?" I ask.

"No, we'll just quarantine them for a bit then we'll help them rebuild. They'll survive the plague and the bombings to wipe out the rest, well, some of them will. Population control is too good to pass up. Think of the cut down of traffic and the sympathy money we'll have pouring into our broken borders to help the victims."

Population control? How was this woman allowed to

breathe air? I was going to strike against her but I was worried about Tara, about the others. Should I even free them if their will wasn't their own? I know what I saw but she could be lying about how far her control reaches. They were human after all, just like me. She had to be lying.

Still I have to consider what would happen if they were killing machines under her control and I set them out into the world. What if I was a killing machine too? What was the right thing to do here? I didn't know and this psycho was still blathering on about her evil machinations.

"We'll be swimming in charity donations and even more means to manipulate the world, and if we can't manipulate them? We'll destroy them. After all I have an army of bionic soldiers that cannot be stopped. I've built you to be indestructible and you answer to me. Therefore, I am invincible."

"Invincible?" I ask. Then before she can blink I kick out and swipe her feet out from under her. She falls hard to the floor, the sounds of her bones smacking against the solid concrete making my heart soar.

I move to wrap my hands around her throat. "Let the others go. Now," I bark, squeezing tighter.

Again, this woman laughs. Who laughs as they're being strangled? Her fingers come out of her pocket, wrapped around a separate control panel remote.

One minute I'm applying pressure, the next I wake up, pressing against bindings.

I'm tied to a chair.

"What the hell?" I gasp out, my breathing heavy.

"Welcome back, Harmony. Did you enjoy your sleep?"

I shake my head from side to side and fight hard, my entire body bucking against my restraints. I test the ropes for any point of give but there's nothing.

I quickly realize there's no use. I need my strength because my adrenaline will only last me so long.

"What did you do to me?" I yell and show her the edge of my teeth.

She freaking tsks at me again.

"You're not listening, dear. I'm afraid I like you better as my mindless pet. I may flip this switch again just so I don't have to hear your inane questions."

I eye the remote and reality crashes down on me. It's true, all of what she'd threatened. She can control me, everything I am and can do, with a single silver remote. I'm her moldable weapon. I'm a monster.

My blood begins to boil with my anger, with my utter lack of ability to stop this. I've never been this hopeless. A hollow darkness sinks deep into my bones, making me immobile.

"How long was I out? Did you drag me here?" I ask, my voice empty and monotone.

She stays quiet and assesses me.

"Come on," I taunt. "You've put all this work into creating me. I know you're dying to share the details."

An ugly grimace covers her normally pinched face before a smirk replaces it.

"You were only out for a few minutes, no need to become hysterical, and as for what I did to you? Absolutely nothing but finish the knots as instructed. You did as I commanded from standing up to grabbing that chair and the rope. You gave me the directions of how to secure you completely. You're quite good at trapping yourself, made sure there was no way you could get out."

"I told you how to trap me?" I ask, not realizing that I'm speaking out loud. I'm too lost in my thoughts and fear.

She lifts one dainty shoulder. "Yes. Now you see why your intelligence and previous skill sets will be a vital component for me. The others can be trained of course. In fact, you can train them. I believe you'll be much easier to deal with than the odious colonel. I can't stand that man."

This was infinitely worse than I thought. I'd moved and spoken and I hadn't even known it. I spoke the truth too. I doubt I could've lied even if I'd wanted to. And Croft? He was definitely in on this then. Milano could overpower me. She could have me do and say anything she wanted.

Did I tell her about Jonah and Adam? Did it matter? Surely Bran had betrayed us all by now, given out Jonah's location if he managed to stay behind and hide.

Bran probably told the colonel and senator our every plan. I had to pray that he just made his bargain and bolted for the other side of the wall without another word. I also had to pray that

Milano hadn't thought to ask me about them when I was under and lastly, I had to keep her from flipping that switch again. There were a lot of prayers and luck I was banking on but there was nothing else I could do.

Another person enters the room and I can hear his cold laughter before he comes into my view. I don't want to see him, to face him again while I'm trapped and helpless. At that moment I make a decision.

I close my eyes and relax every part of my body as the colonel's words hover over me like a black cloud.

"I can't stand you either, Milano but until our goals no longer align you keep your trap shut and I won't slit your ungrateful throat."

"Lovely to see you, as always, Croft," Milano replies in a bored tone.

I hear the heavy click of her heels as she walks away, towards what I didn't know, but I hear her feet stop eventually without the sound of the door opening or closing. So I know she's still in the room.

I can feel Colonel Croft assessing me and I make sure my breathing is even.

"Shit, of all my recruits this worthless maggot survived the bite. I was hoping she'd die slowly. She was dumb enough to get bitten after all."

I hear him and feel the air around me as he moves in closer.

"It'll be fun making her lick my boots though. She always

thought she was so much better than me because of who her father was." He kicks me, hard, with the edge of his steel-toe boots but I don't react. I'm playing dead and forming a plan.

Truthfully, I didn't know what I thought I'd achieve other than the fact that I didn't want to face him but maybe I can come up with something. These two hated each other and maybe I can use it against them somehow.

"Wake her up. I think some training is in order," the colonel barks in that ruthless tone of voice that has haunted my nightmares.

"What are you talking about? She's awake, you ingrate," Milano says with another bored sigh but despite her words I can hear her drawing nearer again.

I'm unprepared for the slap that comes across my right cheek and a small moan escapes me but otherwise I don't move. Whatever happened I was riding this out as long as I could. If I were awake, or worse, put in the zombie trance by the remote, he'd do this to me anyways and more.

"Looks knocked out cold to me and covered in blood. Are you sure you didn't kill her?"

Milano's voice drifts over me from right above me now. They must be nose to nose.

"Of course I didn't kill her. The blood is not hers. They tell me it was some old man's. Insignificant. However, if this were her blood drawn by your hand then you would be dead. You do not touch my specimen until I say so. Her body hasn't been calibrated to be indestructible yet. Now get away from my property before I break the rest of my soldiers out and let them tear you apart."

I do a mental eye roll at their bickering. Maybe she would follow through and one of my problems would be solved. I also found out that she hadn't done a lot of work on me. Maybe I haven't been here long. Maybe there was still time to save-"

"Don't threaten me, Milano," Croft replies, cutting off my thoughts.

"You may pull the purse strings but I lead the few military personnel that actually know what's going on, the ones you paid off, and they'll still listen to me over you. You forget your plans could go up in smoke if anyone higher up finds out about this and I'm not afraid to go down just so I can watch your face as I take you down with me. Better yet, I'll inject the antidote serum into every last lab rat you managed to get. There's 73 of them, isn't that right? Isn't that what you've been bragging about all day? That wouldn't take more than an hour. I promise I can knock you out of commission for that long and you can kiss this all goodbye."

My body jerks the slightest bit before I can tamp it down. Antidote serum? Holy shit. There is an antidote serum. I can't believe it. Where is it? How can I get it? Honestly the details didn't matter. I just knew I had to get it if I ever had a shot of getting out of this alive in order to save my friends, maybe even to save the world.

Hope infuses my veins. I have a purpose now and I can't afford to fail.

"Alas, you won't," I can hear the smirk in Milano's voice as she calls his bluff.

"My money benefits you greatly, as does this revolution so I suggest you get out and let me tend to my lab rats. There's much to do before my next press junket. Go make yourself useful and prepare to release the bombs. Midnight approaches. Only a few hours now. Surely that much destruction will give you the pleasure you lack."

Almost midnight? How was that possible? It had been morning when we'd come to the wall. How long was I knocked out for the first time?

How the hell did I lose so much time in here? I was too late. It was all I could do to keep my breathing steady.

Ever the levelheaded man, the colonel kicks me again, to piss Milano off as well as dig at me once more before I hear him storm off too.

CHAPTER 23

Jumbo Slice

"Get up, you little fool. Don't pass out on me now," Milano says as she shakes me. I decide I should quit pretending now but before I can sit up within the bounds of my restraints I hear her say, "Oh to hell with it," and I know she's going to flip the switch. I attempt to scream out my protest but I'm too late. The me who is still me passes out for real.

I wake up again and my arms move up on instinct as my body jerks. I feel so strange. I feel like I don't even know myself anymore, and maybe I don't. I don't know what's been done to me and I don't know what I've done. Dread fills me, making it hard to breathe.

I lift my hands and they feel like a stranger's hands. I examine them, feeling off in a way I've never felt. Even after the time Bran stabbed me and I changed, I still felt like my skin was my own.

I hear a commotion behind me and I spin around to face it, immediately realizing I'm free from the ropes. I jump out of the chair but freeze to take in the scene before me.

What greets me is something I can't begin to comprehend. Two people are locked in the heat of a battle. "Jonah," I cry out.

Jonah's eyes meet mine for the barest of seconds, his face unreadable, before he faints left and is out of the way of the senator's hand.

I stop at the sight because Jonah is here, breathing, alive, and unhurt. He was fighting Milano and he had the remote. He must've woken me up.

I watch him, stunned and I spy a very large syringe in his front pocket. I bolt towards him. I'm so blown away with relief that I can't believe my eyes. "Jonah," I cry again.

Milano takes that moment to push Jonah off his feet. He falls over. I'm quick, I know I am but even as I head over, I know I'm not quick enough. He's getting up but I see the remote back in her grasp.

"Senator Cookie," I yell and she turns to me, "You don't want to flip that switch."

Milano just frowns, a small wrinkle deepens in her forehead between her eyes. "What a clever little nickname. Remind me to punish you later. Anyways I do want to flip this switch and I will. I'll watch as you slaughter this boy. Jonah, is it? You don't mind giving me a little demonstration on Jonah here, do you?" She laughs. "Oh, of course you don't, you won't have any control over that mind."

With the senator distracted, I watch as Jonah runs to the computer and within seconds the only door to the room closes and locks. My God, I loved that boy.

He looks up and walks over to us after checking out the system on the door. "That'll buy us some time, I'd say," he says to Milano. "Your guards might still catch us but you're a horrible person and you'll be dead, so there's that."

Ok. Seriously, I loved him.

"That's enough. Don't move," she yells to both Jonah and I, her finger right over the switch. I stop dead in my tracks. We both know she's not bluffing.

Jonah slowly points to his pocket. "The antidote," he says, his voice cracking only slightly. "I found plenty of jars of the stuff in this needle in the other lab, as I'm sure you know. I broke into the cells in that lab and I injected about half of the people in there."

He'd found the antidote? And he'd injected some of the test subjects like me with it? He'd been busy. I wanted to throw my arms around him and thank him. His actions would help in whatever war Milano was planning. It would lessen the damage with less super soldiers to contend with.

"I'm willing to leave you the other half," he continued. "Just let go of the remote and let go of H. We'll walk out of here. You'll have your soldiers. You'll have your war."

"You did what?" Milano screeches, her uptight, unaffected facade finally falling away. "You think you can take away my soldiers and negotiate with me? I will not stand for it."

"Jonah," I mouth as my eyes meet his perfect green ones across the cold, sterile room. I motion to him to keep talking so I can steal the remote again and take her down.

He can inject me, inject the rest of the people in the labs and we can be free.

Milano takes a shuddering breath and then an odd grin smooths over her features. "A trade then. The remote for the antidote."

I don't understand the turnaround and I don't trust her. "Don't do it, Jonah," I say but Jonah stares hard at Milano for a moment then nods, not looking at me once. Before I can stop him, he walks over and, in a breath, they've traded items.

Jonah holds the remote gently, like my life depends on it, and it does.

"Well then," Milano, says as if she doesn't have a care in the world, "now that we're on track, I'll leave nothing to chance." She spins and faces the computer, holding down a button on her earpiece. "Deactivate the brain of number 73 and put it into destroy mode," she says, her voice projecting clearly.

"I'm just guessing here but that sounds like it would be about me," I say.

"Deactivation of test subject number 73 commencing," the speakers from the largest screen up on the wall report back. "In 30 seconds, 29 seconds, 28-"

"No," Jonah shouts, "cancel request," he continues as he runs toward the computers.

"My technology doesn't answer to you, boy." She ignores him and turns to me as she tries to make her way to the door but I dog her every movement. "You've got 25 seconds until my machines take over your brain, Harmony. Try to stop me and I'll only have the computer deactivate your brain sooner and you'll kill him sooner. I'm giving you the chance to say goodbye. Don't waste it."

I eye Jonah, over by the computers. If anyone can stop this, it's him. Maybe getting her out of the room isn't a bad thing. I make a decision and throw my arms up, pointing them toward the door. "Get out then."

She nods wistfully at me. "I'm your maker and your master and in time you'll see this is the way things were meant to be. Soon you'll hear my voice over the speaker in these rooms. You will obey me, you will kill him, and then you will crawl back into your broken cage like a good little pet. When you awaken you'll be reprogrammed. We will discuss your punishment then. For now, I'll be watching. Do try to make the goodbye mournful and the killing bloody. I've been bored for days."

I want to hurt her, maybe even kill her but I don't. I do one of the hardest things I've ever done and I let her go. I don't take my eyes from her until the door slams shut.

"23 seconds, 22 seconds, 21 seconds," the speakers yell at me as I race toward Jonah. He's frantically trying to make it all stop as he types away. I kick at the monitors, breaking them and shattering their screens but the voice of the computer continues through the speakers, "15 seconds, 14 seconds,13 seconds."

"It's no use," I tell Jonah, "you have to leave here," I beg.

"I can't," Jonah says, and I notice his eyes are wet, "I can't hack this system. I don't have enough time, H. I didn't plan for this. We were supposed to have more time, damn it. I'm sorry. I'm so sorry." He pulls me into his arms and holds me tight. I can see this is killing him. It's killing me too. "I have a plan B," he says. "Don't worry."

"6 seconds, 5 seconds," the monotone voice continues calmly. I have a plan B too and it doesn't involve hurting the amazing person in front of me, not ever.

I see the monster I've become and everything that means. All the consequences it holds burns a hole right through me. I'll kill, maim, and torture easily without thought, without remorse or restraint, without morals or discrimination of age or character, without even knowing I'm doing it. I will be a blind weapon, unstoppable and at the mercy of a mass murderer.

"I'm sorry," I tell him as I pull away. I know what I have to do. "Get out of here, Jonah. Please save yourself. Promise me you'll fight like hell, that you'll get out of here. You'll try to help the others."

I was a lost cause but the others? The others Jonah hadn't gotten to yet with the antidote? What would become of them? What would Tara be forced to do? We'd promised her sister we'd try to help her and we failed her.

Even if we hadn't gotten to everyone in time, there was an antidote. Maybe somehow Jonah could help the rest of them.

"I won't have to fight you, baby. That's what I'm trying to tell you-"

I put my hand on his, I have no time left and I want him to hear me. "Not me, Jonah. The guards. Fight them, even after I'm gone. I love you and I'm sorry," I say again.

Jonah is grabbing something from his back pocket and I

don't mind knowing that the last thing I'll see is his face.

Then I raise the knife I swiped from Milano. I watch Jonah's arms come toward me in a blur. He must be trying to stop me but I won't let him. I hear the countdown turn to one. I won't be her monster.

I plunge the knife toward my chest and everything, everything goes black.

CHAPTER 24

Delivery

I wake up groggy and aching like I've never ached before. That's saying something. I'm lying down on what feels like a firm, downy mattress with plush sheets that I've sunken into for all eternity.

It hurts to breathe, like needles are being strategically slammed into my chest and throat with each inhale. The exhale doesn't feel too good either. I want that to stop and I'm now noticing that either I'm blind, I'm in pure darkness, or the whole opening my eyes on command thing isn't happening.

I'm also wondering what freight train hit me, or if it at least ended up on the news when I was trampled by a stampede a la Mufasa? Maybe I was in a plane crash? That would suck. With another painful breath, I realize I'm probably still in the facility at the wall. Why didn't I die? Maybe I can't die.

Had the bomb gone off? Is my city gone and I'm trapped here forever as a cyber psychopathic murdering machine? Why can't I remember anything? With that thought my eyes pop open.

The fact that I'm not blind is definitely a relief but I'm not sure I want to wake up. The room I'm in is dimly lit. My eyes scan it like my training has taught me. There are two doors and to my surprise there's a window. The walls are white, the room is ice cold and everything looks state of the art and yet, barren. As I'm planning my escape, finally my memories begin to flood my brain.

Last thing I remember is plunging the knife in so that I wouldn't kill Jonah. I had to sacrifice myself for him. God the look on his face...a mournful sob escapes my throat and I quickly try to cover the sound with my hand.

I don't know where I am or who's watching. I don't even know how I'm alive but I have a bad feeling about it. I bet I didn't stab myself. I bet the switch flipped before I could.

I feel around my stomach and see that there's a bandage over my abdomen but it doesn't feel like I've been stabbed. Did that Senator Cookie psycho keep me alive?

Of course she did. God, how could I be so stupid? I'm her precious test subject. She and her people wouldn't have just let me die. Tears fill my eyes as I realize they've probably killed Jonah. In fact, they probably had me kill him anyway.

A wave of nausea overtakes me and what little progress I've made in sitting up is deleted as I fall back. I've failed him. I failed everyone. My next thoughts are of death and they're dark and painful and all-consuming.

I try to block it out because I need a plan. I always need a plan. The darkness will have to wait for me, and I know it will. I don't want to live as a tool for my enemy. I don't want to kill any more innocents. Who knows how many I've killed already? I need a plan to bring this operation down. This isn't over.

The familiar sound of footsteps fills my ears and ignoring the way my whole-body groans as I move, I leap off the bed and grab the first thing my hand finds to use as a weapon. I look down and realize it's a TV remote.

Wow. My first thought is that I've worked with worse. My second thought is that I guess they want me to be entertained in between my murdering sprees. How hospitable of them.

The door swings open and I'm ready to chuck the remote at someone's nose or stab it through their eye if they get close to me when Jonah walks in. He sees my position and quickly covers his head to block the incoming attack.

The remote falls limply out of my hands and crashes to the floor. Jonah and I stare at each other, his emerald eyes taking every inch of me in. I want to do the same to him but I can't look away from his perfect face. His freakishly long eyelashes are blinking at me like I can't be real. I know the feeling as I scan the way the dim light flashes on Jonah's prominent cheekbones as he slowly shakes his head in disbelief.

His strong jaw is as hard and unyielding as ever but I can see the endless words that he wants to say in his eyes. "H," he rasps, finally.

The sound of my name on his lips nearly has me falling to the bed again. How is this possible? Where are we? A billion and one questions pound at my brain but all I can do is stare.

"You're awake," he continues into the silence.

I nod and want to tell him he's a real observant one for stating the obvious but I can't. Then Jonah smiles, making the room fall away.

Before I know it, Jonah's long legs are moving and I'm pulled gently into a standing position in his arms. The feel of his warm, hard body around me is the most comforting thing I've ever known.

I breathe him in and our hands roam all over each other to make sure the other is real. We stand there so long until one or both of us fall to our knees but our embrace never breaks.

Finally, after I'm not sure how much time passes I lift my head from one of Jonah's broad shoulders and smirk at him. "So, are we alive or is this some weird afterlife for stinker killers?"

"What? Like some zombie warrior Valhalla?" he asks, laughing as he brushes a strand of hair out of my face.

"What? We totally earned a spot, I'd say."

"You don't know the half of it," he replies.

I gingerly sit back on my heels and look up at him. "What happened?" I ask.

Jonah pulls me closer to him again and adjusts us until we're comfortable leaning against the bed. We stay on the floor and as near to each other as we can get while still being able to look at each other as we talk.

"After they took you down with the taser gun, things got confusing. Bran ran off but without his people. Bran's goons started bashing heads in then they ran back to our hideout with stolen guard uniforms. They realized quickly they still needed me to walk them through the wall and locate the exit. Only I had the coordinates. So, Adam, Roxie, and I got stolen uniforms too. I walked in and made it out the exit door with Adam, Roxie, and some of Bran's goons. Adam's safe," he reassures me.

"He's staying with his friends in the government but I'll get to that in a minute. As for Bran, he's disappeared and as far as I know he's still got the Hope Diamond. That bastard has it coming for what he did to Bill though. Roxie started the job."

I look at him quizzically.

"She shot him," he continues. "I think it only grazed him because he got away. I'm glad she did it anyway. I just wish she'd had a better shot at him in the confusion of things. We'll find him, H. Mark my words," he says fervently.

I nod and wait for him to continue.

I'm oddly silent for once but I really want to know what happened and I really, really like the sound of Jonah's voice. Still I have to ask. "Why the hell did you come back for me?"

Jonah looks at me like I'm insane. Fortunately, I'm pretty much immune to that look due to the amount of times I've received it over the years. Jonah acts like I never asked that question and continues.

"I came back once I had all of the cameras inside the facility broadcasting to every United States armed services base. Adam went to get help from an old government official he trusted in the army. Meanwhile, I made damn sure the president and every person of power was seeing what was going on under Senator Milano's hand. The fight between you and Milano? The one between Milano and that Croft guy? That footage was gold. They practically admitted to everything. You were amazing, H. Watching you break out of that cell, it was inspired."

He just stares at me, dreamily, like he means every word.

I smile and raise one eyebrow.

He does this adorable half-cough thing then shakes his head before speaking again. "Anyway, I also uploaded every file she had and broadcast that too. I figured it was icing on the cake when she kept saying her plans out loud. Classic villain behavior, really."

"You read too many comics," I say.

"Do you want me to finish this story?" he asks sardonically. I remember the first time he asked me that and I realize there's so much more feeling in his voice when he asks it this time.

"Continue," I say, biting my lip not to blurt out everything I'm feeling.

Jonah huffs like he's mad but he's totally not then he says, "I needed time and a distraction and I needed to get you out of there. I knew it was risky to show myself but it was the only way. I couldn't guarantee she wouldn't flip the switch on you before help would arrive. I had to make a distraction to buy time. Obviously, I didn't know what would happen, what Milano would try to do..." Jonah's voice drifts off, sadness evident in his every word.

"Not your fault," I say and reach up a hand to caress his face.

Jonah seems to take strength from my touch because his voice picks up and he continues. "Adam came through and he'd made contact with the president's head of security. They had people on their way but they didn't know who they could trust who was close by and they didn't have the means to shut it down from offsite."

"So, what happened when I...when I," I couldn't say it. I cursed my weakness. I could damn well do it but I just couldn't say it out loud.

Jonah suddenly squeezes me. "Don't you ever do that again, H." He tilts my chin up with his hand and he forces me to look him in the eye. "Do you hear me?"

"I'm not going to apologize. I would do it again. To save you. To save innocent people."

"Don't say that," he growls. "I know why you thought you had to but you don't. Not ever. Never again. Your life is worth more than that. I don't care about anything else and I don't care if it makes me selfish. Promise me. Never again."

"I'd say the same thing to you if I were in your place," I admit, "and you would've done the same things in my shoes. We won't ever have to be in that place again so it doesn't matter." He looks so fierce and he wants to believe we won't have to be in that situation ever again too so eventually he nods. I swallow hard and look back to him. "So, what did happen?"

"She was watching and saw what you were about to do so she flipped the switch and you turned rabid. Fortunately, I had the antidote serum. I kept more in my back pocket and only gave her one of the syringes I had. That's what I was trying to tell you."

"Why didn't you say that the moment she left?" I cry.

"I knew she'd be watching and I only wanted to use it as a last resort. When you turned rabid, I only had a moment but I injected it into you where you held your knife. You immediately dropped to the ground. God, I thought I'd killed you, H. You have no idea how freaked out I've been. I didn't know how you'd react to the antidote after the switch had been flipped. I thought you died," he repeats. It's then I notice that he's shaking. With rage or fear, I wasn't sure.

I run my hands up and down his arms. "I'm fine, Jonah. You didn't kill me. I'm right here."

A moment passes while Jonah seems to suck some air into his lungs. Then he exhales loudly. "Senator Milano thought you killed yourself. She thought she was too late and that you had stabbed yourself before she could turn you. She freaked out and came for me. I don't remember anything except staring at your body on the floor. I thought about Bill and my family and my mom and my past and I couldn't stop staring at you. Everything just kind of hit me. I went a little crazy."

I take in Jonah's words and smirk at him reassuringly. "Yeah, I've been there. So, you killed her?"

"Almost," he says through clenched teeth. "Then Adam came back and he brought guys with really big guns. Everything got shut down quickly. The senator got taken away in handcuffs. She was arrested for a shit load of counts of treason, murder, conspiracy and terrorism."

"Hell yeah," I shout but I'm too weak for the fist pump that I feel like doing.

Jonah laughs and I'm so grateful for the sound. "I ran back to you and felt your pulse. I picked you up and I've never left your side. I promise you. It's been three days. I've been through about a hundred debriefings and we traveled here to New York. I never let you out of my sight."

Something warm tingles down my spine and I fight a shiver at how it makes me feel.

"It's too bad you've been passed out though," Jonah says, disrupting my body shivers. "You missed flying on Air Force One."

I blink. "Are you kidding me?" I shriek. "Tell me you're joking!"

He lifts two fingers. "Scouts honor. It was the coolest damn thing. I would've taken pictures but they're pretty strict about that since what we went through is being classified as a secret."

I punch him just because I really have no other way to process this.

"Anyway, yeah," he says rubbing his shoulder but he's smiling. "We have another meeting tonight and then tomorrow we're meeting with our families."

My breath ceases in my chest but I'm too afraid to even believe.

Suddenly he smiles at me. "They found your mom and brother, H. They're alive.

They were in a shelter that one of Bran's goons was assigned to. I checked the maps we made. Just another thing I want to kill that bastard for. I bet they were keeping it from us on purpose."

"Take a number, killer," I say. "We can take him down together."

Jonah stands up and begins walking around the room and I stretch out my aching legs. "We will. Adam got his buddies to get your mom and brother out of the shelter and fly here to New York. My family is here too."

"Good," I reply.

I'm in shock that Mom and Justin are alive. I just keep blinking, unable to process it. Every part of my body exhales in relief. I don't even know what else to say.

"Right, so we're here in a penthouse suite. You've already gotten several offers to work for the government while you were unconscious," he laughs. "It's all very impressive."

"Very funny. Anything else?"

"We're heroes, I guess. Unofficially, that is. Still we're going to be very busy." He runs a hand through his hair as if he's thinking about how to say something. "D.C. is still recovering," he says lightly and I nod for him to keep going. "They had to bomb the city to kill off the remaining stinkers. They didn't have much of a choice. They didn't go nuclear or anything but the D.C. we knew is gone. Everyone, the entire country is devastated. It's been difficult and people are still grieving over their dead, not to mention their homes and livelihoods. Some people are still finding out each day if their loved ones made it to another shelter or were one of the bitten."

"I'm surprised the evil bastards were even going to let the people in the shelters live," I added, remembering how Milano wanted the people who would be grieving, because of what she'd done, to worship her.

"They used the shelters as ways to find the super soldiers quicker. They wanted everyone identified and once the super soldiers were captured, they would've used the remaining survivors in the shelters as test subjects to further the study. They'd do that under the premise that they couldn't leave because of the bomb."

"That's insane," I say.

"Yeah, the rest of our government thought so too. I'm glad it's over now," Jonah says and then he kisses me and I kiss him back. When we pull away, out of breath, he brings his hand next to my eyes and traces my lids slowly. "I like the brown," he states. "Your natural color is even better than the contacts."

I jump a little. "My eyes are back to normal?" I scramble up best I can and find the door Jonah came through, guessing correctly that it's the bathroom. I turn on the light and notice absently that the bathroom is huge and amazing but I'm too focused on the mirror when I stand in front of it.

I stare at my reflection for a long while, drinking in the sight of my eyes. My brown eyes. I didn't realize how much I missed them. I also realize how awful I look. Three days in bed is not my best look.

Jonah comes up behind me and I watch him in the mirror as

he takes me in his arms.

"This bathroom is awesome," is all I can manage.

Jonah nods. "We're staying in this penthouse until our families come tomorrow. Don't worry though. I wouldn't have let them separate us. I'm just glad you're awake now."

Someone knocks on another door that I'm assuming is outside of the room we're in and I turn to Jonah as he brings us into the massive living room. There's a giant window with an incredible view of New York City to my left and I'm gaping.

Another knock sounds and I follow Jonah to the other door.

"I thought you said we'd be meeting our families tomorrow?"

"We are," he says with a smirk.

"Then who?" I demand, my hands on my hips.

I hate not knowing things and Jonah is totally milking this moment. I feel like punching him and his stupid way-too-hot-smirk. I'm picturing the president, maybe Oprah. I really wished I'd had time to shower.

Jonah shrugs as he answers the door, gives someone some cash and then he walks back in with what I would describe as the most beautiful box on earth.

He turns back to me. "I got us some pizza."

I blink up at him in awe as he slides it onto the table and opens the top for me to inspect.

"You wouldn't wake up and I figured the smell of this would get you up or nothing would."

I walk quickly over to the box, my mouth watering as I spy all my favorite toppings on a gloriously large pie.

My eyes shift from the decadent pizza to the boy in front of me. “Jonah?”

“Yeah.”

“I love you,” I say. And I really freaking do.

Jonah just laughs and kisses me.

“I thought you might say that too.”

CPSIA information can be obtained
at www.ICGtesting.com
Printed in the USA
LVHW021212140920
665924LV00002B/114

9 780578 747606